THE IMMORTAL'S UNREQUITED BRIDE

KELLI IRELAND

MILLS & BOON

First Published in Great Britain 2017
By Mills & Boon, an imprint of HarperCollins*Publishers*
1 London Bridge Street, London, SE1 9GF

© 2017 Denise Tompkins

ISBN: 978-0-263-93004-7

89-0417

Our policy is to use papers that are natural, renewable and recyclable products and made from wood grown in sustainable forests. The logging and manufacturing processes conform to the legal environmental regulations of the country of origin.

Printed and bound in Spain
by CPI, Barcelona

Kelli Ireland spent a decade as a name on a door in corporate America. Unexpectedly liberated by fate's sense of humor, she chose to carpe the diem and pursue her passion for writing. A fan of happily-ever-afters, she found she loved being the puppet master for the most unlikely couples. Seeing them through the best and worst of each other while helping them survive the joys and disasters of falling in love? Best. Thing. Ever. Visit Kelli's website at www.kelliireland.com.

This book is an epic love story, one that transcends the bounds of everything we claim to know with certainty about the hard lines of time and space. Turns out we don't know so much. It is with intense joy, immeasurable love and the understanding he's my One Thing that I dedicate this book to Mr. Kelli Ireland. You're my always and I'm your forever.

Prologue

The Year of Our Lord, 1485

"**Y**our personal powers of destruction paired with your sense of justice may yet bring about the end of the world." Isibéal Cannavan, wife of the Druid's Assassin and powerful white lady in her own right, crossed the great hall and stopped beside the massive oak table, shaking her head in wordless censure. "In the time it took me to gather fresh herbs and root stock for the infirmary, it seems you have agreed to mediate a grievance between a god and two demigods while in the presence of the All Father, Daghda. Quite the morning you've had, husband."

Though nothing compared to mine.

She gripped handfuls of her skirt, and her heart seized as Lachlan Cannavan—dark blond, thoroughly sensual, immensely powerful—slid low in the large, ornately carved Tuam chair situated at the head of the table. The worn leather protested his movement with a sharp creak. Indifferent, he folded his hands over his abdomen. The dark phantom of negotiations—his and hers alike—hovered between them, a divination she alone could see. Again Isibéal thanked the gods that it was she who held the power of visions, not her husband. For if he knew what she'd done…

She'd had no other choice, though. Not after the vision had struck her unannounced, revealing that the strife brewing between divine beings would rip her husband from her grasp.

Lachlan was engaged in an authentic struggle. This was no training exercise or sparring session. This was a battle where those who had lifted sword or fist would either claim victory and, as such, live, or they would suffer the highest loss and make restitution in death.

The fight grew more brutal with every passing second. Men shouted and metal blade beat against metal blade so that the whole of the battle was reduced to harsh sounds that stung the ear. But it was the two men in front of her who claimed the whole of her attention. The swing of the men's blades whistling through the air, steel impacting steel and making her teeth ache, the harsh declarations of extreme effort as each combatant hoisted his respective weapon—each sound was horrifying when singly wrought. Together? They overwhelmed her mind and shouted at her to flee.

Sweat slicked Lachlan's arms and trailed down his bare chest. He gripped his sword hilt so tightly his knuckles appeared skeletal beneath his sun-kissed skin.

A vicious blow and he knocked his opponent back, down, and afforded himself a brief advantage. But that

small triumph changed neither the tenor of the fight nor
its probable outcome.

The strength and valor of the honorable could not
hold its ground in the face of malicious deception and
heartbreaking betrayal.

Lachlan would not, could not, fight an opponent who
was possessed with such disregard for honor, but this
particular opponent hurt him on a deeper level than
any other. The blood tie between them demanded as
much. And that, Lachlan's inability to double-cross the
man who would have his head before he'd even hear
his brother's plea?

That would be the cost of Lachlan's pride and a
brother's love.

Lachlan would lose this fight.

His attacker rose from the ground and charged.
Swords clashed. Men shouted unintelligible words. The
battle raged. These two men were pitted against each
other, a violation of nature's intent. Their animosity was
so strong it fouled the air even as it clung to them, a
sticky cobweb of hatred that spun from one and bound
the other, back and forth as they moved through the
steps of death's dance.

Lachlan's opponent lunged at him, and, with what
could only be described as willfulness...nay, willingness,
Lachlan stepped into the man's blade. It struck true, the
resulting sound disturbingly similar to a butcher's meat
cleaver striking the thickest part of a mutton's leg—
heavy, viscous, dense.

Lachlan stumbled back and the damning sword slid
free with a wet, sucking hiss. Eyes bright in a fast-paling
face, Lachlan grinned with grim satisfaction. He coughed
once. Twice. "I will thank you for this."

"Then you are far greater a fool than I believed," his

attacker, killer, *said, voice muffled as though he spoke with a rag over his mouth.*

Lachlan shook his head. "I said I will, not that I do. Not yet."

"And what, then, is the difference?" came the arrogant reply.

Lachlan lifted his long sword in his dominant hand, stealing his opponent's attention. Then, his nondominant hand yielding his short sword with untraceable speed, he raised his weapon and swung down as hard as he could. The blade was smaller but not lesser, proving sufficient to near cleave the man's head from his neck in one blow.

The man dropped his sword and fell to his knees. Defeat fouled the air around them.

"The difference," Lachlan said with cold indifference, "is that I will thank you for striking my deathblow, as it afforded me the opportunity to reciprocate and offer you the same, save one significant difference. The wounds I bear will end me, but they'll send me into the welcoming fields of Tír na nÓg. The wounds I deliver shall not afford you the same. They will carry you straight to the Shadow Realm." Gritting his teeth, Lachlan yanked the shorter blade from deep in his adversary's neck and then swung again. This time the man's head separated cleanly, hit the ground and rolled free. "You cannot escape your fate," Lachlan said as sweat ran freely down his brow and into his eyes. Swaying, he blinked rapidly. "It did not have to be this way...brother."

Lachlan's fingers straightened spasmodically, his swords clanging off each other as they fell. The grass muffled the metal's impact with the earth. He clutched his side, breath wheezing. His eyes lost their intense, sharp look, growing unfocused between blinks.

Isibéal screamed at him to hold on, admonished him

to fight, threatened to see that his cherished knarr—the long boat his Viking great-grandfather had sailed—was used as his funeral pyre should he die. All to no avail, for the living held no dominion over the dying, and Lachlan was dying.

Without acknowledging her, Lachlan slipped sideways, caught himself with one hand and, in fits and starts, eased himself to the ground.

Then it was done. The headless body of Lachlan's enemy lay mere feet from where the Assassin had fallen. Both men's souls had been set free with their last breaths.

Isibéal knew with absolute certainty that Lachlan's soul had begun its journey to the heavens. It was no consolation.

She fell to her knees at his side. And while she alone seemed to hear the impact of her husband's death, hear it she did.

Her heart broke with a thunderous crack, *much like a heavy foot on thin ice.*

Life as she knew it was over.

Desperate to hide the tear that burned her eyes, Isibéal spun away from the hale and healthy man who watched her now.

She could not, *would not*, stand by and watch Lachlan enter into a conflict he wasn't slated to walk out of. She'd seen his death and held suspect one man who should never have been suspect at all. Still, it seemed he would strike the blow that would rob her of her heart's blood.

How? How could he do this to me?

This vision was the first to reduce her to a shivering mess of skirts and tears. Throat too tight to scream her refusal of what she'd been shown and now revisited, she locked her knees and forced herself to remain standing. The original imagery and consequent sounds had left her a collapsed heap of emotional devastation. One truth had separated from the thousand questions she'd been left with. That truth?

Isibéal wouldn't survive losing Lachlan. Therefore she'd do whatever was necessary to stay with him. If it meant sacrificing herself so he carried on and met her in the afterlife? So be it. Where he went, she followed.

The affirmation wasn't based on the melodramatics of a weak-minded woman, but rather a simple, if brutal, truth recognized by her as one of the realm's most powerful witches. Should she be forced to take matters into her own hands, should she be required to end her own life, she would do so. And gladly.

To that end, she'd sought out a solution in the early-morning mists that silently rose from the floor of Caher-murphy Forest. It meant she'd had to break her *geis*—the oath she'd taken to honor her magick's gift and never use it to try to change fate to suit her—but it mattered not.

Isibéal would follow Lachlan into this confrontation.

She had set aside the convictions of her faith that bade her not interfere in the workings of free will or destiny's machinations. That done, she'd set her circle in place, retrieved a small bowl she carried in her pack and then filled it with water. Settled in her circle, she cast it and worked the deep magick required to scry. She would use the reflection of the water's surface to look into the future with intent and the belief she could secure Lachlan's safety.

What had appeared had not been foresight. Yes, the answer to her initial summons had appeared on the water's surface...but as a reflection of the man who stood behind her.

Lugh, God of Vengeance and Reincarnation and one of

the aggrieved parties at the meeting slated for Lachlan's involvement, had sought her out.

Discussions resulted in a bargain struck in the forest's ominous hush, sans the whisper of the wind through the trees or the subtle rush of wings fluttering between branches…a bargain that had not settled well, given Lugh's reputation for trickery. But if it saved Lachlan's life?

"Isibéal?" Laughter colored Lachlan's deep, charming voice. "Where did your bonny thoughts take you, my love?"

She forced herself to turn around and face her husband, swallowing repeatedly. Her regrets were far too many, the memories she'd count on to see her through far too few. Worried he'd recognize something amiss, she arched an eyebrow and waved him on. "Out with it, then. Tell me what I know."

"And why would I?" he asked, humor flashing through his eyes.

"To spare yourself the tongue-lashing you'd receive should you think to withhold information from me?"

Lachlan grinned, his dimples flashing. "Lucky am I that you're not inclined to harp. Now, this tongue-lashing…"

She snatched a mushroom from her collecting basket and hurled it at him playfully. "Lecherous wretch."

He fielded the mushroom and absently tossed it back into her basket. "These premonitions of yours are helpful only in that they tend to save me having to repeat myself in order to keep you informed." He reclined again, resting large hands over his muscled abdomen. His eyelids fell to half-mast, and what little she could see of his irises' color deepened. "You realize, wife, that we finally have a few moments alone. Surely you wouldn't waste such a boon discussing politics."

She pulled the pins from her hair and let the mass tumble to her waist. "I'd rather not talk at all, and well you know it, but you're the Assassin and these are dire times."

"When discussions of the War of the Roses, the Tudors and the gods' petty differences come between, or before, my sworn duty to see to my wife's needs?" He grinned. "Dire times, indeed."

All those who recognized this man as leader of the Assassin's Arcanum, the elite group of men the Druids selected within their own to protect all they revered, knew well enough that his lazy slouch was for effect. Isibéal understood this better than any other.

Her husband was dangerous in a thousand ways that were visible and a thousand more that were decidedly not. Deadliness didn't render the man entirely immortal, though. A killing blow would take him as it would any other. His skill sets only ensured the blow would be more difficult to deliver. More difficult did not translate to impossible.

And he thought to bargain with gods and demigods alike.

Foolish man.

And how are you any better? her conscience whispered.

Perhaps she wasn't *better*, but there was a difference. Lachlan's service to the Arcanum meant that, should she die, he would have to go on without her. Obligation necessitated his leadership, even in the face of unassailable hardship. She had no such requirement. If she were to lose him, she would be less than the shell of the woman she was. There would be no living. Breathing in and out would not constitute life. Her only choice would be to follow him through the Veil into eternity. The end result would be two deaths on the side of Light instead of one.

The gods would never condone such a thing.

Staring at Lachlan now, she felt an ache in her chest with the sense of loss too vast to comprehend. He never had realized the charm he wielded or what a beautiful man he was. Instead, he forever seemed unaware of his appearance or the effect he had on people, particularly women. She would always appreciate that about him. Like now, as he lounged in the grand chair, his blond hair tied back with a leather thong, his everyday clothes fitted and fine but far from formal. Restrained violence settled around him like a cloak, but the teasing laughter never left his face. How he managed to rein in both was beyond her.

Her heart raced and her breasts tightened with arousal.

What she wouldn't give for an hour alone with him.

And had he not just said they had time to themselves?

Her very soul sighed, the rush of relief highly tangible for all it was inaudible. She would steal that precious time with him—experience his mouth on hers, his hands in her hair, the weight of his body pressed against hers, the way he moved within her with control and purpose. She would seek, and take, everything he offered, and all with the crushing knowledge that this turn of the wheel was nearly over for her.

She laid the back of her free hand against her cheek. Gods save her from her thoughts, both carnal and mortal. They'd been married more than four years, and the overwhelming desire she had for him had never faded.

Memories teased the corners of her mouth, coaxing a smile like a daylily, its bloom fading as soon as it was born. Laying her fingertips over her lips, she pressed the sensitive skin against her teeth until it hurt, all in an effort to allay the pain and fear of choices made.

"Iz?"

Her eyes snapped into focus and she looked at him, blinking rapidly. "Yes?"

Lachlan pushed out of his chair and closed the distance between them with purposeful strides. "You're far too canny a woman to allow your good conscience to be fraught with worry over political machinations."

"Mankind has no idea what they've wrought upon themselves."

Stopping before her, he cupped her face and dipped low for a swift kiss. "You and I are well aware that things are rarely as they seem. I've been asked to be on hand to apply that wisdom to a group of men who bicker like six children given five marbles to share. History will record these events justly, provided mankind does not gloss over the outcome. Either way, we must do our duty to the gods. Then?" He traced a thumb along her cheek. "Justice will surely prevail."

"Is there no other way? No way for us to refrain from becoming involved?"

"You know there is not, Isibéal."

She blinked through an unwelcome sheen of emotion.

The corners of his eyes tightened as he thumbed away a tear from her cheek. "What's this, my lady?"

Her throat burned as if she'd gulped down a flagon of raw alcohol. "What has been set into motion cannot be stopped."

But what if she was wrong? What if her vision was flawed? What if she'd been led false? Or…what if the bargain she'd struck this morn did, indeed, change this man's free will? Could she save him?

She gripped her husband's forearms, fingernails digging into sun-kissed skin pulled taut over defined muscle. "You must cancel the meeting, Lach. Please."

"It…and I…will be fine, *mo chroí.*"

"You call me your heart and ask me to have faith, but what of you? Have you no faith in my gift of seeing? Of knowing? I am certain this will not go well, Lachlan." She gripped the back of his neck and pulled him down until their foreheads touched. "Would you declare me naught but a foolish wife and incompetent witch in this matter?" she breathed.

"Neither is true, and I would take to task any man, woman or child brazen—and ignorant—enough to speak such nonsense." His gaze bored into hers. "You must trust me in this, Iz. Daghda himself has ordained that this meeting is both just and necessary. By the gods' own laws, this is the appropriate venue for the parties to issue their grievance. Yet he cannot preside over a hearing involving his own kin. They asked for my time and opinions, and I'm of the belief that this is right and fair. The Arcanum is, and always has been, the gods' sword arm to justly wield."

Isibéal shook her head slowly. "Neither you nor the Arcanum should ever be ordered to strike out in revenge, particularly on the gods' behalf."

Lachlan stilled his caress. "I have not been called to fight but, instead, to listen. To mediate. The All Father would no more lead me blindly into harm's way than he would manipulate my service to render it unjust. I've served him more than a mortal lifetime, and he has seen the Druids through the worst of Ireland's troubles."

"So far," she interjected.

"So far," he conceded. "But if he has done so thus

far, what grounds do I have to deem him unwilling or unable to continue on this path he's forged?"

"You cannot believe... I never meant... It's only that—"

He kissed her quickly, shushing her sputtering objections. "You love me just as I love you, and that makes life a wee bit harrowing at times, yeah?" Then he turned away and started for the Elder's Library. "Rest easy, wife. I will see this handled and return to you."

An idea struck her. "Promise me, Lachlan. Please."

He spun and walked backward. "I give you my word that I will see this handled and return to you, Lady Isibéal Cannavan."

With a nod, she turned and took a couple of steps forward before glancing back and finding that her husband had already passed through the library door.

Perfect.

She reached up to smooth her furrowed brow even as anxiety, weighted with irrefutable knowledge, settled over her. Lachlan was not meant to meddle in the gods' arguments, be they petty or just. And while he might feel obligated to participate in this hearing, she held no such compulsion. Her first duty, now and always, was to look out for her husband and see him safely returned to her. It would have been so even had her heart's mate been a shepherd and not the Assassin.

She would do what needed to be done to ensure that she did not lose Lachlan in this, or any, lifetime.

Bowing her head, Isibéal threw open her ties to the elements and the magicks they heralded. Threads of color whipped around her with dizzying speed, colors only she could see. The magicks were as bright as they were ethereal, raw power drawn into her hands and shaped to her will alone. Few witches had come before with more power than she wielded even now, decades before the zenith of her power was forecast to arrive.

Lachlan's parting words were still so new that the memory of them would be strong enough to cast and weave around, and she would do both, and more, if it meant tying his promise to her intent.

With few movements and naught but whispered words, Isibéal created a sphere that raced across the deepening shadows of time that grew between his words and the present. The sphere reached back and retrieved the promise Lachlan had made her, captured the words and then sealed them inside the crystalline ball. Threads of color wound around the exterior at ever-increasing speeds until the motion was a blur. Colors fused in a bright flash of light that made her eyes water. Magick receded with very little in the way of a dramatic exit. Shimmering inside the orb was the essence of the words Lachlan had gifted her with.

Isibéal cradled the sphere between her cupped palms, one above the globe and one below, the strength of her magick suspending it. Dipping her chin, she spoke over those harvested words—words that represented her future, her hope—and infused her voice with both her will and power. "Protect these words, heartfelt promise man to wife, keep the promise alive for me, that we might again share a life. His spirit shall not cross to its final resting place, but will remain in limbo, affected by neither time nor space. My soul shall serve as sacrifice, to bind us where we fall, only love's inherent power will be enough to break the thrall. Hear me now and mark my plea, for wait I shall, across years or centuries."

The bespelled orb flared bright. A flash of heat passed into her hands and made her gasp, but she managed to hold on to it until the heat dissipated. Then, with a subtle glance around the stairwell, she tucked the living spell into the depths of her basket and bade it reduce in size until it was no larger than a small stone from the streambed.

Peace warred with fear at what she'd done. It was unnatural to bind a single soul, let alone two, to this plane when their physical bodies died. Their souls could go on indefinitely, though whether madness would take their minds had yet to be seen. To be freed would have to be an act of love. Nothing else would suffice to bring the two souls back together. That didn't bother her, though. Their relationship was, and always had been, ripe with love and heavily decorated with lust. If two souls were ever to find their way back to each other and reunite, their souls would.

Gathering her basket of naturals, she resumed her trek up the broad staircase that would take her to the third-floor infirmary only to pause at the first landing, her hand on a newel. She could not let him go. Not without knowing him one last time.

There was no shame in her request, no remorse or hesitation when she said, "Join me, Lachlan. Steal that wee bit of time we've tripped over, time alone to…" She looked down demurely only to glance up at him through lowered lashes. "There will be plenty of time to see to the intricacies of mediating under Thranewyn's Law after I've had my way with you."

She started up the staircase again, swaying her hips back and forth suggestively.

Booted footsteps closed the distance between them and sounded as if they took the stairs two at a time. Hard hands wrapped around her upper arms and pulled her back against an even harder chest. "The deepest prisons of the Shadow Realm couldn't keep me away."

"Never in a thousand lifetimes will such keep me away from you, husband. Never."

He followed her up the stairs then, to her room, where he loved her as passionately as she loved him, and with almost as much manic fervor.

Almost.

For Isibéal knew what he did not. This would be the last time they would lie wrapped in each other, loose-limbed and sated.

She stayed as long as she dared, watching the late-afternoon sun paint Lachlan's skin in warm colors as he drifted into a deep, quiet sleep. Then she rose, wrapped her robe about herself and crossed the hall to her infirmary, where she set about gathering a basket full of fresh bandages, salves and healing ointments she'd made. They would be needed on the coming morn when mediation turned to war.

Dressed and packed little more than an hour later, she tried to leave. Truly, she did. But she craved one last look at her husband's face, peaceful in sleep, long lashes fanning over his cheeks. This was how she would remember him, always and forever.

Emotion welled, filling her chest until she could not breathe.

"From my very first breath until time ceases, you have been and will always be the heart of me. I love you, Lachlan Cannavan."

Isibéal shut the door and then headed down the stairs and toward the stables. Pausing at the keep's huge front doors, she swung her traveling cloak about her shoulders and raised her hood against the misting rain.

She had a long ride ahead if she were to die before the sun's zenith as agreed.

Chapter 1

Ethan Kemp forced himself to keep his pace slow as he made his way down the castle's long, forever-chilled hallway. He'd been called a lot of things over his thirty-four years—warlock, physician's assistant, American expat, friend, lover and, on occasion, fighter—but he'd never been called a coward. That was a moniker he refused to sport. So he would *not* allow himself to walk faster, speed up or, gods forbid, run. He would not curse. He would *not* look over his shoulder. Again, anyway. Why bother? He knew what would be there. What *had* been there for the last several months. Always following him. Always just out of reach, that shapeless smudge on the air. Nothing tangible. A mirage.

Hand at his side, he held the dirk with apparent disregard. Looks could be deceiving. He was under no illusion the blade would help him fight something he couldn't see, but the weight of the weapon was better than nothing.

Besides, if the Assassin's Arcanum—the biological outcome if 007 met *Highlander* and had unprotected sex with *Practical Magic*—found out he was running from shadows and tricks of light? Gods save him. He'd rather have his balls waxed than take the endless ribbing he'd receive from those five men.

While the heart of Druidism centered on a high regard for life and peaceful existence, the Assassin's Arcanum, protectors of the Druidic race, were an entirely different breed. The Arcanum was composed of men who did whatever was deemed necessary to ensure that their brethren could live within their chosen—peaceful—parameters. But the assassins? From manipulation to murder, they *were* the things that went bump in the night. No mark would ever take notice of an assassin's approach any more than he would the assassin's departure. Dead men don't hear a thing.

And while Ethan had developed a deep appreciation for the assassins' mad skills with both weapons and elemental magicks, he wasn't part of their inner circle. Not really. They'd gone so far as to jokingly label him their mascot—or resident pain in the ass. The moniker depended on whom he'd either helped or irritated at the time of conversation.

There were places Ethan had found he fit better than others. When *the* Assassin, Dylan O'Shea, had made the decision that compelled Ethan to participate in both weapons and hand-to-hand combat training, no one had been more surprised at the outcome than Ethan himself. He'd done well. No, not *well*. He'd excelled in a way that defied logic. That was when Dylan had begun involving Ethan in some of the Arcanum's less risky ops, inviting him along as an extra set of hands to manage the element of earth, since none of the other men possessed that skill. But it didn't change Ethan's status among them. He was an outsider, a man without legitimate purpose, and it bothered him far more than it should.

A weighted stare settled between Ethan's shoulders, and he clenched the dagger handle tighter. Last time he'd experienced something like this, assassins—*junior* assassins—had bagged and tagged him, hauling him from Atlanta, Georgia, to the Irish countryside in County Clare. That still irritated him. The purpose for his warlock-napping had been legit, though. His closest friend, Kennedy, had asked for the chance to say good-bye before the assassins or, more specifically, *the* Assassin, killed her. Ethan had arrived in time to see her beat the odds, and the gods, and then marry the man she'd fallen in love with.

That her new husband, Dylan the Ass, had been her appointed and questionably willing executioner?

"'Love is blind' and all that crap," he muttered as he rolled his shoulders. "More like it encourages perfectly sane individuals to perform in certifiably *in*sane ways."

After the dust finally settled from that little magickal brouhaha, Ethan hadn't wanted to leave her.

At least, that was the public version of events.

Privately? There was another chapter in his play-by-play living memoir. One he hadn't discussed with anyone.

Ethan hadn't been *able* to leave.

He'd tried.

Sure, he could pack his bags and buy his airline ticket and make noises about going back to the States. But when it came time to go? He would stand at the largest window in his small suite and stare out over the cliffs as the clock ticked past his boarding call, past his departure and *well* past his scheduled arrival.

He would stand there listening. Looking. Waiting. For what, he didn't know.

Then he'd unpack and start the cycle over, trying to live until he could manage to leave.

No one said a word to him about the number of times this had happened. The Arcanum simply carried on as if he'd be there. The Druids' healer and surgeon, Angus, never moved Ethan's supplies or the medical files he kept on each patient he'd treated. His place setting was always laid out on the dining table. And the tyros, or assassins-in-training, never questioned him as he moved throughout the castle or across the grounds. He wasn't one of them, but he had become part of the familiar landscape. They'd accepted his presence if not him.

None of that was what kept him ensconced in the Arcanum's inner circle, though.

Truth? All he knew was that his heart was here. Not in Kennedy, although he'd suffered a moment of sheer panic right after she'd married, wondering if he'd unwittingly fallen in love with her. The revolting idea was too close to incest, though, and he'd been relieved. Yet that relief hadn't translated to anything near understanding.

He'd had to accept that knowing his heart was here and understanding what that meant were two unrelated things. He had no idea what it meant that he couldn't make himself go back to his former life. Didn't understand how this drafty old castle, known among Druids as The Nest, had somehow become the GPS location labeled "Home" on his phone. Couldn't explain how, after only days here in this foreign land, it wasn't foreign at all. There was no logical explanation.

Despite his gifts in magick and his intimate ties to the element of earth, Ethan didn't appreciate things that defied logic. Not like this. And definitely not when the heart—*his* heart—was involved. He loved this country, this keep and the very land beneath his feet. Loved it with absolutely no reserve. It was as if Ireland was his, and he was hers, logic be damned.

A touch, colder than a thousand-year-old grave, skated across the nape of his neck. Despite his conviction to stay focused and reach his rooms, he spun and staggered as he ripped at the shimmering form with his short blade.

"Show yourself," he demanded, chest heaving.

The visual disturbance winked out, leaving behind record of neither its presence nor its passing. Innocuous dust motes danced on the air where the thing had been.

Like every other time he'd demanded a confrontation with whatever it was that followed him, he experienced a moment of awareness, a sense of soul-wrenching despair, before abject solitude wound its way around and through him, strangling limbs and organs and emotions without differentiation. Every bit of him was put through the wringer and left feeling crushed.

As he rubbed his sternum, Ethan's wild gaze skipped around the hallway, floor to ceiling. "If I trip and fall and get murdered, I'm filing a grievance with management." Irritation saturated his mutterings as he whirled away from the emptiness and resumed the trek to his rooms.

That he'd been reduced to what felt like the sacrificial starlet doomed to be the first one taken out really pissed him off. Sure, he loved a good slasher flick as much as the next guy, but he strongly preferred fiction to fact when personal threat was involved. This real-life emotional-torture-cum-horror-fest was messing him up. All he needed to round out his physical retreat was a tension-building score filled with haunting piano music accompanied by ominous strings. Maybe pipe organs...

"Organs." He snorted. "Bad word choice."

A huge shadow rose in his peripheral vision.

Ethan's lungs seized as if a massive, invisible hand had gripped the pair and squeezed them like they were the leather bags on a bagpipe. A choked wheeze of alarm was the most he could manage. Whatever was stalking him had never rematerialized so fast and with such density. Intent on rending that shadow in two, Ethan swung out.

His short blade met the heavy metal of a proper sword, the shock singing up his arm until his nerves vibrated like a tuning fork. His hand spasmed and his dagger fell to the stone floor, striking with a metallic clatter.

"Shit!" He cradled his numb arm to his chest and glared into the shadowy alcove. "You scared the ever-living hell out of me."

"The gods of light and life will be glad to hear it." A dark looked passed over Rowan's face. "If you intend to strike out at a larger man carrying a much bigger sword, you need to either arm yourself better or get faster. Preferably both."

Ignoring the chastisement, Ethan let a slow, wicked grin spread over his face even as he fought to bank the fury he knew filled his eyes. "Frankly? I'm more interested in what you're doing tucked away in a lovers' alcove with nothing but your sword than I am in hearing you criticize my mad fighting skills."

"It's not a lovers' alcove, witchling. It's an archer's lookout." Rowan stared down the hall in the direction Ethan's mysterious stalker had disappeared. "As for the other, I was doing exactly as you asked—trying to see if whatever it is that you claim is following you might be visible to me in the spirit realm."

"Tell me you finally saw it." Coarse and strained,

Ethan's demand sounded like it had been squeezed through a vise.

Rowan's nostrils flared. Then he gave a single, sharp dip of the chin.

Hope warred with terror. Ethan wanted—*needed*—to know what was going on. With the banished and damned gods rallying as the Shadow Realm's power shifted, the appearance of this otherworldly stalker had him unnerved. He waited on Rowan to speak.

Nada. Nothing. Niet.

The assassin just continued to stare down the hall, his eyebrows drawn together.

Ethan scooped up his dagger and, to hide his trembling hand, gestured with the blade as he spoke. "Tell me, or the next time you end up in the infirmary, I'll set up an account and profile for you on www.hotmenofDublin.com and tie the account to your phone so it posts your location…no matter where you are."

He fought to keep from flinching when the man's arctic-blue gaze refocused and landed solidly on him. The vacancy in those eyes made it seem like Rowan was no more than a husk of a man. A shell. Soulless. His response did little to dispel the impression. "I'd refrain from referring to the being as an 'it.'"

Ethan tried not to grin and failed. "You're telling me I've picked up a…what? A ghost? As in, an incorporeal stalker?"

"Of a sort."

Grin fading, Ethan couldn't stop the sudden buzzing in his ears. "What 'sort,' exactly? And how do I get rid of it?"

"'It' is a woman," Rowan answered softly. "And I'm not sure you want to be rid of her."

"Why?" The buzzing grew louder as something heavy pressed against the corners of Ethan's mind.

"Because it would seem she's your wife."

Isibéal Cannavan quite literally hovered around the corner and out of sight of the assassin with the terrifying eyes. The man had seen her. *Could* see her. But that wasn't what had scattered her so and left her suffering with uncontrollable palsy. She'd touched the man now known as Ethan. The man she knew as Lachlan. And the terrifying man who could see her had either heard her or read her lips when she uttered that cherished yet damning word. "Husband."

Nor was her admission what had sent her careening down the hall. All she had wanted was to touch Lachlan. Nothing more. So, after summoning every ounce of will she possessed, she had concentrated on Lachlan's bare neck. And she'd done it, had *felt* him. But the very second the sensation registered, an excruciating pain had ripped through her and torn an involuntary, albeit soundless, scream from her throat. Nothing, not even the sword strike that had taken her life, had ever hurt so badly. She had been catapulted away from him as if she'd taken a far more violent blow to the midsection. Even now her hands hovered over the sight of the original deathblow. She looked down, half expecting to find blood staining her gown.

There was nothing there.

Isibéal rubbed one thumb and forefinger together, still convinced it should be blood-slicked. Her other hand she held clamped against her side. Despite the fact that she didn't need to breathe, her chest heaved. Pain still ricocheted through her, pinging about like a maddened hornet trapped in a jar. It was of no consequence, seeing as she refused to regret her actions. She wished with fierce intensity that she'd been able to retain the sensation of Lachlan's warmth. A fitting reward that would have been worth the lingering pain. Such was not to be. Touching her husband had taken every ounce of available concentration and more than that in bravery to master her form and create the brief connection. To retain it would have taken the very thing she did not possess.

A mortal body.

That she would never again realize the intimate feel of Lachlan's form sliding beneath her hands, stroke the stubble along his jaw, experience his lips against hers or his arms cradling her... The realization, both compounded and comprehensive, had been enough to do what the pain had not done, driving her from the keep.

She raced to the cliffs, teetering to a stop inches from the edge.

Wind whipped through her.

Her simple gown did not so much as move.

If her sacrifice had not saved her husband's life, it had, at the very least, saved his soul. She must remember that. Never would she regret her choice. How often had she sworn from her cursed grave that she would suffer a hundred eternal damnations to simply be able to see and hear Lachlan...now Ethan...after all these centuries? Someone had heard her fervent prayers and granted her this boon. If that single touch meant she was forever removed from Lachlan, so be it. It was a price she would pay a thousand times over to know he lived once more.

She pressed her fingertips to her lips before whispering his name in reverent invocation. "Lachlan."

Recognizing her husband on sight had been a matter of no regard. Even now her heart called to his, just as it had the first time they'd met. Lachlan Cannavan looked much the same as he had before her death. He who had once led the Assassin's Arcanum had been an attractive man with dark blond hair, a strong jaw and merry blue eyes more inclined to shared laughter than somber weight. Broad-shouldered with muscle layered over muscle, he had commanded any room. She had watched him long enough in this life to know that he still did. His modern clothes struck her as odd, but he looked so similar to those around him that she had to assume what he wore was fashionable. None of this was truly relevant, however.

What mattered most was that, after an innumerable number of centuries, she had *touched* him, touched the man she'd thought lost to her for eternity. Her hand dropped from her lips to hover over the quiet at her breast. She might not possess a heartbeat, but she still possessed a heart. Of that she was certain. Otherwise, her chest wouldn't ache with such vacancy.

A soft but persistent tug behind her breastbone drew a small gasp from her.

"I will *not*," she snapped. "You do not command me."

Though she spoke to the air, she had hope that *he* heard her—the God of Vengeance and Reincarnation, once known for far greater things than cold-blooded murder.

Lugh.

He summoned her yet again, this pull on her being stronger as his will forced her back a step.

Pressure in her chest eased.

She so was not ready for this.

After she'd risen from her grave, nearly a moon's cycle passed before she understood what the pull meant. The more insistent it became, the more certain she was that the curse Lugh had laid on her at death had been consequent.

The wordless command intensified.

She resisted giving in and doing as bade, instead stepping forward. The summons caused her limbs to ache as it evolved into a silent demand. No matter. She was not his to order about. Not now. Not ever. Still, the sensation grew.

She set her jaw and leaned forward.

When the pull finally stopped, the release nearly drove her over the cliff. Not that it would hurt her, but it still unnerved her when she ended up hovering in midair.

There was no way to predict how long Lugh would leave her be this time. Every day she remained free of the grave, the god grew stronger and more insistent she answer his summons. He fed from her freedom, siphoning it like a leech. She resented his presence, despised the fact that she had no control over what he took from her. That resentment was nothing compared to the vitriolic hatred she harbored for *him*, though. His death curse had stolen more than her life. To say she had suffered through the centuries would be like saying a blacksmith's forge burned hot.

"Understatement." She huffed out a sharp breath, at the same time absently tucking a loose curl back into the hair piled on her head.

Not once had she ceased her pleading with the gods of light and life, beseeching them to find mercy and release her from the hell to which she'd bound herself. She'd had no idea what that spell would mean long-term. Darkness had blinded her. Her corporeal and incorporeal bodies had been trapped in her grave. But by some small grace—damnation?—she'd been able to hear everything that happened in the castle. It had nearly destroyed her mind even as it shredded her heart, hearing that Lachlan had died despite the bargain she'd struck and the subsequent sacrifice she'd made that summer night.

Her life for his.

She swiped at the tears that tracked down her cheeks at the memory of hearing that Lachlan had perished, the heartache as fresh as ever. "Fickle gods have no care for those whose lives are destroyed by their impetuous choices."

And now both her sacrifice and Lachlan's death would amount to naught. With the disturbance of Isibéal's grave, the very grave to which Lugh had linked his binding to the Shadow Realm, Lugh's confinement to the underworld would begin to deteriorate. While she had been bound to her grave, so had he been to his. But now that she was free? That freedom would empower the god to begin his own resurrection process. Once he manifested, she had no doubt he would rain vengeance on those he deemed enemies, past and present.

And Lachlan, nay, Ethan, would be at the very top of his list.

Chapter 2

Thoughts raced willy-nilly through Ethan's mind as he crossed the threshold into his room. *Wife. Mine? No. Married. Me? No. No, no, no, no. Crazy-ass ghost. Rowan's wrong. No other explanation.* And then he was back to *Married. Me? No. No, no, no, no.* At some point in what had evolved into a mad dash down the hall, his feet had gone inexplicably numb. With a little luck and some staunch medicinal Irish therapy, the rest of his body would follow within the half hour.

He shoved through the door to his rooms and crossed straight to the small bookcase with the bar on one end. With the tip of his dagger, he performed an impromptu game of eenie-meenie-miney-mo. The blade landed on an unopened bottle of Midleton Very Rare. Ethan grinned without humor and pulled the bottle off the shelf. No glass needed.

"Waste of fine whiskey."

The deep voice nearly drove Ethan out of his skin. His knife clattered to the floor, and he fumbled the expensive whiskey. Sunlight flashed through the bottle's rich amber content as the decanter went end over end, its impact with the stone floor forecast in horrid slow motion. Ethan lunged for the bottle. His knees scraped the uneven floor, the burn advertising that he'd taken the first layer of skin off. But by the gods' grace, he snatched the bottle out of the air before permanent damage—the kind that involved curses and broken glass and bandied accusations—occurred.

Rounding on the intruder and light-headed with a wild cocktail of anger, adrenaline and something too close to fear for comfort, Ethan gestured with the neck of the bottle. "*Stop* sneaking up on me!"

Rowan shrugged and, with his heel, shoved the door to the suite closed before zeroing in on the bookshelf. He plucked the Very Rare from Ethan's hands as he passed. "I realize you're not Irish and, therefore, are arguably ignorant, so I'll tell you once. You don't get fluthered on Midleton's. It's too fine a drink for that. Choose a bottle of Jameson's, Blended."

"What? Why?"

Rowan placed the Very Rare on the shelf from whence it came and selected a nearly new bottle of Jameson's Blended, handing it to Ethan without pomp or flourish. "Why?" He blinked once. Twice. "Easy. Midleton's is a rare whiskey made for sipping, not drinking. It's a whiskey for celebration, not obliteration. And while Jameson's is also an admittedly fine whiskey, it's half the cost. Your guilt won't be so pricked when you're puking it, and your toenails, up come sunrise."

Ethan blinked at Rowan. "That was a speech."

The muscular man rolled first his shoulders and

then his head, rocking the latter back and forth until he paused to stretch and his vertebrae made a popping sound. "Made my point, didn't I?"

"Sure, but it seems there were extra words in there. Some might even say they were compassionate words."

Rowan shot Ethan a bland look before plucking a glass off the shelf. "Shut up and pour."

"You too good to drink from the bottle?"

The larger man didn't respond, simply held out the highball glass. When Ethan didn't move fast enough, Rowan snatched the bottle and poured a solid two fingers of whiskey. Neck corded and hands trembling, he passed the glass to Ethan, picked up a second glass and poured again.

Ethan swirled his drink, staring at the play of light against fine crystal. "I'm not sure what to think, seeing as the ghost got to you. *You.* She must have been terrifying, horrid even. Dude, I bet that was it. She's a hag, isn't she? Proof she's not my wife. I mean, looks aren't everything, but when you take your marriage vows? That's it. You're waking up to that mug for the rest of your life."

Rowan lifted his chin and locked his stare with Ethan's. "Did you just call me 'dude'?"

"Maybe?" He shrugged. "Okay, fine. Yes. But it was my second choice. First would have been Special Agent Supernatural—SAS for short—because of all the freaky shit that goes on around here. 'Dude' slipped off the tongue easier." Sure, Ethan could have been a little more couth, but it would have been wasted effort. Besides, he wasn't in the right frame of mind to worry about offending the centuries-old Druid. Let Rowan turn him into a toad. With any luck, Ethan could counter-curse the other man on the way down. Gulping down the contents of the proffered glass, Ethan took the last swallow and gasped as powerful fumes rushed out his nose, cauterizing the tender skin. "I'd turn you into a gnat."

Rowan's eyebrows drew together for a split second. "A gnat?"

"Well, you're turning me into a frog."

"I am?" Rowan shook his head and tossed back the two fingers he'd poured. "I haven't had enough to drink for you to make sense."

"I always make sense," Ethan countered. "Sometimes."

Rowan grunted as he poured himself a second shot.

"So, let me be blunt." Ethan set his glass down, commandeered the bottle and took a long draw, his breath exploding from his lungs as if he were a mythical fire-breathing creature. He wondered that the room hadn't been incinerated. Voice raw, he managed to wheeze, "Why are you here?"

Rowan shrugged and sipped at his glass. "Personal reasons, I assure you."

"And here I thought you cared," Ethan murmured before taking a less aggressive pull from the bottle's mouth.

"Don't think that my presence here is any type of indicator that I give a personal damn about what you do or don't do." The barked response bore an accusatory tone. "I don't leave my friends in trouble."

"By your own admission last Thursday after sword practice when I cut you like a little bitch, I'm not your friend. And as far as my troubles go?" He lifted the bottle in toast and took another pull. "The only one I have involves a crazy-ass ghost-hag-stalker no one but *you* can see. Soon as I banish her? Life's golden."

Rowan stepped closer to Ethan. "You won't banish the woman until we're sure she's not your wife."

Ethan's temper snapped like a mousetrap. The victim here, though, was his common sense. Pushing into Rowan's personal space, he glared at the Druid. "Get it through your thick, geriatric skull, *dude*. I've never *been* married. Won't ever *get* married. So the only thing I know for sure is that the woman wants something bad enough that she's motivated to lie in order to get it."

Rowan pushed Ethan back with enough force that he stumbled.

"Asshole."

The bigger man set his glass down and, moving faster than thought, closed his hand around Ethan's throat. "Leave it be."

Simple words issued with such hostile overtones didn't steal the underlying truth. Rowan gave a shit about him on some fundamental, purposeful level.

Wrenching free of the assassin's grip, Ethan spun and stalked to the window. He braced a hand against the casing and leaned into it, pressing the pads of his fingers into the rough stone. He watched the waves rolling into the cliff face and took a drink.

This time the whiskey burned slower, spreading through the middle of his chest before radiating down his legs and along his arms. Lingering surprise at Rowan's roundabout admission stole Ethan's sarcasm. His fingertips twitched around the glass. Shoving off the window's frame, he forced himself to face the man who inexplicably considered him a friend. "What do we do to get rid of her?"

Rowan retrieved the bottle of Midleton's and poured himself a clean shot.

Ethan's eyebrows drew together and he absently rubbed his furrowed forehead. "I thought that wasn't the whiskey you drank to get drunk."

Ice-blue eyes met his. "You're getting drunk. I'm only

here in a support role. Plus, you drank from the bottle. I prefer to keep my glass to my person."

"Whatever." Ethan took another sip, appreciating the ease with which the strong alcohol now went down. "Why are you so supportive of my intent to get blotto? You don't even like me."

"If you'd been paying attention to the gossiping hens around this place, you'd have heard I don't like anyone or anything."

"Gossip is for little girls and old women. Oh, and doctors. You wouldn't believe how doctors gossip around their computer monitors in a hospital." He shook his head. "Crazy."

Rowan snorted. "Don't be a fool. Gossip is limited only by one's ability to communicate, be it by mouth, hand or other method." Lifting his glass to his lips, he paused. "So, how long are you going to avoid the specter in the room?"

Ethan's hands spasmed and the bottle he'd claimed fell to the floor, shattering on impact. "Where?" He glanced around wildly. "Where is it? She? It? She's here, isn't she?"

Rowan watched him through those notoriously shrewd, dispassionate eyes. "I haven't seen her since she took off down the hall."

"You said she was here. You said, 'How long are you going to avoid the specter—'"

Rowan interrupted with a sharp look. "It was a question similar to 'How long will you avoid the elephant in the room?'"

With a ragged curse, Ethan picked his way across the glass-strewn floor and back to the bookshelf where he blindly retrieved a third bottle. "And if I'd been an elephant handler traumatized by a crazed elephant, I'd have reacted the same."

"Lucky for us you don't have any elephants in your past."

"It's far more likely there's an elephant—maybe even two—hanging around in my past than there is a woman who can claim with any legitimacy that she's my wife." Ethan pulled the cork free of the new bottle with a sharp *pop*. He took a long draw and coughed, his response as harsh as if the words had been run over a coarse cheese grater. "Trust me."

Isibéal slipped unseen through the doors of the castle. That she could pass through walls of glass and stone, doors of wood and iron, still bothered her. For all that she'd been dead for centuries, she'd been trapped in her own personal hell. This? Moving free in the world? It would take some getting used to.

Wandering across the massive foyer and toward the stairs, attention wandering as she stepped from stone to stone, she didn't see the man in time to keep from passing through him. She shuddered as she emerged, a sick sensation stealing through her middle even as a muffled *whump* had her looking back.

The man she'd passed through had collapsed and now flopped about like a flightless chick cast from its nest too early. The paroxysm he suffered proved severe as he smashed his head against the stone again and again, his arms and legs alternately flailing and stiffening as straight and rigid as an arrow's shaft.

Isibéal moved to kneel at his side. She wanted to help him, to ease whatever pain he suffered, but without a body?

She sat back on her heels.

Useless. I'm entirely useless.

Men rushed to the foyer and headed straight for their felled brother.

Isibéal scrambled away, determined not to touch another soul until she was sure what the consequences were—for *both* parties. Summoning her focus and touching Lachlan…*Ethan*…had cost her mightily, but it was a pain she would gladly pay if only to touch him again. Yet this particular discomfiture proved powerful enough to sway her from any desire to touch any other human being. The consequences were a bit unnerving.

Moving like the wraith she'd become, she climbed the broad flight of stairs that would take her to the guests' quarters in the northern wing.

Ethan's quarters.

She remembered this castle as it had been before her death—stones rough from recent hewing, glass smooth in the windows that had been afforded such luxury, peat smoke already marring the hearths, and what had seemed like miles of hallways.

The stones were smoother now.

Glass, even resplendent stained glass by the most skilled artisans, filled every window and overhead opening.

Hearths were generally cold, replaced by strange flameless stoves.

Yet not everything was different, thank the gods. The floor plan had remained largely the same, from dining hall to observatory to sleeping quarters. She knew these halls. Remembered them. Had spent the last several months rediscovering nooks and crannies all around the castle as she observed Ethan.

Husband.

She couldn't believe she'd laid claim to him in such

a forward, arguably brazen manner, let alone in front of another assassin.

He's mine.

Her heart's objection to her mind's reserved behavior coaxed a smile from her. She'd always had a bit of a problem with what men deemed appropriate for women to say and do. Seemed death hadn't changed that.

Perhaps Ethan would still find that part of her as appealing now as he had done all those years ago. He used to tease her, once even threatening to do away with her dresses and make her wear men's breeches after he found her riding astride her horse, voluminous skirts tucked around her legs. She'd stumped him when she begged him to follow through.

A soft laugh escaped her.

Gods, she had loved that man. That he might not be the same man he'd once been terrified her. Fear didn't change the fact that simply seeing him had elicited from her the same response as in their previous life together. Being in Ethan's presence made Isibéal want to be more, do more, rise to any challenge, fight harder— all the same feelings, emotions and reactions Lachlan had roused in her.

Not all, silly woman.

"Silly woman, indeed," she murmured, pressing the back of one hand to her cheek.

Honesty, then. The other emotions Ethan roused in her were the very same Lachlan had discovered. Longing. Fervor. Lust. Passion.

"Love," she amended for no one save herself. "All based in love."

The emotions were there, regardless. She wanted Ethan as a woman wanted a man. No, not just "a" man.

Her man. For that was who he was, and would always be, to her.

"Husband."

She trailed unfeeling fingers along the stone walls out of habit, pausing when she reached Ethan's door. She heard two voices. One belonged to her husband. The other could only be the large assassin who'd seen her. The latter gave her pause.

She laid a hand on the door and took a deep, unnecessary breath. "No matter what you've heard over the years, Isibéal, no matter that you know bits and pieces of his…Rowan's…history, he's given you no cause to fear him."

That didn't mean her inanimate heart wasn't lodged in her throat. Some physical reactions, it seemed, were unaffected by death's strict parameters.

Tucking a stray strand of hair behind one ear, Isibéal drifted forward, through the door and into Ethan's personal space.

Luck was with her as she found Rowan with his back to her. That allowed her to enter unseen. She'd take whatever boon the gods deemed appropriate, particularly if such resulted in her being able to observe Ethan without fear of discovery.

The men were in a hushed but heated conversation. Like as not, she wouldn't have paid them any mind, would have simply watched Ethan, had she not heard the word *ghost*.

She shifted her attention to her husband, and what was left of her heart seized on his next words.

"I don't care if the woman claims she's my wife any more than I'd care if she claimed she'd once been the patron saint of sheep shit and goat cheese."

Sheep shit and goat cheese? She shook her head, irritated but equally amused. His next words stripped the amusement away in mere seconds.

"She goes, Rowan. She's out of the castle. I won't have her here." He shoved the fingers of one hand through his hair as he lifted the whiskey bottle with the other and took a hearty swig.

"You'd use your magicks to cast her out of this realm without knowing if her claim holds even an ounce of truth?"

"*Our* magicks. It'll take us both, as I'll need you to open a path into the spirit realm. I've more than enough magick to handle casting my...her...*the woman*—" Ethan's eyes narrowed and his body swayed as he leaned into Rowan's space "—out. And I'll say it one more time, since you're obviously deep enough in your cups to no longer make easy sense of the English language. *I'm. Not. Married.* Never have been. Never wanted to be."

Rowan crossed his arms over his chest. "And just what have you got against marriage, then? What is it that scares you? The commitment, I'm guessing."

Isibéal moved around the men and into Rowan's field of view. She knew she had to look a sight with her temper up and her tenuous claim to her magick flaring. Strong emotion fueled her response and afforded her the wherewithal to rein in the wind that swirled around her. Not entirely, though. Her hair crackled and popped and her dress whipped about as her temper brewed.

Ethan carried on, totally unaware of Rowan's raised eyebrows and the cause for the Druid's response.

Her.

"I have no issues with committing but every problem letting the Fates take control when the heart gets involved and logic is replaced with emotion. And to do marriage right, you have to set logic aside. You have to allow yourself to fall. You can only hope the landing doesn't break something critical."

"It's not like falling in love leaves you with broken bones, you gobshite."

"It's not broken bones I was referring to, but rather irreparably mangled hearts." Ethan grinned, but the affectation was so dark as to be disturbing. "Love is for children and fools, Rowan, and I'm neither."

The Druid's shoulders stiffened even as he lowered his arms to his sides in a controlled move. "Tread lightly, darkling, seeing as I, myself was married and yet never counted myself a fool."

"Why don't you talk to your wife, then?" Ethan shot out. Rowan flinched and Ethan's shoulders hunched. "Forget I said that—that was out of line. But know this, Rowan. I'll not 'tread lightly.'" Ethan's lips thinned into a hard line even as his jaw took on a familiar, mutinous set that made Isibéal long to stroke the skin just there. "It's been hundreds of years since you lost your wife and you still suffer with the mangled heart I referred to. You're as dead inside as the incorporeal stalker who's mistaken me for someone who would have *ever* said 'I do' to her or anyone else."

Isibéal fumed at the thought that there would be someone else for her husband. The man she'd known would never, ever have operated with such blinders on, let alone have even joked about forsaking his vows to her, his wife. This man, Ethan, might have been the spitting image of her lost husband, but she wondered if she'd misjudged his character. Worse, had she mistaken his soul for Lachlan's simply because she so desperately wanted it to be so?

She sagged, and Rowan caught her eye with a sharp move of his hand. Glancing up, she met that cold gaze and couldn't help shivering. Then he gave a sharp shake of his head and laid his hand over his heart. Isibéal was lost until he mouthed the word *patience* as Ethan rambled on.

"The only time you'll find me wearing the one suit I own and standing at the end of *any* aisle is right after Easter and Halloween when the grocery stores put the good candy on sale. I take my Toblerone acquisitions seriously, man."

"Ethan." Rowan dragged the name out, clearly a warning.

"Rowan," Ethan mimicked, irreverent as ever. Then he held up his free hand, palm out. "The psycho-stalker came after me. That makes her mine. As such, I reserve the right to have the final word in this. She's to be banished, *dúr, caorach-grámhara duine cac.*"

"And when, exactly, did you pick up the Irish?" Rowan asked quietly.

Ethan paled and shook his head, mouth working silently.

His shock at having spoken the old language fluently didn't settle Isibéal's ire. Ethan had done far too good a job at ensuring she was…what was the common vernacular? Ah, yes. Pissed off. He'd ensured that his words had enflamed her temper and pricked her pride. She knew she should step outside, give herself time and space to settle, but damned if she would. Ethan couldn't be allowed the time necessary to create the banishing spell that would send her away. Permanently. For an unanchored spirit neither belonging to nor claimed by Tír na nÓg or the Shadow Realm, banishing her meant her soul would splinter. *He* would cause it—her—to splinter. The result? She would be little more than a recorded birth and death. She would have no more substance than a dandelion's head blown into the wind by a temperamental child, its fluff carried a thousand different directions by the mercurial wind.

So, yes, while she should have stepped outside and centered herself, should have done whatever it took to subdue her wrath, she didn't. Not even hearing Ethan slip into the Irish and call Rowan a "stupid, sheep-loving shit face" tempered the violence brewing in her.

Ethan could say what he would and call her whatever names soothed his black heart. None of it hurt like his explicit objective. If he thought she would sit around and passively wait, hands folded in her lap like a simpleton, while he gathered the means to *banish* her? He had another think coming.

By the gods, she'd survived this long. She wouldn't give up the fight not only to carry on but also to make her way back to her husband's side because of one imbecile's unencumbered conscience. Even if that man was her husband. For all that she wanted to doubt, she'd seen too much to believe otherwise. Period. If it took her a thousand lifetimes of fighting her way back to him to convince him that that was, in fact, his role? So be it. But there would be more than a little hell to pay for his ridicule.

Isibéal looked at her luminescing hands and basked in the stinging power that traced her nerves. Skills long bound by the grave crackled to life, her long-neglected senses sputtering.

Holding her arms away from her body, she let her power run unchecked for the first time since she'd died. She pulled on her cursed tie to Lugh, the god who had bound her thusly. For the first time she was glad she could summon more power from her tie to the god than what now seemed such a paltry sum at her immediate disposal. She felt him stir, felt his interest in her wrath. So be it. If teaching Ethan a little respect meant she had to draw on the damned god's strengths? She would do it, and without apology.

For if delivering a little retribution would feel good, certainly raining undiluted hell would be grand.

Isibéal raised her hands above her head.

Her hair whipped in an incorporeal wind.

And she called the brimstone and rain.

Chapter 3

Ethan had no idea where the native Irish language had come from when he insulted Rowan. Had no idea why he'd called him a "stupid, sheep-loving shit face," either. It had to have been a fluke. Something he'd heard before. Surely...

Intent on terminating the conversation and getting Rowan out of his rooms, Ethan opened his mouth to speak. And stopped. Gooseflesh decorated his exposed arms as the temperature in his living room dropped from comfortable to for-the-gods'-sakes-someone-light-the-fire cold. His breath condensed on the air, small clouds chugging from between his parted lips. He lifted the whiskey bottle, intent on drowning the last of his urge to argue. A scattering of light caught his attention, and he paused. "What—" he tipped his head toward the door "—is that?"

Rowan turned with great care. "It seems 'that' would be your hag-stalker-ghost-wife. You probably shouldn't leave off the moniker of 'witch,' though. It seems rather relevant. Particularly now that you've pissed her off." He inched around the flashes of pale orange light that cascaded like a Fourth of July sparkler from roughly four feet off the floor. "You're the one who pissed her off, so you're the one responsible for settling her down." He reached the door and slipped out, peeking back around the door frame to deliver his parting shot. "Preferably before she does something like, what was it you so randomly accused me of? Oh. Right. Turning you into a frog. Good luck." He ducked into the hallway then, pulling the heavy door closed with an authoritative boom. A split second later, the iron latch dropped with an ominous *clank*.

"Coward," Ethan called.

Interpreting Rowan's muffled reply proved impossible.

Sure, Ethan could have gone after him, asked the man to repeat himself. He could have argued a bit more. Or he could even have…found one of a thousand more ways in which to avoid the inevitable confrontation with the invisible woman.

He sighed.

Avoidance was no longer an option. Intentional evasion would only allow things to escalate and leave Ethan hiding behind the Druids' proverbial skirts. And Ethan did *not* hide behind anyone's pleats and folds, maxis or minis, round gowns or kilts.

Taking a deep breath, he focused in the general direction he thought the woman stood.

Or did she hover? Crouch? Float? Whatever.

"This is going to be awkward, seeing as I can't—" he gestured at the cascading sparks "—you know, *see* you. So I'll just talk in your general direction and hope for the best."

A book flew from the shelf and careened off his shoulder. "Ow!"

He spun away from the next book only to be pelted across the abdomen with the contents of the slag bucket from the hearth.

Ash billowed around him and created ephemeral clouds, the dark mass ballooning as it was pushed toward the ceiling, driven by an unnaturally pernicious wind. The gritty residue destroyed his white shirt and khaki pants, covered his exposed skin and burned his eyes. Racked with chest-rattling coughs, he covered his mouth and nose as he tried to steal even a single deep breath.

He needed to shut Sparky here down. Now. Her sparkler display had evolved from orange to a deep crimson. Ethan couldn't envision a situation where that could possibly bode well.

Pulling his shirt up over his lower face, he squinted through the worst of the fallout and moved forward. The gritty stuff was everywhere. That wasn't what had his ire up, though. It was the idea that she'd come into *his* space in what had become *his* home and wrecked *his* stuff that thoroughly pissed him off. Not only that, but now there was this monstrous mess to contend with. He coughed, and the ash in his throat seemed to congeal. A second wave of ash rushed over him as the winds stirred with more aggression, whipping against his skin.

Who the hell does this ghost think she is?

Oh. Right.

My wife.

Ethan's temper spiked. He'd reached his limit with this nonsense. Whipping his free hand out, he cupped his palm and made a scooping motion toward the ghost's colorful display. He *felt* her. Felt the shape of her bare feet and ankles. Felt the grave's chill countered by the hum of elemental magick coursing through her form. Felt the electrical charge that made her twitch and jerk in his grip. Felt the slight weight that powerful magick always carried, that touchable, tangible thing. And it was that weight, that substance of understanding, that confirmed she knew what havoc she could wreak and with minimal effort. His acceptance that she had to be sentient forced him to rethink how he approached her.

Forcibly shedding the cobweb-like strands of temper that had woven around him and now clung with what seemed like pernicious intent, he tapped into the last of his tolerance. "I will afford you one chance to control your temper, woman. That chance is now."

The mirror above the fireplace gave an ominous, otherworldly groan, bowed outward and then shattered. Shards bounced off each other, the tinkling sound eerily similar to that of a thousand crystal flutes simultaneously toasting a single event.

"Enough!" he bellowed. Tightening his ethereal hold on her feet, he nearly lost his tenuous control over her when the urge to caress her ankle stole over him. "Magickal manipulation," he spat, "not authentic feelings." A harsh twist of his hand to the right and he pulled her down, anchoring her where she stood. Holding his other arm out parallel to the floor, palm down, Ethan let loose the barriers he kept in place, barriers that held his earth magick at bay so he could live, think, breathe, even just exist without bringing about destruction. He was beyond thinking now, driven to respond. "Rise!"

The stone floor, an extension of the element he controlled, responded by cracking and shattering in such rapid-fire succession his room sounded like a war zone. Rock and mortar heaved and blew apart, only to reform to Ethan's will. He commanded the floor upward, drawing more and more stone to encase the unseen woman where he had pinned her struggling form.

"Bind and hold," Ethan breathed, infusing the word with intent, with elemental magick, as he curled his fingers into his palm. Made a fist. Melded the rock together to form an impenetrable, airtight, inescapable prison created by his will and his element. He wouldn't have her waltz out of here without consequence.

Materials continued to fly toward the column he created, exposing the castle's wooden support beams as the rock adhered to Ethan's orders and reformed, horizontal floor to vertical prison. And then a room appeared below—a classroom by appearances. Its occupants, students and instructor alike, could be seen through the dust. Shouts resounded as the young assassins in training—tyros—scrambled to avoid falling stone and other debris even as they adhered to their instructor's shouted instruction to "Get out!"

The instructor, Niall, was one of the Arcanum. Controller of the element of air, he thrust his hands out and used his element to deflect a large rock that had broken away and careened toward him. The assassin's eyes narrowed and his lips began to move in what was, Ethan assumed, a summoning spell wherein he called his element to heel.

Invisible though it was, the physical barrier the air created could be seen because of the thick dust on this side of the boundary and the clear space surrounding Niall on the other side. The world behind the artificially created wall shifted, papers blowing all about, as Niall commanded the air to lift him straight up and deposit him at Ethan's side.

Cool. The first of the cavalry has arri—

Niall's fist connected with Ethan's jaw. The impact sent him lurching across the wrecked floor, where he slammed into a damaged stone wall. Bracing one hand against the windowsill, he shook his head and tried to clear his muddled thoughts.

Didn't see that *coming.*

His concentration broke and the stones he'd been directing began to fall, creating a deadly shower. Rock ricocheted around him. Chunks large and small plummeted into the room exposed below. Larger stones took out the ancient wooden tables the tyros used as desks as well as the hodgepodge of both archaic and modern lab equipment, the podium Niall had lectured from and the computer that had been open atop it. Niall's computer.

Oops. Again.

Smaller stones, mortar and personal flotsam from Ethan's living room continued to fall through the floor and fill in voids until the classroom below looked as if destruction had rained, and it had been a torrential downpour.

Ethan worked his aching jaw back and forth as he slowly straightened.

Niall crossed arms sleeved with tattoos over his chest. "Ask me why I hit you and I'll do it again."

Normally, Ethan would have poked at Niall simply because the man had a fantastic sense of humor. Today wasn't a normal day.

The door to Ethan's room crashed open in a shower of splinters. The Druid's Elder and the entire Arcanum, some with spouses hot on their heels, crowded the entrance, weapons raised.

For a second, Ethan's heart swelled. They'd come to him believing he'd been in danger, intent on ensuring his well-being and ready to fight beside him or cover his back if the need arose. It floored him to realize he mattered to them, filling a vacancy he hadn't realized existed—an emotional vacuum in him that had craved that sense of belonging and genuine camaraderie.

He was on the verge of blurting out his gratitude, a sentiment that hovered somewhere between wildly emotional and unquestionably fervent, when Dylan shoved forward and glanced around the room.

"What. The. *Hell.*" The leader of the Arcanum, *the* Assassin, gazed around the room and took in the total destruction—from the giant hole in the floor to the classroom below, to the absolute devastation of what had been Ethan's living room. "This castle has stood for well over half a millennium. Eight hundred years, Ethan. Eight. *Hundred.* You've been here…how long? Not even twelve months. Less than a bloody *year!*"

"No need to shout, Dylan." Ethan looked around the room. "I'm pretty clear on what went down, seeing as I was in the middle of it."

"'What went down.'" The Assassin shook his head as he gestured for everyone else to lower their weapons. "What you wrought is more like it."

Rowan wove his way through the crowd. "Where is she?"

"Who?" Dylan asked at the same time Ethan said, "Taken care of."

The icy-eyed assassin closed in. "What did you do to your wife, warlock?"

Before Ethan could formulate an appropriate answer, an ominous rumble sounded.

Every gaze in the room shifted to the heavy stone column that now stood near the hearth.

"Out!" Dylan shouted, and they all dove for the hallway.

Everyone but Ethan. He was on the opposite side of the room and couldn't get across the gaping hole in the floor.

He was exposed. Defenseless.

The columnar tomb he'd created exploded, and like organic shrapnel, stone shot in every direction.

He spun and ducked. Wrapping his arms around his head, he intended to get as low as he could and protect his head.

But a large rock caught him at the base of the skull before he was down.

The last thing he remembered was the floor rushing toward him as darkness crowded out his awareness of both the moment and his concern over the simple truth.

I'm so screwed.

Pain wedded panic and scrambled Isibéal's wits. She wanted to scream but couldn't manage to create a sound under the deluge of pain. Everywhere he touched her, her skin burned and blistered with life's inherent heat. Light equated to life, death to darkness, and light always ate darkness's chilled shadows. The two were ne'er meant to mix. They were disparate things that could not coexist without consequence. For Isibéal, that consequence was immeasurable, mind-shattering pain.

Then the walls to her personal prison were up, solid and unyielding. That was when he finally released her.

She shook violently. Experience with panic told her she would ride this out. There were no other options available. Her knees gave way as she sagged against the stone before slowly sliding to crouch on the tiny floor space. How could Ethan do this to her—reduce her to shreds while he locked her inside another tomb, one his magick built? Centuries she'd spent in a cursed grave and he could do this to her without a second thought? How?

"Trapped." A small sound of despair caught in her throat. "I can't be trapped." She flattened her palms against the walls and fought the constriction in her chest. *Claustrophobia.* It came from spending centuries buried yet fully cognizant, aware of her circumstance and unable to do anything about it.

Beneath the pads of her fingers, magick coursed and pulsed. But it was neither her magick nor any she had intentionally borrowed. This magick had a flavor so familiar she ached to dip her hands into it, to savor the sensory pleasures and memories created and shared when breath had still been necessary. Had she been able to truly experience its strength, it would have smelled earthy and rich. Organic. The taste of green grass would have rolled across the front of her tongue even as the smell of pungent soil, a loamy smell underlaid by the warmth of sunshine on barren rocks, would have tickled her nose.

Lachlan's magick.

Yet there was something there—an undertone of thyme and sage—that created enough difference, enough unfamiliarity, that she was reminded it was *not* Lachlan's power.

It was Ethan's, and he was not truly Lachlan.

She beat at the rock like a madwoman.

Be at ease, a deep male voice whispered through her mind.

"No." Clutching her head, she pressed the heels of her hands to her temples. "You're not welcome here."

Calm yourself, the voice breathed. *Freedom is within reach, yours to claim if you will.*

She held her head as the full-body shakes took over. "Can't."

Isibéal!

It wasn't the command issued in the darkest reaches of her mind any more than it was the fathomless depth of the voice itself. That her name had been shouted was what startled her.

Break the ties that bind, woman. Shed the unnecessary fear. Then, and only then, will your way forward be unfettered. Until you choose to do so? You will be a slave to anyone strong enough to ensure your bondage.

"I am no one's slave, nor do I belong to anyone. That includes you, Lugh." Her upper lip curled. "And I am strong enough to do what needs be done. Stronger than *you*." Funneling all her rage and fury into her fists, she drove them into the wall with unmitigated force. The moment before impact she realized she had an emotional vagabond who had stolen along, piggybacking on her riotous feelings. That letch magnified her power, increased it a hundred—nay, a *thousand*fold. And she was too far gone, too committed to her emotional purge, to cast the unwelcome tagalong aside.

Stone exploded outward as if compelled by a will, and magicks, that far exceeded what she could, in all reality, call her own. But there wasn't time to question. Only act.

Isibéal rushed from the crumbling prison, clearing the wreckage in time to see Ethan whirl away and take a large stone to the back of his head. His entire body fell forward before it went lax like a marionette whose strings were severed. The man landed in a heap and began a slow slide down the sloped floor, heading straight for the gaping hole between this level and the next.

"Ethan!" The man might not be Lachlan in entirety, but there was so little difference between who he was and who he'd been that she couldn't let the warlock go.

If this man were dead, though, he would be with you. We could both have at least some of what we have yearned for—you, your companionship.

That voice. Not hers. And it lied.

"And what of you?" she absently asked the male presence. She began to inch her way around the ledge toward the fallen man.

I seek the truest form of revenge.

The sliver of floor on which she stood rumbled. "And what is revenge's truest form?"

Vengeance.

Ethan slipped several inches in a rush.

She bit back a vile curse.

Angry and terrified as she was, a whole new emotion stole over her, one that trumped what she'd only just called fear. This? *This* was fear. And it demanded she either act or react. Whichever would save her husband from the potentially deadly fall.

"Don't you dare let go, Lachlan Cannavan," she bit out, considering every option that would get her to his side faster.

Lachlan Cannavan.

Her husband's name was a smear across her mind, the caustic acknowledgment so heavy and full that she instinctively cradled the crown of her skull for fear it would crack under the pressure.

Then she realized what she'd done.

She'd named Lachlan in front of Lugh, confirming her husband's return.

Oh, gods, what have I done?

She couldn't have been so stupid as to hand her husband over to the god who believed he'd been betrayed, and damned, by Lachlan.

Ethan slipped another fraction, and she lunged forward, teetering on the unnatural crevice's edge.

She had no time for this, no time to dally with might-have-beens, empty promises made in the heat of the moment and new threats based on a mythology that had been rewritten so many times over the centuries that there was no one still alive who knew the unbiased truth. No one but Lugh and, to a point, Lachlan. She wouldn't allow the god to ruin Lachlan's…Ethan's…best chance at finding his way back to her.

"No," she responded aloud.

The thread between her and the god who had damned her was severed so abruptly that Isibéal collapsed. Throwing out the hand nearest Ethan's body, she strained toward her man, willing the earth to shift with everything she'd ever possessed.

It wasn't enough.

His limp body slid faster as he inched his way toward the floor's edge and a fall that would, at the very least, leave him broken of body. At worst? She couldn't fathom the outcome where she would lose him again. The spell she'd bound their souls to had been released. If they died now, they would move on, though not necessarily together. And she'd just been returned to him. If anything more than the plane of life and death were to separate them? Well, that would be her version of humanity's Purgatory. But if that separation were to last an eternity?

That would be her version of hell.

Driven by a new kind of madness, one that demanded

she save her husband's life, Isibéal launched herself across the expanse.

A spectral hand shot out of the bowels of the damaged classroom. Skeletal fingers widened and smoke roiled around them, leaving a vaporous but inconsequential mist. Snatching Isibéal midflight, the hand encompassed her waist with the speed of a viper's strike. Translucent and yet as solid as the confines of her grave, those bony fingers curled into the soft flesh of her belly. She might have been a ghost, but to this thing she was as tangible, as malleable, as she'd ever been. The hand clamped down. Squeezed. Flexed. Tightened further still.

Something within her torso, something that would have been labeled "Fragile: Handle with Care" if she were still alive, gave with an internal snap.

Excruciating pain scored not only the heart of who she was but also who she had been—child, daughter, wife, friend, witch, lover. It was as if every nuance of life that had ever wounded her—from minor bruises and scrapes to the final and fatal blow that had taken her life—now reoccurred, and she experienced the pain of each one all over again. The reality of the moment transcended everything she thought she'd known about pain across the centuries, from birth to mere moments ago. This, this breath-stealing, heart-stopping, soul-breaking torture that amplified every nerve's response one hundredfold? Everything else was reduced to a precursor to this.

This was pain.

She bucked and flailed, desperate to break free.

Something else snapped.

A sound eerily similar to gale-force winds erupted from lips parted in a scream.

Her lips.

Her scream.

Windows shattered.

Glass rained, creating pinpoints of light that sparkled brilliantly against the inverse sky.

The hand that held Isibéal flexed, relaxed a fraction and then began to withdraw from Ethan's primary room. Though her mind was hazed with pain and her stomach had lodged in her throat, she still made an effort to strike at her bizarre assailant. She didn't want to go anywhere this thing would thrill to take her. Yet nothing she did— fists, kicks, curses—slowed her macabre abductor. She had the strangest sensation of being cradled and crushed, unsure which experience would prove most accurate as she was hauled through the gaping hole in the floor.

She flinched as piles of debris fast approached, not convinced she wouldn't hit them with a firm form. But as she flew through solid materials, she had to accept that whatever physical attributes she'd temporarily assumed when "the hand" snapped pieces of her were now gone, the changes temporary.

The speed of her descent increased.

Isibéal sagged in her captor's grip.

Who would see her through this? Who could intervene on her behalf? The answer was redundant. She had no one. Not really.

She passed through the familiar into the unfamiliar, leaving behind wood and stone and dirt, descending at an ever-increasing speed. Topography changed. Nothing was recognizable any longer, and she was oddly grateful because this new land was terrifying. She moved beyond what human geologists knew and into the birthplace of every mythological tale ever told.

None of it mattered. Not when Isibéal realized what was happening.

"Stop this. I said stop!" she shouted, verbally at first. Then she let the objection rage through her mind. Nothing she said, no threat she made, carried the weight or consequence to slow her abductor's retreat. No magick she possessed was enough to halt this.

Absolute darkness wrapped itself around her. She fought not to panic as memories of being entombed threatened to steal her sanity. She couldn't go back to that, to the silence and unyielding isolation with only her voice to keep her company, not without losing the tenuous hold she had on her sanity. Straining to listen, she heard nothing. There were no voices from the keep. No shouted curses from the god responsible for this mess. No benediction from the gods of light and life. She heard nothing, saw nothing and yet felt everything.

Her struggles renewed and she fought viciously but to no avail.

The hold she had on her sanity, precious and revered, slipped. It was arguably an incremental move, but, for all that, it made her feel as if there were fathoms between the woman she was now and the woman she'd been so long ago. Never had she thought to lose her mind. Never had she considered it to be the remotest of remote possibilities. Isibéal had always been the sound one, the reliable individual, the practical woman. No longer.

Anguish that she had survived so long on the fundamental hope she might see Lachlan again, that she might know his touch even once more or hear him call her name, blew through her like a caustic wind. The emotion scoured her throat. Tipping her head back, she opened her mouth and loosed the most raw, animalistic sound ever to cross a woman's lips.

The cry went on and on until she was jerked upright and set on her feet with more force than finesse.

"By the gods, woman. Enough already." Clothing rustled. "You weren't this difficult the day your soul was bound."

Chest heaving on the tail end of the scream, Isibéal dropped her chin and opened her eyes. Blinked in the small room's low light. She turned in a slow circle, fighting the fiery opposition in her ribs.

So the damage had been real.

Her gaze landed on a man whose appearance was hidden in the room's shadows. Propped as he was in the corner, she was only able to make out the quick flash of his smile.

"Welcome to the Shadow Realm, Isibéal Cannavan."

He leaned against the wall behind him, his face hidden deeper in shadows.

She'd heard his voice, though, and it was enough. Unless judgment had been severe, he would still be far more than fair of face. His beauty would be so undiluted that he would be hard to look upon, a god among mortal men. She didn't need bright light to confirm that he possessed hair that mimicked the complex colors of a fox's pelt and eyes so green that their very existence would challenge the spring grasses to grow brighter or forever look dull in comparison.

His body would be that of a warrior's—honed and hardened. Wide hands. Smooth knuckles. Broad, heavily muscled chest. Gods, he had been lovely to look at, his full lips curling with seductive intent he used to aid powers of persuasion. He'd also been cunning—would still be cunning if centuries in the Shadow Realm hadn't tipped him over the edge from lacking any identifiable conscience to malicious insanity.

She'd learned all this the first time she faced the red-haired, bright-eyed Lugh. That meeting had cemented her preference for blond-haired, blue-eyed men. Rather, *one* such man in particular. *Lachlan.* Beautiful this cast-off god might be, but he would never be more attractive than her husband, nor would Lugh ever overrule Isibéal's all-consuming love for the man she'd pledged her life to. This god, discarded by the heavens for one violent act and cast to hell for subsequent carnage delivered, hadn't understood her sacrifice centuries ago. And she knew time wouldn't have changed his ability to understand or even accept that she would willingly die a thousand painful deaths, suffer century upon century of maddening incarceration, if it meant her husband would live on and find his joy. There was nothing she wouldn't do to secure that payoff.

Lugh startled her when he chose that moment to break the silence. "It is admittedly good to gaze upon your fair face after all this time, witch."

She opened her mouth to speak but had to close it as she cleared her throat and fought to keep her wits about her. Histories, both written and oral, had warned those dealing with Lugh to tread lightly. She had once boldly tromped into the bog of negotiations with gods and mortal men, believing herself capable of managing their trickery. She'd promptly sunk to her neck.

The god shifted enough in the shadow's depth that he regained her attention. "I have a proposition I'd present for your consideration."

"I have no desire for anything but a severance of the ties that bind us," she said evenly. "Let me go."

"Not yet." He rose to his full, impressive height, his head approaching what had to have been a nine-foot-tall ceiling. "I would that you hear me out."

"You would dare to ask me for, what? A favor?"

"I intend to see myself out of this prison and settle

the score that landed me here, but the act of breaking free will require the assistance of one already tied to the mortal plane." The cast-out god dipped his chin. "I would ask for your help, though not as a favor. I'm fully prepared to compensate you for your efforts."

"'Compensate' as if I'm some two-bit floozy whose 'services' you can buy on a whim?" Hands curling into fists, Isibéal shook with unfettered rage. "Should you ask, I would vehemently decline…right before I cursed you to hell."

The smile that had been convivial darkened, Irish-green eyes turning blacker than an ironmonger's tongs. With precise movements, Lugh stepped toward her, the shadows hovering around him like vapor to a hot spring. "Would you like to know what being damned truly looks like, Isibéal? Are you strong enough to see what it is to be cursed to an eternity in the Shadow Realm? Would you like to know what it is to crave the heat of a single taper as one burns with a cold impossible to replicate in any other realm? Would you be able to stomach the truth of damnation, fair lady, and will it upon me again? Aye, again. For I am already there." The subtle threat in his words provided the only warning she received before he dropped the little glamour he'd held as a shield to his vanity.

Hardly an outline of the man she remembered remained. Still tall, he was more cadaverous than brawny, more specter than solid form, and far more nightmare than dream. Semitransparent from head to toe, his skeletal form flickered beneath translucent skin that had taken on a hideous gray color, a color seen in those for whom death was imminent…or had already called. Most of his scalp was revealed, and what hair remained hung in thin, brittle clumps. But the vacancy of his eye sockets, the fathomless pits of misery that were exposed when his skeletal form flickered over the ghastly remains of his human countenance? She dared believe she could close her eyes ever again and see aught but that terror.

Lugh grabbed her wrist before she could move. "Tell me, witch, that you could, in good conscience, damn me to this existence for a crime I did not commit."

"I—" A cry of sheer agony escaped her when he tightened his grip. Cold burned through her where their skin touched, the experience excruciating in its severity.

"I live with this every day, Isibéal. *Every. Day!*" he roared. Looming over her, those vacant eye sockets arrested her attention once again. "Every day," he repeated, this time in little more than a whisper. "For a crime I again assert I did not commit."

He released her, and she stumbled back, clutching her wrist to her breast. "You killed me."

"I did not strike the blow that ended your life."

Isibéal's gaze snapped up and she searched his face, disturbed to find no sign of prevarication. "If not you, then who? For no one else stood at my back."

"And that, my dear woman, is the point of contention, is it not? For how would you have known, how would you have *seen*, if anyone else approached you from behind?"

Chapter 4

Ethan pressed the heels of his hands against his temples in an effort to silence the brutal noise in his head. It was like a band of drug-addled musicians had been released to tear through his gray matter with the goal being total annihilation. Whichever maniac was hammering out the drum fill was doing a hell of a job. The thrash-metal rhythm filled his head until the sound pulsed behind his eyes. He would give anything for silence. *Anything*.

Blinking rapidly as he fought to bring the room into focus, Ethan glanced at the group who hovered around him. "Fifty euro to the man who shuts down the noise," he slurred.

"What noise?" a familiar, feminine voice asked.

"Kenny?"

Kennedy Jefferson, the woman who'd been his best friend for years, moved close enough that her thigh brushed Ethan's bare arm as she settled the covers over him, pulling them up to his chin.

He rolled toward her, craving the comfort and compassion earned through years of friendship. Unfortunately, his stomach opposed. The movement sent it flipping over again and again, bouncing from one side of his belly to the other. Easing onto his back, Ethan closed his eyes. "The noise—it's like amplified drums played by a nine-year-old boy hyped up on gummy bears and Gatorade. And the child has no musical talent. What he *does* have is a hell of a lot of time on his hands. And enthusiasm. Did I mention he's nine? Nine. And he's in my head."

Kayden laughed. "Sorry, mate, but there's neither music nor drummer. We just aren't that posh a place to offer live music to our recovering patients. Budget cuts and all." He winked. "Sure an' ye understand."

Niall clapped his hands before rubbing them together briskly. "Your head's no place for children. I, however, am willing to chase the little criminal out for the money. Hand over the euro and we'll talk. Sure and ye understand this is business and all."

"Doing my best to understand," Ethan said around his thick tongue. "Recovering?"

"How hard did you hit your head, mate?" Kayden moved into view and winced as he looked down at Ethan. "You're in the infirmary. With any luck, your vanity will be preserved and you won't scar."

Infirmary. What was it about the infirmary that made him want to lie down and be tended to?

You're injured, you idiot.

The quick, subconscious answer was true, but his conscious self rejected the idea that a singular truth could serve as such a comprehensive explanation. There was more to his desire to seek out the location of the old infirmary and discover the comfort that lived there—

a bone-deep comfort that superseded anything offered via simple first aid.

There was an answer there, and he intended to find it.

Clearing his throat proved pointless. It was raw and swollen and refused to give any quarter. Regardless, he managed to scratch out a few words. "The infirmary upstairs. Is it still in use?"

"There isn't an infirmary upstairs." Dylan's cold voice and sharp enunciation were unwelcoming at best. "How hard did you hit your head, warlock?"

"Not hard enough to convince myself I'm fond of you," he responded with saccharine sweetness.

Dylan's eyes narrowed. "You try my patience." A slow grin spread over his lower face. "But you're entertaining enough."

Gareth, second in charge of the Arcanum, moved into Ethan's field of view. "Anyone know how to knock this bowsie out just a wee bit longer so we might tend his injuries? You die now and you'll ruin our survival statistics."

Ethan huffed out a semblance of a laugh. "I wouldn't trust you to keep Sea Monkeys alive, Gareth, so hands off my person." Eyes squinted, he flipped the covers back and swung his legs over the side of the bed. The room swam.

I had to choose Sea Monkeys.

His stomach surged, and he swallowed convulsively at the rush of bile that pushed up the back of his throat. The effort wasn't enough, though, and the fraction of control he'd held disappeared. Without his consent, his stomach rejected the little bit of lunch he'd managed to get down before the showdown with the ghost. Someone appeared at his side sans commentary. The figure, male by form and aura, offered a bucket and settled a cold rag on the back of his neck.

Moments later, when Gareth was confident there was nothing left to offer, he sat up. The washrag slipped, but he managed to snag it before it fell out of reach. He wiped his face and then set the rag and can aside with a soft "Sorry. Thanks. Both." He gently shook his head. "You know what I mean."

With the men hovering and shifting to keep an eye on him, Ethan wiggled his way back into bed. The whole third-floor-infirmary thing was still nagging at him. He *knew* there had been another infirmary, but he didn't know how he knew, only that there wasn't a single doubt in his mind that he was right.

He needed irrefutable proof. What he would do with it, he didn't know. He wasn't even sure what difference it would make.

A sharp stabbing sensation deep in both ears made him shout, surge to a sitting position and grab his head.

"Ethan?" Kennedy appeared at his side and slipped an arm around his waist.

Her voice rang in his head, tinny and unnatural. Scooting forward, Ethan swung his legs over the edge of the bed. Every muscle protested and he swore he heard his joints creak. "If I don't start moving, I'm going to freeze in place. I…" He glanced at Kennedy. "I need to get out of here."

The Druid's Elder and Dylan's father, Aylish, stepped into the room and, seeing Ethan sitting there, crossed to him with long, strong steps. "Rowan sent for me."

Ethan scowled at the room in general before his gaze rested on Rowan's. "Thanks, *mate*."

"Seriously, don't mention it." The large warrior didn't smile. "Ever."

Aylish raised a hand between the two men. "Something is happening here, and the puzzle is ours to piece together. Rowan, give me some space." Aylish turned to Ethan. "Warlock, tell me of the infirmary you referred to."

Ethan managed a small shrug. "Not much to tell. I just wondered if it was still used."

Aylish laid his hands on Ethan, one over his heart and one around the back of his neck. Soft but persistent power pushed into him, through him, and rendered him mute as it filled him, searching, seeking.

"Not to worry." Aylish's eyes drifted closed. "This will only take a…" His brow furrowed and then, without warning, he whipped his hands away and stumbled back from Ethan. "Oh, gods."

Ethan couldn't help looking over his shoulder. Nothing there. Spinning with infinite care, he faced the Elder again. "Based on your reaction, I'm going to assume what you found is more significant than an emotional hangnail, bigger than the proverbial bread box and more lethal than Conan over there—" he glared at Rowan "—without his double espresso shots in the morning." He tried to smile—might have—but his lips were so numb he couldn't feel them. When Aylish said nothing, Ethan stood and rolled his shoulders, ignoring the pervasive drumbeat still hammering through his head. "If no one is inclined to tell me what the hell is going on, I'm going to my room, stripping to my unmentionables and catching some z's. This cat's nine lives are shot."

Aylish grabbed Ethan's arm just above the elbow and turned him around. "You won't make light of this, warlock. It impacts each of us on some level."

Ethan started to ask how the cacophony in his head could affect anyone other than him, but the riff grew louder. The drumbeat burrowed deeper, a parasitic sound he couldn't shake. Each note was hammered out before burying itself deep in the center of who he was, into his very psyche.

Panting through the excruciating headache, Ethan bent forward, rested his forearms on his knees and dipped his chin to his chest. "How does it affect... How?"

Aylish stepped closer, gently shushing everyone with a wave of his hand. No magicks but rather absolute authority. "Ethan, you are not as removed from us as you, and we, have believed."

His heart tripped over the hope he'd carried without comment—hope that he might one day find his place and identify that piece of him that was forever absent. That it could be here, in Ireland? In a country that sang through his blood? His heart lurched. Was it possible that there was more to him than his bland history? More than a middle-class American kid who went to college and did everything he'd been expected to do? More than... *this*? *All* of this? Because he wanted to be more. Craved it. Needed it in the worst possible way. He wanted an identity that thrilled and challenged him, a reality that pushed him to be better and do more. When his last breath came, he needed to take it knowing he'd made a marked difference in the world—a difference somehow more significant than the practice of medicine afforded him.

And your stalker? his subconscious whispered. *Where does she play into this?*

Ethan didn't know. Not for sure, anyway. The only thing he knew for certain was this: she had shown up after he arrived at the keep. She'd stayed close to him despite his threats and muttered annoyances. She was somehow bound to this place and, she seemed to believe, to him. Above all this, though, was one disturbing fact that he'd kept to himself, a fact that he hadn't wanted to accept, let alone embrace, but one that could only be ignored to his peril.

Every time his ghost was near, Ethan was more and more sure he recognized the feel of her, the tenor of her presence and, earlier, the touch of her skin to his. This ghost, *his* ghost, resonated through him with this awareness he couldn't describe. It was like she knew something about him—something so intimate and significant and large that mankind had yet to create a word sufficient enough to describe it. Whatever it was, if she spoke it, it would change him on a molecular level and there would be no unknowing the truth she carried. Scary realization, but one that didn't change that he had no clue how she'd come by this *thing*.

There was also a prescient connection between them. Warlock or not, Ethan had never been one to buy into the woo-woo-psychic-connection-third-eye-visionary-master thing. It just wasn't him. Could visions occur?

Yes.

His subconscious answered, swift and decisive.

Whatever.

The thing with the ghost was that his connection to her, almost metaphysical in nature, had been forged without his understanding or consent. Yet, for all that, there was no denying the truth. When she touched him today, when their skin made contact, and when he later touched her, Ethan had experienced the briefest yet most undeniable sense of awareness.

He'd never felt more alive than he had in that split second.

Somehow, somewhere and at some time, this ghost, *his* ghost, had been someone to him.

He shuddered.

More than someone.

She'd been his everything, and he'd lost her.

Isibéal hadn't yet regained complete control of her shaking limbs. She had—finally—been returned to humanity's realm without warning, her soul ripped across planes of existence until up had been down, left had been right and she'd lost all sense of control. Dropped onto the moor, she now rested on her knees, her face angled to the sun hanging low in the western sky. For a moment she pretended she could feel the setting sun's warmth upon her skin, that the warmth seeped into her bones and chased away the chill she thought might never leave her. What she wouldn't give to experience the sun's intensity even once more.

Getting back to the keep needed to be her priority. Rising, she made her way across the turf and through the overlarge front doors, all the while rolling between her fingers the little stone Lugh had given her. Without anything else to occupy her mind, her thoughts raced to the conversation that had precipitated the gift, a conversation she had no idea how to process, let alone assimilate.

She hadn't been able to contain her disbelief when he asserted his innocence in her death. Her derision had irritated him. Badly. He'd clutched his head and walked in a tight circle, muttering the entire time about trust willingly given, life duly earned and vengeance warranted but waylaid. Without warning, he'd swept low, picked up a pebble and, cupping it in his palms, whispered to it a bit…maniacally. Then he'd rounded on Isibéal.

"You trust me no more than I trust you."

"You *killed* me," she nearly shouted.

"I did not." He waved a hand at her, stymying her rebuke. "Regardless, you have access to the world that I no longer have. I'd pay you for your assistance."

"Assistance," she said a bit dumbly.

He'd offered her the small stone. "This is my initial deposit, as it were. Its lifespan is short, as I've little to offer in the way of magicks, but I believe you'll find it sufficient enough that you shall return to me of your own accord to discuss terms."

"Terms?"

Lugh sighed, the sound heavy in the oppressive silence. "You have language skills. Use them."

"Terms. Yours," she said more firmly. "Spell them out."

"Carry the stone with you and hold it when you next face Lachlan."

She'd arched an eyebrow. "Better a pebble in hand than in my slipper, I suppose. And what then? What great boon should I expect that will have me racing back to 'discuss terms' with you?"

"Irreverent chit," Lugh had muttered. Then he'd waved her off with a single word. "Return."

Now, stepping into the great hall, she paused and took in the rocks strewn about and the dust wafting from fractured walls.

The fight...

"Ethan!"

Isibéal sprinted across the floor, up the stairs and down the hall. She didn't hesitate when she reached his chamber door but instead rushed through. The room was so crowded she was forced to twist this way and that to avoid slipping through living flesh and burning alive even as she stripped the body of its life force. It was a complicated dance on a good day, but in a situation like this? It was nearly impossible.

It proved unavoidable that she would brush against several people as she worked her way through the room's occupants. Their resultant complaints ranged from small shivers to sharp comments, all of which were understandable, as well. She didn't begrudge anyone the distaste of her passing touch. The trace of the grave's spindly fingers over living skin reminded even the longest-lived and near-immortal souls that they couldn't deny death's summons.

Still, she pressed forward until she reached the end of the bed.

Ethan sank down at something said by an older man of immense power.

The woman nearest him sat at his side and slipped an arm around his shoulders. "You need to lie down, rest," the dark-haired beauty said softly. "Want some help?"

Isibéal wasn't one to operate on untempered jealousy, but the woman would do well to remove herself lest Isibéal thoroughly lose her temper.

Clutching the fabric of her pockets, the small pebble Lugh had offered pressed against one palm, the force of her grip sure to bruise, Isibéal considered the woman's offer, Ethan's lacking denial and then she bit out her own answer. "No."

Ethan's chin whipped up and he surged to his feet, shedding the woman's supportive arm. "Did you hear that?"

"Hear what?" the elder man asked as he moved closer to Ethan's side.

"Someone just said, 'No.' Not conversational, but—" Ethan's gaze skipped around the room. "It echoed. Not a normal voice. Soft but firm. Familiar."

Isibéal's entire world stopped. Her hands went limp in her skirt pockets. *He heard me.*

All she could manage was to stare at her husband in wonder.

The men shuffled about, looking at each other one at a time.

Rowan's eyes narrowed.

Desperate, she tried again, softer this time. Pleading. "Ethan."

He didn't move. Didn't react. Just waited.

"Ethan," she said, this time with more focus.

Again, nothing.

Digging through the depths of her pocket, she found the small stone caught between stitches. She picked it out and held it tight.

Faith, Isibéal.

Holding her hand over her heart, she looked at her husband and pleaded, "Hear me, Ethan."

He lunged toward her, eyes wild. "There. Again." He spun around. "Tell me you heard her!"

Rowan closed the distance between them. "Elder, I'd ask that you empty the room save for me and the warlock here."

Aylish considered the older Druid and, without comment, strode toward the doorway. Pausing, he looked over his shoulder. "Let's allow these two the time and space to do what needs be done."

Isibéal's stomach plummeted as everyone filed out.

The moment the heavy door shut, Rowan rounded on her. "Your name."

"M-me?" She stepped away from him and the violence he projected.

"Gods save me from fainting females," he muttered.

"I beg your pardon," she said, standing straight. "I

am no—" A small movement caught her attention. She looked over at Ethan, and her heart nearly broke.

Her man, her husband, stood a dozen feet from her, skin gone waxy, full lips parted. He worked through each hard inhale and shook through each tremulous exhale. Knees locked, he clenched his shaking fists at his sides. His shoulders curled forward as if the weight of the world rested on him and him alone. But his eyes... Gods, save her. His *eyes.*

His gaze ricocheted around the room in a frantic manner. "Show yourself," he croaked.

"You truly hear me." Her words were hardly whispered, but he jolted as if she'd screamed.

"I do."

She squeezed the small stone in her palm. Lugh had said it was not a powerful item, so she had no way to know how long it would work, how long she would be able to speak and be heard. She didn't care, because she didn't intend to waste a single moment.

"Lachlan... That is, Ethan..." And for all her good intentions, her throat tightened around the thousand things she wanted, even needed, to tell this man.

Ethan's brow furrowed. "Who *are* you, and why won't you leave me in peace?"

Isibéal looked at Rowan, desperate to find support in some corner, *any* corner, of Ethan's everyday life.

The tall warrior crossed his arms over his chest and spread his feet, waiting.

She'd find no help there. Acknowledging the giant with a sharp nod, she focused again on Ethan. "I would never voluntarily leave you again."

"Again? How can you leave me *again* if you've never left me *before*?"

"I…have. Left you, that is." She clutched the stone harder. "I won't leave you again. I can't."

"Why, damn it!" he shouted, lurching forward.

She leaped aside and he passed her by. His nearness made her fingers twitch with the urge to touch him, but mere inches might as well have been miles between them for all that she could satiate that fierce craving.

"You are my heart," she answered, her tenderness an emotional counterweight to his anger.

"No matter what you seem to think, I don't *know* you. You're a stranger to me. If I were the person you believed me to be—"

"My husband," she interjected.

"If we truly held such intimate ties, wouldn't it make sense that I'd remember you?" He swiveled, following her voice and reaching out with a single hand. "If your claim held any validity, why would you alone retain every shared moment? Why would I not be able to lay claim to even a single memory? Why would you be a total stranger to me? Because I have nothing…woman. Female? My lady?" He snorted, the sound both derisive and self-deprecating. "I don't even know what to call you. Do you have a title? A call sign?"

She chanced a glance at the other assassin.

"A call sign is current vernacular. He wants to know your given name," the man clarified.

She faced Ethan again, closing the distance between them. "I am Isibéal. Isibéal Cannavan."

He gave a terse nod. "Fine."

"I would that you say my name."

"Why?"

"Names have power, and it's within the confines of that power that you will, I believe, recover the memories of your former life."

His lips thinned. "I'm shocked. That doesn't make me stupid. I know names have power."

She fought the urge to grin at the familiar lines irritation still wrought on her husband's face. "Please. Call me by my given name. Just once."

He shook his head as wildly as a bear emerging from a deep, cold lake. "I have no former life. I've never been married. I don't…" Shooting a look at Rowan, he lowered his voice. "When this all started, when you showed up, I tried everything I could think of—scrying, regression therapy, temporary magicks. I even went to Dublin and was hypnotized. I came up empty every time. There's nothing there, no memories for me to reclaim."

"Why try so hard to remember something you don't believe in? Why not just rid yourself of an inconsequential woman?"

He glared. "You felt *real*. But when no one could turn up anything at all?" He shook his head. "You have the wrong man."

"I don't." Her chest ached as if someone had attempted to carve out her heart with a butter knife. That was what this did to her, being so close to him and yet so incredibly far away. "You simply haven't remembered yet. Start here, anew, with me." She fought the urge to reach for him, to find a way to soothe him, but she could no more touch him than she could touch the sun. "Please, Ethan. If I'm no one to you, it will mean naught. Just… call me by name."

He opened his mouth, but no sound emerged. A visible shudder rippled through him, head to toe, and he blew out a hard breath. Lifting his chin, he looked at Rowan. "Stand behind her. It'll take two of us to summon the physical form."

The larger man silently moved into place. "You sure you want to do this?"

"I'll call her forward." Ethan raised a hand, palm facing out. "You know the words?"

"You're *sure*, warlock?" At Ethan's fierce stare, Rowan shook his hands out and raised them to mirror Ethan's. "Aye, I know the words. I'll no' be responsible for the outcome, though."

"Understood." Ethan shifted to align himself better with Rowan.

Isibéal gasped as the sheer weight of magicks rose, pressing against even her incorporeal form. "You needn't do this. Simply say my name and—"

Her husband took one deep breath. Two. And then he called his magick, commanded it, wielded it, bending it to his will. Both men spoke at the same time. Ethan's voice overlaid Rowan's even as each echoed with unfettered strength. *"Ostende mihi verum sui, Isibéal Cannavan. Nec infernum, nec in tempore nec foedera ligabunt te."* *Reveal to me your true self, Isibéal Cannavan. Neither grave nor time nor covenants bind you.*

The men's magicks folded in on each other until they formed a dense stream that flowed first over and then through her. Like a living, sentient thing, that power sparked along each nerve pathway in her body until she was locked in place but vibrating with the magick's force. Her hair crackled. Her skin luminesced. The world came into living color, and for a handful of seconds, Isibéal felt the ground beneath her feet, the chill on the evening air, smelled the peat fire and even the underlying pungent tang of the sea.

Overwhelmed, she closed her eyes and gasped as impressions rolled over her one right after another. There were smells and sensations and familiar comforts she'd not experienced in centuries. What she wouldn't give to turn back time. She would never have taken so much for granted.

"Isibéal." Ethan's voice rang with power. "Isibéal Cannavan."

She slowly opened her eyes and met his blazing gaze. "I am."

He slowly dropped his hands to his sides. The connection was broken then between the men's hands, and the blended magick separated with a sharp crack.

The sound was a tangible whip that lashed through Isibéal's abdomen. Clutching her stomach, she staggered.

Ethan lurched forward, hands outstretched, but it was too little, too late.

She faded out of sight, returned to the miserable existence of a monochromatic world punctuated by bone-crushing cold. But not before she heard him. Two words—the most powerful two words she'd heard since she'd been bound to the grave.

"I remember."

Chapter 5

She'd only been visible a few seconds, but it had been enough. That moment of recognition, the rush of memories that had washed over him, undid him. From her long auburn hair to eyes that flashed an eerie gold before the deceptive hazel settled in, from the slight swell of hip flowing out from such a narrow waist, the elegant column of her neck, slender arms and graceful hands...

I remember.

And he did. Not a brief glimpse into a life he hadn't recalled, but more. No. Ethan remembered everything. From their first meeting as children to their fumbling first kiss as young adults to the day she'd worn a pale gown and adorned herself with a halo of blue forget-me-nots in her hair before she said, "I do." The way the sun had flashed through her hair and colored the long curls with shades of deep red as the steady breeze pushed the mass about, much to her consternation. She'd been naught but a bairn the first time she threatened to shear it off. Then there was the way her magick had come on her at age nine, thrilling her with its first influx of power even as it had terrified her that it was too much for her to control. The way they'd snuck out to meet in O'Mallory's barn, first as friends and, late in life, as lovers. And those memories led him to recall the countless nights spent wrapped in each other's arms, whispering shared wants and wishes and dreams.

Then there was the loving. She had given herself over to him, body and soul, settling for and demanding no less in return. So he'd given it, given all of himself into her keeping, knowing he could trust her as he'd trusted no other.

And then she'd been killed.

Ethan sank to the floor, heart threatening to stop beating even as it tried to break the confines of his chest in order to go after her. But nothing would move. He was stunned by the weight of recollection, rendered immobile by the vivid imagery of a past he could not deny. The most he could do in the present was contemplate his predicament. He had passionately loved the woman he'd glimpsed. He knew it. His heart knew *her*. He wanted to hold her tight and discover her all over again, to reaffirm the connection they'd had all those centuries ago. Yet for all that, his mind couldn't accept the idea that time and fate had seen fit to reunite them in such a macabre manner. His heart, though? Oh, gods, his heart. It shouted at him with every rapid, thunderous beat to seize the moment, grab the girl, steal the happily-ever-after they'd set course for all those years ago…and been denied.

Denied then.

She lost her life far too young.

Denied now.

She's a ghost.

He went to his knees, the snap of impact between flesh and stone unrelieved. His grief was so raw he could hardly breathe through its massive, dense weight. Each inhale rattled and each exhale wheezed. Sharp fist-to-chest thumps did nothing to knock the strangling emotions loose. For a split second, he'd seen her. In only a moment, he'd known her. For lifetimes, he'd loved her.

And now she was gone.

Kneeling where the woman, his *wife*, last stood, he mentally shuffled through the flotsam of time, considering the memories that afforded him a look at the life he'd lived well over five centuries before.

So long ago.

He raised his face, cheeks unashamedly dampened with regret, his attention on the room at large and any flicker of movement he might catch. Lifting his hands, palms up, he pleaded with the gods for the first time in this lifetime. *Let her be here. Let her hear me.* "I married you, Isibéal Cannavan, on the spring equinox in the year 1481."

Silence met his declaration.

"You've been here ever since, haven't you? You never left. Why? Why didn't you move on?" He waited, swallowing around the emotion wedged in his throat. "I know you hear me. Answer me. Please."

More stolid silence.

"I remember you, Isibéal. Everything about you. About us… Iz. I called you Iz." Mind awash in memories, he fought the undertow of a past he didn't recognize as Ethan but one that resonated through the very core of the man he'd been. He couldn't let go of the present lest he end up swallowed by the past. But he couldn't deny the past, either. He didn't understand it, couldn't make sense of it. It was as if he were two separate men with one common tie.

Her.

"We were inseparable. Always. Come back to me. Please." His voice broke on the plea. He didn't care. She needed to hear him, needed to know he remembered, needed to know he couldn't make sense of this without her there beside him. "I'm begging you. Focus. Try to materialize for me. Or talk to me. You don't even have to materialize. I need to hear your voice, Iz." He choked on the emotion wedged in his throat.

Leaning back as he knelt so that his butt rested on his heels, he tilted his face to the ceiling. "I can't help you materialize again," he murmured, despair pouring from him in a quiet, confessional rush. "The summoning spell I just used, the one that calls a spirit forward, only works the first time the magick practitioner calls an entity by name. After that? The cosmos seems to believe the two—summoner and summoned—are at least fundamentally familiar." A small smile pulled at the corners of his mouth. "I guess the cosmos is right, isn't it? We're more than familiar."

He tunneled his fingers through his hair, gripping handfuls at the crown. "I need to know you're still here, Iz. With me. Because I have no way of making you visible again. Give me something. A sign." Nearly rendered mute by all the things he wanted, *needed*, to say, he managed to choke out the most important. "I need to see you again. Hear you." A flash of memory struck—her face above him in the dark of night, a candle the only light to be had, rain pattering the hide over the tall, narrow window. She made love to him, rode his arousal with abandon, loved him, whispered things he didn't quite hear but that resonated like a tuning fork to the soul. He had known she was his everything, but it had been then that he truly understood that life without her would be no life at all. "There's nothing I wouldn't give, nothing I wouldn't do…"

A soft squeak had his chin jerking up, his attention drawn to the nearest window. Condensation coated the wavy, single-pane glass. Slender spectral fingers flashed, there and then gone, as character after character formed until three distinct messages were displayed.

1481
Husband.
Love you.

More damnable emotions welled in Ethan, settling in his chest and making it nearly impossible to draw a single breath. Anxiety wove a heavy thread through the complex tapestry that represented his life so far. The unwelcome filament spread through his ribs, over his shoulders and up the back of his neck, pulling, tightening. He ran a hand around the base of his skull and dug his fingertips into tense muscles. "I…" Shaking his head, he dipped his chin to his chest.

More squeaking on the window didn't make him look up. The lamp she knocked over, however, did the trick.
Lachlan.
Ethan.

"Isibéal." One word, a simple name, had never carried more anguish. Sharp corners of life's adversity that had honed in him cut through anxiety's thread, and the pattern Ethan had long considered his own began to rapidly unravel. Everything he thought he'd known about himself—his past, his present and his future—began to blur as what had been and what was tangled together.

He couldn't pick a single color and identify it, assign it value, save one.

The color red.

Isibéal.

She was the most brilliant ruby, a deep, earthy color he recognized for its strength, passion, loyalty and constancy. And for its love.

Ethan moved to the glass and laid a hand beside her words. Burning cold stole over his skin. And then a smaller handprint appeared beside his, less than a hairbreadth away, the little finger on the phantom print almost touching his little finger. Moving with care, he slid his hand across the glass until his shortest finger lay over the imprint of Isibéal's.

My...wife's.

The familiar presence that had dogged him for months was there again, but the tenor was different, more intimate now as her desperation saturated the air. Or maybe the desperation was his. One thing was for certain: if he had to work through every day with the knowledge that she was right there, within reach, and entirely untouchable, he was going to lose his mind. Probably before Tuesday.

Ethan watched with irritation as the condensation Isibéal had written in slipped away one drop at a time, trailing down the window to first obscure her words and then her handprint. "While this smoke and mirrors stuff is cool, it isn't enough." He breathed as deep as he could and swore, for a second at least, he smelled sunshine on boiled wool. "I need to talk to you again, Iz."

Ethan stared intently at the glass before facing the area he thought she occupied. A small movement in the corner of his eye kept his gaze traveling until he found Rowan standing against the room's door. He'd forgotten the other man in the thrill of magicks accomplished, memories revealed and Isibéal's presence established. "Can you see her?"

Rowan's response translated to a single dip of the chin.

"Can you hear her?"

"I believe she just said she'd 'like some orange juice before I tan your hide.' Or was that 'like some more of you or I'll eat you alive'? Can't be sure. She's talking so fast I can't read her lips." Rowan arched an eyebrow and snorted. "That, Mrs. Cannavan, was as clear as day." He glanced at Ethan. "She flipped me off."

Ethan couldn't help laughing, the release of tension washing through him in an emotional rush. The humor passed like a spring downpour, there and then gone. Shoulders sagging, he leaned against the window casing and crossed his arms. "I need to talk to her. Window frost isn't going to cut it."

"How much do you remember?"

Ethan pressed the heels of his hands to his temples and slowly shook his head. "So much. All of it? At least most of it." He slid down the wall at his back until he sat, knees bent and feet flat on the floor. "I need to talk to her to be sure, though."

Rowan's eyes narrowed. "Explain."

"I'm not sure how."

"Try."

Cool air brushed over his forehead, and Ethan knew she hovered at his side. Listening.

Letting his head fall back, he gently thumped his skull on the stone wall. "I remember her, us, growing up together. I remember days playing by the loch, nights by the campfire telling scary stories. I remember Iz curling up next to me for protection. Gods, I ate that up." He smiled. "She knew it, too. She always seemed to know.

"There was my first magick and then hers, our skills growing in tandem. There was our first kiss," he murmured, closing his eyes, "and the night I proposed to her, thinking to be romantic. Our wedding day...and night.

"Four years we were married, Rowan. Before that? I called her my own for every day I knew her as Lachlan. Marriage only added another level of knowing. Of... intimacy." Ethan couldn't stop the pained, animalistic sound that escaped him.

"And then?" Rowan asked.

Grief and rage and loss warred within him, none more dominant than the other, until revenge settled into the mix. "She was taken from me," Ethan said with cold quiet. "Her life was cut short by Sean, a man who thought it his right to give and take as he saw fit. My brother," Ethan spat even as he clutched his shirt over his heart and pulled. "He... Gods, save me, I saw..."

"Enough," Rowan said gently, not looking at him but, seemingly, at nothing.

Ethan knew better. He looked in the same direction, resented that he couldn't see her, hear her, touch her. Pressing his hand flat over his chest, he bowed his head. "I can't even kill him, seeing as he's probably already dead." He sighed. "I can't remember."

A heavy, male hand landed on his shoulder. "Sean Cannavan was cast out of the Arcanum and shunned by all Druids when I was a wee lad. It was never known why by any of the elders. There's a chance your brother lives, but if he does? He's lost everything, Ethan. Sean was infamously banished. The decree set down by the Elder's Council said he was never to be acknowledged by a Druid again. He was sent into a life of absolute exile, Ethan. Not much you can do that's worse than that."

Ethan smiled, slow and sure. "You've never seen me lose my temper."

"No one's heard from him in centuries. As far as I know, he's presumed dead. How do you intend to avenge someone who's already dead?"

He glanced at Rowan. "Helps to have a friend who sees dead people."

"I won't be responsible for helping you strike out blindly. Only heartache comes from foolishness."

Ethan shot to his feet and gripped Rowan by the biceps, ignoring the man's pointed look. "If she was yours? If you could set to rights your own loss? And if not that, at least deliver some semblance of justice that might, *might*, let you sleep at night?"

Rowan went rigid as he closed his eyes. "Aye, man. I'd do whatever was necessary." Then he looked at Ethan. "*Whatever* was necessary."

"Then you'll understand that I need to borrow your power. I need to talk to her."

The giant Druid's eyebrows shot to his hairline at the same time a cold gust of air blew over Ethan.

He spun toward the disturbance. "Isibéal?"

The window to his right exploded outward and rained glass down the side of the keep, the merry, tinkling sound in direct opposition to the violent war of emotions that raged within him.

Isibéal was gone.

Ethan stared out into the night sky and rested one hand over his heart.

He would find a way to touch her, hold her, save her from an eternity of nothingness and avenge the wrong done her—*them*—if those were the last things he did.

And they very well might be.

* * *

Isibéal raced across the field toward the cliff's edge. She didn't fret about running versus flying. She simply flew. The faster she could put space between herself and Ethan, the better. She needed to think. Had to think. Couldn't think at all.

Why had she never considered what it would cost Ethan to remember? The crush of emotion would be overwhelming to anyone, but when that person had been part of a fated couple? When that person had been handpicked by the gods themselves to see the Druids through a horrible era and had paid for it by losing first his wife and then his life? How could he make it all make sense and stay rational, keep himself focused on the life he'd been given, the second chance, versus the life he'd lived…and lost?

She slowed as she neared the top of the hill. The odds of Ethan accepting the second chance he'd been afforded were heavily weighted by his admission that he now remembered her death.

Murder.

Ethan remembered his older brother striking the blow that had killed his wife.

Sean.

Isibéal tipped her head back and screamed. The sound, equal parts fury and despair, came from the very depths of her and sliced the air to ribbons. It was one thing to lose her life based on her choice to accompany her husband to a fight she'd foreseen. But to have her life cut short by a member of her own family? That was something else altogether.

My life, stolen. And for what?

Rowan had hesitated in repeating Sean's fate, clearly wanting to believe the dark warlock was dead, but the

Druid hadn't been able to convince himself any more than he'd convinced her. Or Ethan.

And with good reason.

Sean, Lachlan's older brother, had defied death more than once. It wasn't that he was hungry for life but rather, power. He'd craved it far more than anyone—even Isibéal—had realized, casting his lot with, and support to, the All Father's grandsons in the very conflict that Lachlan, Sean's younger brother, had been called to mediate.

From the beginning, Sean had been unwilling to listen, posturing and carrying on about Lachlan's inability to see justice through. He'd alleged that, as the gods' own Assassin, Lachlan had lost his ability to differentiate between might and right. Sean had poked at poorly healed emotional wounds even as he provoked short tempers, pushing at both until the conflict erupted. Isibéal had stayed on the periphery until the battle shifted and she'd been caught up in it. Sean had set himself on opposing sides to her since she allied with Lugh, but had he killed her over it? And if so, to what end?

The answer didn't change the outcome. If Ethan went after Sean now, he had no way to know the depths to which his brother might have sunk. The fundamental laws of magick, and this law in particular, couldn't have evolved so much over the centuries as to be untrue. The longer a soul was exposed to the malignancy inherent to black magick, the more warped the soul became. Centuries of recorded histories had proven this to be an irrefutable fact.

Yet every sixty or seventy years, power would entice some greedy individual who possessed intimate ties to magick to attempt to defy the universe's laws. He would dabble in the darker arts, just a touch at first. Then he would go deeper, and deeper still, until the desire to control that which had never been controllable grew unmanageable. He would fall into the bottomless chasm where the temptation of ultimate power lay, whispering lies disguised as promises of grandeur, and he would be consumed by the malignancy that dined on souls.

It was the greatest show of human ego, the belief that the universe bent to mankind's will.

And it was the very path Sean had set upon.

If Ethan pushed the issue, insisted on doing whatever was necessary, by magickal means or other, and faced off with Sean? The universe would reestablish the cosmic balance it demanded at all times and in all things. Nothing given was ever free. The universe would always take something equivalent from the recipient of its gift. This had been the first rule of magick she'd learned as a wee girl at her mother's side. She'd watched the woman she'd cherished above all others work over a healing poultice for Isibéal herself as she was sick with a wicked cough.

Invoking blessings as her mother added her naturals to the steaming water, the woman had moved the small pot off the fire. Placing her hands over the steaming pot, she'd begun to murmur. Isibéal had only caught a few words, as she'd been young enough that her Latin had still been atrocious. What she knew with certainty was that, as her mother's magick grew and expanded, it filled the room and made Isibéal fidgety. She'd been anxious in the knowledge that whatever spell was being cast, it had approached its zenith.

Then her mother had taken her small herb knife and sliced her thumb deep enough that the wound bled freely.

At Isibéal's small sound of despair, the woman's loving gaze had rested on her even as she directed the blood to drip into the iron pot. "Heed this lesson, darling. Nothing is free. If you ask the universe to provide you something, you must be willing to give something in return. This ensures that you will never take more than you are willing to give and that you will always recognize your obligation to maintain balance in the face of the universe's benevolence."

Using her undamaged thumb, she'd wiped Isibéal's tears. "As you grow and your powers increase, it will be your job, little witchling, to ensure that balance is always preserved. The sacrifice one makes must always equal, or exceed, the gain one seeks. Ne'er allow the two to be disparate lest you wish to offend the cosmos. Rest assured she will find the means to rebalance light and dark, thus containing Chaos, and she will be indiscriminate in her choices." She'd winked down at her then. "And I refer to the grand Chaos, not the trouble you stir when you run through the chickens in the yard."

"But…blood?" Isibéal had asked, scrubbing dirty hands over her tearstained face.

"Blood magick is the strongest, darling. It is used when you absolutely must ensure the results."

"Why use it for my cough?"

Her mother had turned away then and begun dipping linen strips in the poultice and setting them to cool in a clay bowl. "Perhaps I'm just a worried mama." When the bowl was full, she'd directed Isibéal to bed and laid strip after strip across her bared chest. Iz had stayed there for hours, her mother entertaining her with stories of the gods and goddesses and their feuds and battles and love stories, as the medicine, and magick, silently worked.

The lesson Isibéal learned that day had stuck with her as she grew, but her mother had never failed to reinforce it every chance she got: the sacrifice one makes must always equal, or exceed, the gain one seeks.

Now, as Isibéal stood at the edge of the cliffs, her incorporeal form indifferent to the ocean breeze or the chill night air, she had to wonder just how sick she'd been as a child.

Blood magick.

The universe was now, and had always been, a blood-thirsty beast, and had demanded its counterbalance in kind when magick was used. Elemental dark magick was the strongest a practitioner could exercise and, consequently, required the strongest counterbalance. Hadn't she proven that herself when she offered both blood and soul in exchange for Lachlan's survival? She'd been a fool, though, failing to stipulate for how long the bargain would last. He'd died violently within a fortnight.

Her sacrifice had been for naught.

The weight of her choice still hung heavy around her neck, an emotional yoke she alone bore. Had her life been sufficient recompense for Lachlan's, he shouldn't have died. Clearly, her life had been of less value than Lachlan's in the grand scheme, since the universe had claimed him as its due despite her best efforts to offer herself in his place.

The truth chafed no less now than it had then, leaving a bitter, familiar and unwelcome aftertaste she'd never been able to overcome.

What could she have offered that would have been enough to spare her husband? If blood magick hadn't been enough then, what options were left her now in the face of his mad insistence he confront her killer? *His own brother.* She struggled through her options, weighing each idea against the next, as she sought to come up with a sufficient bargain she could strike with the universe—a bargain that would spare Ethan the consequences of death revisited. What did she have to offer that she hadn't had before?

Sean.

She stilled.

He was certainly at the heart of the issue.

Sean.

Again, the universe dropped the dark mage's name at her feet. What was she to do with…?

"Sean." Understanding dawned clear and bright. The banished Druid comprised her options, the heart of her plan and, ultimately, the answer. He had ended her life, and that meant he had created a tie between them. Such a tie might allow her to trace to him, to navigate the various planes of existence and root him out. It would take time. Provided she could keep Ethan occupied, she had nothing *but* time.

Help would make the search faster. Yet who to ask? She had no means of communication, save with Rowan and…*Lugh.* She was fair daft! Of course Lugh was the answer!

The thought took shape and became a roughly defined plan that was either sheer brilliance or complete madness. She wasn't sure which, and wasn't sure it mattered. If she was going to navigate the Shadow Realm, she could potentially seek out Lugh, the God of Vengeance…and Reincarnation. She could make her case with him, a case that would see her returned to her body to love Lachlan as she'd been meant to love him.

Forever.

Lugh had been part of the original infrastructure of her plan. She'd bargained with him originally, intending to secure his protection of Lachlan in exchange for her assistance should things get out of control with his accusers, and the god had failed.

You both failed, her conscience amended.

So it would seem they'd ended up bound together in death, the magicks surrounding her agreement with him and her intent to manipulate outcomes having intertwined. She hadn't planned for this, hadn't foreseen the possibility she'd be allied with Lugh for more than a morning, but as far as she could tell, the ties that bound them together were strong. Those ties ran to and from both of them, not from her to him singularly. That gave her so much more leeway, more control in the negotiations than she intended to need. She would keep this short and sweet.

Now she had not only to get herself into the Shadow Realm, but also to find Sean and then Lugh once there. Nothing would suck more than finding herself delivered to the despairing planes devoid of all that lived. She'd heard tales of the ruined souls that populated the realm and the demons who ruled them with dispassionate cruelty. The stories Lachlan had told her around the campfire when they were naught but bairns still haunted her but, perhaps, would also prepare her for that into which she prepared to descend.

She shivered. Never, in all the years of her life—or the centuries she'd been tied to death—had she anticipated she would need to traverse a path that would take her straight to, and through, the Shadow Realm. There were spells, complex magicks and more that would work, but she would require a physical body. To perform the necessary magick without one? Not an option.

Entering the Shadow Realm as a ghost left her entirely dependent on the strength of the tie between her and Lugh. The tie alone would create a path for her to follow to the god himself. But she would be vulnerable to those entities who picked off undesignated souls, particularly the soul catchers who would render her a slave to her captor or worse, a lost soul. Neither was happening.

To get back? She'd follow her heart and seek Ethan here, in this place that was now, and had always been, hers.

Theirs.

Hesitation sang along her limbs. To allow herself to depend on Lugh, a god consigned to the Shadow Realm for acts of violent revenge that often resulted in murder, registered as fundamentally wrong and criminally stupid. She racked her brain, trying desperately to come up with any option that would relieve her dependence on the god's strength and character. Nothing came to her no matter which route she took or which corner she tried to cut.

There was no other choice.

Spreading her arms wide, she began the process of summoning a god.

Chapter 6

"I have to find her, Rowan." Ethan moved to a supply cupboard in the lower level infirmary and shoved a couple of candles, a flashlight and a first-aid kit into a small field pack.

"Bandages aren't going to help you with this, mate."

"If you have something that *will* help, great. If not?" He mashed his pointer finger and thumb together and squeezed. "Shut it."

Over the last hour Ethan had followed the Druid around, prodding him forward in a hunt to discover where Isibéal had gone. Each nook had been empty, every cranny vacant. The woman was nowhere to be found. Yet Ethan was sure she was nearby, swore he felt her like a subtle buzz humming through his veins.

"I've let you drive me about this bloody keep as if I were a mystical gaming hound whose sole responsibility was to hunt down and flush out...well...*souls*." Rowan's big shoulders hunched. "I'd have thought that was help-ful enough to forgo you shushing me right about now."

"It would have been incredibly helpful if we'd found anything or any*one*. We didn't." Ethan tossed a second pack at the larger man. "Fill this up with herbals and such. We're probably going to be forced to summon her. I don't know what it will do to us. Or her. I want sup-plies on hand."

"'We'? I think not." He tossed the pack back. "She broke the damned *castle* the last time you pissed her off, Merlin. You're on your own."

"Don't be a wuss." Ethan fielded the pack and threw it back with uncharacteristic force. "You're the only one who can see her, so, like it or not, you're in this."

"Pack a bloody mirror for her to frost over. Then you can hunt her down and doodle-chat on your own. I've things to do." Rowan made for the door.

Panic and anger drove Ethan to lash out, his magick silently winging across the room. The spell hit the door hard enough that the metal handle rattled. Iron banding warped. Wood swelled and groaned and threatened to splinter. The door bowed outward. When everything stilled, the door was impossible to open, crammed into a casing that was now far too small.

Rowan slowly rounded on Ethan. "Either you open the door, or I will."

"I..." He swallowed hard. "I need your help."

Empty blue eyes sparked and flared with something too close to compassion to have been real. The calcu-lated stare that followed proved far more recognizable. "The proud warlock admits he needs help, does he?"

Ethan sank into the nearest chair, the aged leather creaking as he shifted to rest his forearms on his knees and let his hands and head hang loose. What could he say that would be honest enough to serve as a suitable answer but wouldn't leave him vulnerable and exposed? He couldn't take being laid emotionally bare. Not now. Not as memories from another lifetime hammered against his awareness. Small fissures allowed bits and pieces of a past he couldn't recall to trickle through and he knew that one good hit at the right weak point would leave him drowning in someone else's life. He hadn't chosen this, any of it, and he resented being caught between memories of what had been and what was. And the one thing in all of it he wanted, Isibéal, was beyond his reach.

He curled his fingers into his palms, fighting the urge to strike out, knowing such action was undeniably futile and yet needing the summation of frustration to find an outlet in violence.

Rowan lowered himself onto the exam table to Ethan's right. "If you want this, *her*, bad enough, you'll put your pride aside."

Ethan lifted his head until their gazes locked. "If you think this is about pride, you're not as smart as I thought you were."

"By all means, what is it that bids you hold your tongue if *not* pride?"

"Don't press me on this."

A midnight eyebrow arched with irreverence. "And if not me, who?"

"You're an ass."

"If you're trying to hurt my feelings, try harder."

Jaw clenched, Ethan spoke between gritted teeth. "I'm struggling with my faith. I see her, I remember her and I…" He forced himself to relax. "She matters. I need to know if what I felt then translates to now, but I don't trust the gods to be fair and just in affording me the chance."

The larger man leaned forward at the admission and

gripped the back of Ethan's neck, pulling him forward until their foreheads touched. "You should have said so."

Releasing him, Rowan stood, snatched up the pack and moved to the nearest cupboard. Bottles clinked as he gently set one atop another, muttering to himself about ingredients, bad ideas and potential fail-safes as he went.

"A single admission of foundering faith and suddenly you're jumping on the one-man, find-the-ghost-and-make-her-visible-again bandwagon. Why?" Ethan heard the skepticism in his question, knew it came through loud and clear, but he didn't care. Not really. What it came down to was that Rowan had pushed him to believe and then threatened to leave when he did. The leaving thing didn't sit well with Ethan. Either Rowan was a friend or he wasn't. A man stuck by his friends come hell or high water. If the giant ass wasn't a friend? Fine. His prerogative. But if he was? He should probably add waders and sunburn cream to his pack inventory because the floodwaters were imminent and hell wouldn't be far behind.

Turning away, he grabbed his field pack and tossed in some gauze and medical tape.

"It wasn't the admission that you're struggling with your faith."

The soft-spoken words hit Ethan between the shoulder blades. Chest-crushing panic—that his weaknesses were there for anyone to see, to manipulate, to exploit—threatened to overwhelm him. "Then by all means, what was it?" he squeezed out, twisting so he could see Rowan when he answered.

Broad shoulders shrugged in a jerky motion. "You remembered her."

"That's the foundation of friendship?" He couldn't subdue his surprise. "Between *us*?"

"Apparently." Rowan shoved a bundle of sage in the pack and pulled the cotton rope tight, cinching the top as much as possible.

Ethan considered the bulging pack. "What did you pack?"

"Stuff. A lot of stuff." Rowan hunched his shoulders. "Maybe a little bit of everything. Can't be over-prepared when we're dealing with ghosts and gods and other realms." Looking up, he grinned unexpectedly. "Ought to be a good fight if nothing else."

"You didn't get enough of that with Gareth and his phoenix?"

"Nah. That was just a warm-up. This? Fighting creatures we canna see? That's the good stuff."

"You're sick."

Rowan looked over Ethan's shoulder and out the window. He hiked his shoulders, the shrug stalling out so he looked rather hunchbacked. "Found your ghost."

"What? Isibéal?" Ethan spun and visually searched the dark, rain-lashed but empty field. "Where is she?"

"Seems she's thinking the cliffs are a good place to perform ritual magicks." The Druid's voice was thick with concern. "We can't allow her to perform such magicks without a physical body. She won't be grounded."

"Won't be…" Ethan's stomach pitched. "But she has to be grounded. If she's not, she won't be able to control whatever magick she summons."

"So we discovered in the early nineteenth century—*after* your woman had been dead several hundred years. She won't know, aye?"

Ethan snatched his pack up but didn't have a good grip. His medical goods scattered across the floor. "Son of a—"

Rowan interrupted Ethan's curse. "Seeing as she just cast her circle of protection, I'm thinking you might abandon your bits and bobs and go to her right fast like."

Discarding the pack, Ethan started from the room. The last thing he needed was someone apparently as powerful as Isibéal calling ritual magicks. Isibéal would lack the anchor of earth beneath her feet. She risked being swept away if the magick's current superseded her control. The aether would claim her magick as its own, absorbing it—and her—into the heart of creation magicks. She'd be irretrievable. Lost to him forever when he'd only just found her again.

No way in hell would he allow her to be taken from him.

Never again.

"Hold on, warlock," Rowan called. "Seems she's done whatever she intended to do. A summoning spell, mayhap?"

Ethan skidded to a stop. "What?" he rasped. Bending forward at the waist, he planted his hands on his knees. Fear had driven his heart rate into the stratosphere. He could hardly hear Rowan over the stupid organ's manic *thump-thump-thumping*.

"A man just stepped out of the shadows. They're talking. He looks familiar." Rowan narrowed his eyes. "All the same, I'm not getting a good vibe here, man. Seems to me she wouldn't look so righteously pissed if she was glad to see him." He glanced at Ethan and then toward the cliffs again. "Maybe we should head out there after all."

"Stay. Go. Run. Fetch the girl. Make up your mind."

Rowan shot him a look so bland a hospital could have put it on the menu.

Ethan pushed himself upright and crossed to the window. All he saw was the immediate darkness backed up by the star-filled night sky that hovered over the endless expanse of midnight ocean. He couldn't see her or the man.

Frustration spiked his temper and he slammed his fist into the stone window casing with a curse before he rested his forehead against the cool windowpane. "Even if I go haring off on a 'Save the Girl' mission, what good am I going to do? I can't see her. I can't see the guy she's talking to. I'm literally blind in this." He drove his fist into the wall again but with less fervor this time. "If she needs help, you'll have to go. Help her." And he hated himself for saying it.

"You truly can't see them?"

"No. Smart-assery aside, is the guy threatening her?"

"No. He's posturing, but your woman isn't backing down. Doesn't look intimidated at all, actually. But he's a big guy—probably pushing seven feet. Threads are prime, but definitely in a way that says he sat for sixteenth-century-GQ paintings. Nothing modern about him. In fact, I'd go so far as to say that he looks like Thor when he was in the pub." His brow furrowed. "He does look familiar, though."

"Great. I finally remember I'm married and within hours the king of Asgard pops in to chat up my long-lost, decidedly dead wife." The last word emerged as a prepubescent squeak. Ignoring the churning in his gut—him? Married? Cue testicle shrinkage *now*—Ethan cupped his hands around his eyes to block out extraneous light and pressed the sides of his hands against the windowpane. His gaze roved back and forth repeatedly, but the effort proved entirely pointless. He was as useless as a trombone player in a string quartet. "And of course they look familiar. If you have a Pinterest account, you've seen a meme or twelve featuring the Asgardian king so fair."

Rowan didn't spare him a look. "Pinterest." The monotone enunciation was as damning as if he'd called Ethan out for possessing a used dental floss collection.

"Not now, Conan." Frustrated, Ethan blew out a hard breath. It fogged the window. "Damn it. Tell me what's going on, would you? Do we need to go out there?" Using his sleeved arm, he rubbed the glass clear and looked again. "I can't see sh—azam. Tell me I'm not imaging things. Did he just go from *being* a shadow to being able to *cast* a shadow?" He pressed the sides of his hands harder against the windowpane and willed his eyes to work. *To hell with it.* A quick spell and he was sporting night vision. There were times he believed it was warranted to use magick in a self-serving manner. This was decidedly one of them.

"Your woman doesn't look happy."

"I can't see her—only the guy who looks very Asgardian-lite."

The conversation between Isibéal and the stranger took on an intensity Ethan could sense despite the distance between them. Then he sensed a change in the air as if the stranger was taking a menacing step toward the woman, lording his height and size over her. He loomed.

Oh, hell *no.*

No one loomed over Isibéal.

Ethan grabbed his satchel and slung it over his shoulders, running for the door. "If he touches her, I'm going to let loose with the kind of magick rain—the kind of shizzle that would have given one boy wizard night terrors well into middle age."

Rowan quickly caught up. "Don't think you can out-dark me, warlock."

"If he puts her in harm's way, even if he's the source of harm?" He glanced at the Druid. "Don't think you can out-dark *me*. Period."

They sprinted across the wide foyer and Ethan flung out a hand. Magick lashed from his palm, the pulsing shimmer in time with his furious heartbeat. His will manifest struck the keep's giant wood and metal front doors and they flew open with a thunderous clap that reverberated across the air. Curious and concerned shouts sounded from the nearby tyros.

Much as it galled him to ask for Dylan's help, Ethan shouted to any who could hear, "Send the Assassin to the cliffs. Tell him the warlock needs him."

His step faltered when he realized his heart had forged ahead into territory his mind had yet to go. Isibéal was his wife. While he couldn't quite grasp the magnitude of feelings he had for her, couldn't differentiate between what he'd felt as Lachlan versus what he felt now as Ethan, he recognized he had taken a vow to protect her. And he'd failed. He didn't need to know more than that. His pride had gone before her fall, her *death* at his brother's hand, and he would see that set to rights. Cost and consequence were of no consideration. He would do whatever was necessary to see her safe.

No. Holds. Barred.

Isibéal braced for the blow she anticipated from Lugh. She wouldn't strike until struck, but then? She would hold nothing back and relish the chance to spread her magickal wings after so long.

"Stand down, witch."

"I will…when you afford me the same courtesy."

Lugh looked at her, cocking his head to the side so

much like a curious bird. "You believe it a courtesy not to strike me?"

She didn't answer, merely lifted her chin and held his gaze.

"Tell me why you believe I would afford you the grace of resurrection." He lowered his hand and clasped one wrist with his opposite hand, taking an at-rest position. "Neither your death nor rebirth is of any consequence to me."

"Then you are certainly no longer the God of Vengeance and Resurrection. Tell me, who should I summon in your stead?"

His eyes narrowed. "Tread lightly, mortal."

She arched her eyebrows with transparent insolence. "But I'm not mortal."

He waved her on impatiently.

"You gain strength from vengeance you coordinate, and my rebirth would afford me the opportunity to exact the truest form of revenge."

Curiosity and interest sparked in his gaze. "Do tell."

"Vengeance." The passion in her one-word answer was undeniable, her desire unmistakable.

"And who would you seek vengeance against? You're a woman. Nothing more. Would you seek my assistance to execute your plan or would you hire a witch to make her bobbles and potions and chant a little hex on your behalf?"

"Do not treat me with amusement, Lugh." Isibéal summoned a shimmering ball of energy, cupping it in her palm. Lugh's pupils turned to pinpricks in the bright light. "I am the very witch other *witches* once feared and only sought in desperation."

"Tell me what you know of the day you died."

* * *

Isibéal sucked in a great, burning breath and curled her fingers into the loamy forest floor. The vision had come upon her so suddenly she hadn't been afforded the opportunity to set her gathering basket down. Instead, she'd collapsed where she stood. Now she lay where she'd fallen, raindrops pattering her face and, on occasion, pelting her in one eye or the other as she blinked and sought to reclaim control of her mind and body, to regain focus.

This wasn't the first time she had returned to consciousness with confusion muddling her thoughts. The onerous weight of absolute knowledge and impending acts often fractured her mind, but time would restore the balance of mind and matter that the present demanded as recompense. Divine visions, imminent and unchangeable as such augury oft was, were much like magicks in that they came with a cost.

But time was the one thing she no longer had in abundance.

That meant the cost to intervene in the forthcoming tragedy would have to be paid with immediacy, and pay she would. Gladly. For if she did not, Lachlan Cannavan—the Druid's Assassin as well as her lover, friend, confidant, husband—would die by his brother's sword as the sun reached its zenith.

The thought, and the despair attached to it, had Isibéal surging to her feet. She stumbled about the small clearing as she collected what she would need for the execution of far more than ritual magicks, for she intended to seek an audience with the gods this day. Only they could chart an alternative course that would spare Lachlan's life.

She paid little heed to that which she shoved in her

gathering basket. As such, she started when she sliced her thumb deep on the small blade she habitually carried when she harvested the forest's offerings. Blood welled and she considered it, saw in it an option, mayhap the only option, she would pursue should the gods deny her request.

She would offer herself in turn.

Setting the basket aside, she cast her protective circle and began to summon the elements to her, drawing on their strengths and feeding the same into the aether.

For a brief moment nothing happened. And then everything happened at once. Sound disappeared. The smell of sap and pine and vegetative death faded, replaced by a spicy, aromatic smell she didn't recognize. Pressure around her increased and her ears ached. Her eyes watered. The forest backdrop softened, colors running together until all she saw was an organic wash of indiscernible color.

And from that scrim, her very nemesis had appeared. The man she called a brother through marriage. Her husband's blood brother. Sean Cannavan.

He circled her, a smile teasing the corners of his mouth. "You seem anxious to gain the gods' attention... sister."

She turned with him, always keeping him in sight. "I seek guidance."

"You are my family. What might I do to offer what you seek?"

Squaring her shoulders and standing tall, she didn't look away when she issued her command. "Do not interfere in Lachlan's life, Sean. He is the Assassin and serves the gods."

He laughed, a bitter, foul sound. "And as I am the

*elder, we are all well aware that the title should have
been mine."*

*"What I'm aware of is that you intend to take by de-
ceit and violence what the gods themselves have deemed
you unworthy to possess."*

*He stopped then, rounding on her, face pale, black
lines spider-webbing through the whites of his eyes.
"You will not stop me."*

*"Perhaps not, but I would offer you alternative rec-
ompense."*

*"What could possibly equal the theft of my brother's
life?"*

*Isibéal ignored the sharp pain in her chest. "The of-
fering of mine."*

*Sean's eyes flared so slightly she wondered if she'd
imagined it until he nodded for her to continue.*

*"You seek to hurt him, do you not?" She knew the
answer, did not need to hear it spoken aloud, but she
needed to persuade Sean that her loss would cost Lachlan more than his own death. It was true. But both the
Druidic race and the people of Ireland needed Lachlan's leadership. He was the man the gods had chosen to
carry Ireland through the imminent blight she'd foretold.
"Death is an insult, but it can hurt but for a moment."*

"And you would lay down your life to spare his?"

"I would, provided you gave me your oath."

*"I am not so much the fool that I will make you blind
promises, but you have my attention...sister."*

Centuries had passed since the day the gods allowed
Isibéal to bargain for Lachlan's life. They had not inter-
vened. They could have. She had yet to forgive them for
it and could not stay the bitter memories. But she'd be
damned a thousand times over if she'd recall the worst

of them and lay those at his feet. Yes, she might have been forced to her knees, even prostrated herself as she pleaded with Sean to forgo his grievance, but she would not fall so low again, would *never* humble herself so completely again.

Looking at Lugh now, he obviously believed himself worthy of her submissive pleas. He would think to lord his power over her. What he failed to realize was that she had lost everything and lived with the consequence. There was nothing he could take from her. Not anymore. He could only give, only flesh out her life, quite literally. She had nothing to lose.

As they faced each other now on the cliffs, the sea creating a dark backdrop to the animosity that created their common ground, Isibéal knew she had the distinct advantage. She was no longer the naive and guileless woman who had believed her brother-in-law's claim that "a" death would satisfy the debt his brother's perceived betrayal had created. She had died to satisfy the debt Lachlan's life had been slated to reconcile, and it had not satisfied Sean's need for blood—Lugh's blood. Nothing else would ever do. Proof? Lachlan, too, had died months later despite the bargain struck to allow Isibéal to take her husband's place, and she knew Sean had been present when the killing blow was delivered to Lachlan. She had, after all, been forced to blindly endure the confrontation, hearing every word exchanged, every sword strike, every shout of rage and every grunt of pain that culminated with Sean's killing curse. And all from the pitch-black of the grave to which Sean had bound her.

In the end, what Isibéal knew to be true was this: Sean's lack of honor and subsequent choices had cast Lachlan's lot in that final mortal vignette.

If the god who stood before her now believed that betrayal had not hardened her, if he did not believe she was strong enough to seek—and achieve—retribution for what had been stolen from her? More the fool was he. A body would make it easier, but the lack of a body did not make it impossible.

Lugh shifted to look over the cliffs, the wind carrying his words to her. "You must want vengeance more than you want anything else. It must be the driving force that causes you to rise early every morning and lay your head late every night."

"And what of my other desires?" she contended. Yes, she wanted a corporeal form, but she also wanted, *needed*, Lachlan's love. She was wild for the chance to see a lifetime through with him. Living without knowing what might have been would hardly be an existence and in no way would it constitute a life.

"Your 'other desires' will be second to your need to deliver your revenge. Many believe they have the fortitude necessary to avenge violence done them. Few are strong enough to carry it out." He looked her over. "You're far too dignified in your carriage to make me believe you would slit the man's throat who did you so wrong."

Her bitter laughter preceded her reaching for her power by no more than a single tick of the clock's hand. Power boiled inside her, fueled by her temper's invisible winds so fiercely she swore she felt the flame's heat. She held her hands out in front of her, palms skyward, and let pools of light coalesce as her rage brewed. "I would not slit his throat, Lugh. I would eviscerate him while he was conscious and leave him to consider his entrails as his heart beat its last." Power as bright as molten metal dripped between her splayed fingers and over the sides of her hands. "I have the strength available to make sure he lives long enough to satisfy the desire to extinguish the voice that has haunted me for more than five hundred years." Magick saturated her voice's low, sultry timbre. "And as for dignified behavior? I shall gladly cast it aside, discard every honorable intention I possess, before I approach my transgressor. I will let nothing impede my decision to see Sean Cannavan dead."

Lugh's chin whipped around, his eyes narrow and lips thin. "Sean Cannavan, the Dark Druid, is the man you think to kill?"

"No. It's the liar and deceiver, Sean Cannavan, I *will* kill." She watched Lugh for a moment and then asked, "You know of him?"

"It would seem that the Wheels of Justice have turned in your favor." Lugh faced her fully. "I have a debt to settle with him, as well, and it isn't a minor one."

"What injustice did he deliver upon you?"

Lugh stared at her, unblinking. "The type that only violence done to him personally will satisfy."

"I would see it done." She took a step toward him. "In exchange for the restoration of my physical body."

"We'll see. Come to me in the Shadow Realm."

"Where, specifically, in the Shadow Realm?"

His grin spread, slow and cold. "Prove to me you want your vengeance."

Her brow furrowed. "How?"

"Find me." He shrugged and could not have been any more indifferent. "You have until the sun sets tomorrow. Fail to cross my threshold and you may consider your petition denied. Until then, I will that you be seen and be well." He looked over her shoulder. "It would seem your man approaches."

She curled her fingers over her palms to protect the magicks settled there, magicks that awaited her instruction. Lifting her chin, she would let him strike her. Then? She'd strike him *down*.

Chapter 7

Ethan's magick raced ahead of him, smearing the air as it homed in on its target. Following in its wake, the caustic exhaust choked him, the smell far harsher than the fumes created by burning car tires. Dense. Oily. Dirty. He coughed and gagged as he fought to breathe through what amounted to the equivalent of magickal emissions. Much more of this and he'd need to start carrying his own oxygen tank, tubing and cannula in order to get the pure O2 hit he'd need to clear his lungs.

The time it took him to reach Isibéal—*By the gods, there she was! He could see her again!*—passed far too slowly, as if Ethan wasn't running as hard as he could but rather had come out for a Sunday stroll. He pushed harder, dug deeper—and moved no faster. *What the hell is going on?* The moment he thought it, his mind grew soft, his rationale heavy. He only *thought* he'd been slow before. Now? Now he moved as if he was doing the breaststroke through a vat of cold maple syrup.

That was when the truth struck him. His magick, light or dark, carried an organic smell. Always.

Whatever the source of this power and whomever it belonged to, Ethan didn't—couldn't—own it.

Eyes narrowing, he sought the responsible party. It took mere seconds for him to pick out the man Rowan had spoken of. He stood near Isibéal. Too close. The strangest combination of indifference and animosity rolled off the stranger in waves.

Ethan watched the man lean farther into Isibéal's space and speak, the conversation punctuated with his sharp movements.

Magick swelled through Ethan's arms and legs, casting off the invisible tenterhooks that had kept him from passing through time and space with ease. He was suddenly moving, then moving faster, his magick propelling him forward through, and despite, the brutally condensed air. Time moved at *his* command now. And yet it still felt as if it took forever to reach his...Isibéal. He did, though, arriving with the intent of putting himself between her and the man who thought to aggress her. Dark power's fumes were heaviest here, sullying the air and coating his throat with a nasty residue he couldn't bring himself to swallow.

The stranger looked up and their eyes met for a split second, and everything took on a surreal tone. Ethan traced the last few steps to Isibéal. She was achingly familiar, but he didn't accept that as the grounds for wild, unchecked emotional overload. He'd honor his apparent obligation to protect her, but he needed to consider where he was in the whole feelers department.

"Step. Off." The tone of Ethan's voice was soft. The tenor of his words, however, was not.

We are so *talking about this. "Stranger Danger"*

wasn't a thing in her medieval life. Now? Looking like she does?

He shook his head. *Focus.* "Touch her in *any* manner and I will return to you a hundredfold any damage or distress or discomfort you cause."

"And what if I were to bring her immense pleasure?" the man asked, antagonistic eyes glinting. "What would you return to me then?"

Ethan didn't think. He acted. Reacted. Whatever. Standing one second, the stranger found himself laid out on the grass the next as Ethan shook out his balled-up fist. "I'd forgo magick and instead pull out my trusty medical degree and a scalpel. That's all I'd need to castrate you before I took whatever vengeance she deemed me take. See, here's the thing. I know she wouldn't leave me, wouldn't go with you unless she was under extreme duress. And if you think she'd *ever* take her pleasure with you?" He shook his head even as he took a short step forward and closed the distance between himself and the downed man. Adrenaline sang through him, a siren's song he adored. "For what it's worth, if you'd done something, *anything*, to cause her so much grief she felt compelled to go with you? Your next breath would be cut short and then cut off. Permanently."

"You are naught but a blowhard, an expendable pawn, a talk-a-lot who was born into your first life just waiting for your day of death. It was your lot. You were never destined for anything more," the man said softly. "But in this turn of the wheel, you have a purpose, though I doubt you're patient enough to discover it. If, somehow, you defy my estimation, I still hold you will not be wise enough to use this life wisely."

"I couldn't care less what you think about me or my wisdom." Ethan moved to stand beside Isibéal. "The only thing that matters here is *your* understanding. She's not someone to be used as a bargaining tool or a pawn. Ever. That's nonnegotiable."

"And what if she were to bargain on your behalf?" the bastard pressed.

Isibéal moved to Ethan's side, and he fought the need to pull her close and shelter her. Instead, he made to drop an arm around her shoulders, surprised when she jerked away from his touch and stepped well out of his reach. If she didn't want public displays of affection, even one so minor as touch, he'd let it ride. For now. Relationships were, after all, about compromise. While they might not have a formal relationship right this second, they had a history. Had taken that particular relationship all the way down the aisle.

Sweat bloomed, decorating his brow.

Lowering his voice and leaning toward her, he tried to ignore her flinch at his proximity. He tipped his chin toward her still-glowing palm. "You want to douse the 'double, double, toil and trouble' you've called to hand? It's a little…" *Hot. Sexy. Too close to foreplay.* "Maybe *threatening* is a good word."

Isibéal shivered, dousing her magick before wiping her palms against her skirt.

"I should probably have asked this first, but with all the posturing and chest thumping, we should probably just be glad he and I didn't resort to marking our territory. Who is he? And you weren't really leaving with him, were you?" She didn't say anything, and his chest seized. "Iz? Tell me you weren't—*aren't*—leaving with him."

When Ethan reached for her hand, Isibéal jerked away from him. "You can't…" She stole a quick glance at him. "Please, Ethan. Please don't touch me. Not here."

The way her voice wavered ripped through him. "Why?"

"That's a private discussion." Despair colored her response.

He didn't understand it—any of it—but he'd honor her request. For now, anyway, because there was no denying that he wanted to touch her. Badly. This thing between them had fast developed an undeniable sexual flavor, an organic draw that pulled at him, pulled him *toward* her, and he wanted to know what it meant. Both to them and for them. For *him*. Selfish? Probably. Honest? Absolutely and to a fault.

The stranger had made his way to his feet as they talked and now crossed his arms over his chest, staring down at them. "If you're done, Isibéal, I believe we've an accord."

Ethan ground his teeth and blew through his nose, forcing himself to moderate his tone mentally before letting it loose to play where others could hear. "I thought I made it clear, but I'll say it again in case you struggle with comprehension. There's nothing between you if you coerced her in any way." There. His response had been sensible and articulate. No one could accuse him of not using his words or, as he tended to prefer lately, reacting with fists backed up with, and punctuated by, magick. No one could ever say he wasn't flexible that way.

The red-headed Thor look-alike actually considered his fingernails and buffed first one hand and then the other against his tunic before turning his attention to Iz again.

Ethan knew he'd do well to leave it alone and keep his mouth shut. He'd just never been one to settle for doing *well* when the opportunity to excel presented itself. Inserting himself between the man and Isibéal, he waited until the guy looked at him. "I'm two steps away from breaking out the finger puppets, my friend. What part of 'leave her be' did you not comprehend?"

The guy's pupils ate up his irises until his eyes were entirely black. Leaning forward, he went nose to nose with Ethan and snarled, "Every. Word."

Ethan rocked forward and back just enough to force the other man to move or make physical contact.

He moved.

It was a victory. Small, but still a victory by definition.

He'd defended her, put himself in harm's way for her and would see her protected from a man he inherently knew did not have her best interests at heart. Her.

Isibéal.

Something unfamiliar welled up in Ethan, a force so strong as to be undeniable, so rooted in him as to have been planted, nurtured and grown, that it would become part of him forever. It would be impossible to remove physically, surgically or mystically. This unfamiliar sense of self was disturbingly strange yet inherently familiar, as if a part of himself had lain dormant all his life and, with this woman's absolute faith, had come to life. He was suddenly more than the sum of his parts. He was greater than the finite pieces that made up who he was. These truths, fundamental yet organic, were now exposed.

Ethan considered himself and the man he wanted to be, not only for himself but also for her.

Rowan sidled into view.

Ethan couldn't help experiencing a sense of relief that the somewhat scary Druid was there and for their benefit.

Hand on his sword pommel, Rowan subtly closed the

distance he'd kept between himself and the confrontation. "It has been centuries since you have come to the Arcanum for anything, Lugh. And come to us you have."

"I summoned him," Isibéal said in a subdued voice. She might have answered Rowan, but her mind was clearly on whatever had transpired between her and…

"Wait. *Lugh?*" Ethan nearly shouted. "As in the God of Vengeance and Reincarnation? *That* Lugh?"

Rowan watched Ethan carefully, apparently gauging his temperament, before responding, "One and the same."

"You did not know?" The god arched a single eyebrow. "Are you a simpleton?"

"Sticks and stones and all that shit," Ethan said, waving the god off before looking to the woman who'd been Lachlan's wife. "Any reason you summoned a dark god, Iz?"

"That's a conversation I'd prefer not to have in the open."

Rowan's fingers twitched against his weapon as if they ached to draw it. "Do you expect eavesdroppers, Isibéal?"

She met his gaze but avoided Ethan's. "One can never be too careful, and…" She worried her bottom lip before seeking Ethan's gaze. "It's complicated."

Ethan had no idea how complicated it was, but he had the distinct impression he was about to find out.

Isibéal watched as something achingly familiar washed over Ethan.

The last time I saw this was the day he was inducted as the Assassin.

This was a mantle of power that came with self-awareness and, even more so, self-acceptance. To see it occur here in this, the central location of his power, gave her an immense sense of relief. He might not understand everything that had come to him, but that would likely come with time. Memories would sort themselves out and he would integrate who he'd been then into who he was now.

That he'd also faced Lugh with the clear intention of defending her stroked a very feminine part of her. No, she didn't need to be defended, but that wasn't the point. That he would do so as a matter of honor was what moved her.

She reached for him, aching to stroke his cheek.

Without warning, he stepped into her touch.

Vitality hummed through him and burned the tips of her fingers, forcing her to yank her hand away.

"Isibéal?"

"I…" Swallowing, she fought to find the words to admit she couldn't touch him, couldn't caress him, couldn't be the wife to him she wanted, above all else, to be. "It is not something I can…" She forced herself to square her shoulders and subdue any sign of weakness Lugh might use against her. Or them. "I won't discuss this with an audience. It's something that lies between us and us alone." Isibéal let everything she'd felt for her husband shine in her eyes. "Trust me when I tell you that what you stir in me is definitely between us."

Lugh crossed his arms over his chest and stared down the blade of his nose. "You need not profess that you cannot touch him, Isibéal." When she opened her mouth to volley a response, he shook his head. "I see the denial ripe on your lips, but recognize to whom it is you speak. I know enough of the living and the dead to know what your limitations are."

"Limitations?" The soft, one-word question held

within it a world of anger, a universe of pain. "You know nothing of what this has cost me, Lugh. I vow to the gods of light and life that I will not rest until restitution is made against the one who struck me down with deceit and dishonor."

"Vow to whoever suits you. The heavens are as rife with political machinations as ever. You think the gods would take note of one decidedly deceased witch's plight?" Lugh snorted and shook his head in apparent disdain. "Your best bet is with me, which is why you summoned me in the first place. I've set the terms of our arrangement. Will you allow this man to speak on your behalf and nullify the bargain so important to you that you delved into the fringes of darkness?" He made as if to leave, starting for the cliffs and calling over his shoulder, "Perhaps you do not want it so badly as you alleged you did. I do not spare my greatest gift on those who would either undervalue or squander them."

Isibéal knew better than to allow herself to be manipulated in any way, but the fear his words evoked pressed solidly against her chest. Could this god turn his back on her? Could the others? Would they? Again? Would they leave her to suffer endlessly? Would they deny her the right to avenge a broken blood vow that cost her so much? Nay, that had cost her *everything*? Would they notice her at all? And if they did, would they think to offer her entrance to Tír na nÓg after all this time or would they leave her to carry on, to exist without form or purpose?

She glanced at Ethan and blinked rapidly as the most daunting reality since she'd bargained her life presented itself.

Could I leave him if the gods offered me the chance?

Fear's invisible manacles clamped down on her common sense and tightened.

Her face must have conveyed her distress, because Ethan's brow furrowed and his lips thinned to a hard line across his face. "What's wrong, Isibéal?"

She shook her head and forced what had to be a pathetic attempt at a smile. "Nothing."

He considered her with shrewd eyes, this man who had possessed her heart for centuries, before nodding once. "Another one for private? Fine. For now. But be prepared to spill when we're alone."

Then he turned to Lugh and, without pause, asked the one question Isibéal had hoped to avoid, if not permanently, then at least while they were in a group. There were things she would have said to Ethan first, things she wanted to explain. That option dissolved like salt dropped in boiling water.

"What's your issue with Isibéal?"

The god stared at Isibéal though he answered Ethan. "If she has not told you herself, I must consider that she may not wish you to know."

Ethan bristled. "It's been a rough day. You might want to tread lightly."

Lugh grinned. "Or not."

His dismissiveness stoked her ire all over again. "Mind yourself, Lugh. You are a dark deity, yes, but that does not automatically afford respect."

"Yet you came to me, little witch. Petitioned me. Pleaded for vengeance against the one who agreed to take the payment of your life in lieu of your husband's. I can grant you that vengeance or deny you. *I* am indifferent. You, however, care very much, and that leads me to believe I can carry on as I see fit."

Ethan clutched his head and bent at the waist, wheezing.

"Ethan?" Isibéal rushed to his side only to stop yet again. That she could not offer aid infuriated her. She glanced at Rowan. "Do something. Fetch your healer."

Rowan's eyebrows shot up at her unapologetic impertinence. "He *is* our healer."

"Then fetch *another*," she ground out as she stalked around her husband. "Be at ease, warrior," she murmured.

"Feels like my head is going to explode." The pain was as clear as the shallows of a narrow stream.

Lugh moved closer, and Isibéal fought the urge to stay out of reach. "I could help him, witch. But nothing is free."

"No," she spat. "I agreed to see your vengeance meted out, but I will not beg you for aid. The gods abandoned me before. I do not trust that they, or you as one of their ilk, will bargain with honor. You are as likely to hold to your word as an unanchored ship is to remain in harbor as the tide recedes."

"You make bold accusations and unfounded assumptions," he volleyed.

"And yet you did not deny them."

"Do you truly not trust me to be fair?" he asked, his curiosity evident.

Her laughter was dark and bitter and so caustic it burned her throat. "'Fair' is for fools."

Lugh looked at her then—truly looked at her, saw her—and his facade slipped. What manifested in his gaze rattled her. *Pity.* Visible for a split second, Isibéal found herself unnerved. Never had she been one whom others would justifiably pity. That it might be warranted now had her twisting her hands in her skirts and fighting not to break eye contact with the god. Her skin crawled.

Her eyes burned. She felt compelled to lash out. But to what end?

Before she could react, the moment passed. Lugh resumed the familiar appearance she recognized and attributed to him, one of absolute indifference liberally peppered with unrefined arrogance. When he spoke, however, she knew that what she'd seen had been authentic. "I will honor my initial offer, witch, but the terms do not change. Your hourglass has been set. The sand falls. Whether you choose to seek that which you requested of me is on your shoulders."

"What did she ask for?" Ethan's interruption drew everyone's attention. Still clutching his head, face pinched, he couldn't disguise the strain of simply speaking.

Isibéal froze. For the first time in her life, she was torn between honesty and deception. To tell Ethan what she wanted would be to admit she would hunt his brother down and see him dead by her hand. What if he asked her to forgo her vengeance? She glanced between the god whose help she needed and the man whose love she couldn't live without and answered the only way she could. The only way she would be able to live with herself.

She faced Lugh and said, "We have an accord."

Chapter 8

Isibéal had asked Ethan and Rowan to give her some time to collect her thoughts after Lugh left. Rowan was easy to persuade. Ethan? Not so much. She'd finally insisted he give her the time she asked for or she would simply take it. Somewhere out of sight. He'd begrudgingly stalked off, mumbling about being emotionally besieged and masterfully manipulated.

She'd fought not to laugh.

Now she stood beneath the brilliant night sky at the cliffs' edge. The heavens would be at their brightest in four more days when the moon rose in her full glory. That would have been the ideal time for her to reach for her magick after so many years. She'd once loved to practice under the full moon, had craved the light. Tonight would have been a reminder of who she was. She would have given anything for the tides to roll in under that full moon, higher and decidedly aggressive. They would have created friction between the elements—earth and water, air and water—that she would have fought to tap into as surplus Earth energy.

However, fretting over what she preferred versus what she had at her disposal would be the height of dishonorable behavior. Such would disgrace the goddess Danu, and that Isibéal refused to do. Instead, she'd give thanks for the strength the moon gave, and she'd joyfully bask in both the glow and the power she'd only been able to call forth in memory as she lay trapped in the dark. To have this opportunity again? To practice magick with so few restraints? She had missed this almost as much as she'd missed Ethan. Almost...

Clearing her mind, she began the process of centering herself. It had been centuries since she last practiced this, or any, spell, and there was a good chance she would forget something. It presented a risk, but she couldn't bring herself to temper her desire to reconnect with the earth beneath her, to feel the electrical currents that ran through the soil. She craved the experience of interacting with even a fraction of the aether's immense power and infinite reach.

She knelt on the loamy soil and let her fingers ghost through grass and dirt and root matter. She focused as hard as she could, pouring her sense of self into that connection. A subtle hum reverberated around her, and then the Earth sang. The soft melody swept through Isibéal, reminding her that she wasn't so far removed as she'd feared from her magicks or the elements that fed them. Humbled, Isibéal offered Danu a short but fervent prayer of gratitude.

With her head still bowed, she began to pull the elements to her one at a time. The Earth responded but didn't come as easily as it once had. Isibéal didn't give up. Magick wove through her voice, projected across the air, and the elements—all of the elements—responded to her. Their response struck her as collectively lethargic, as if commanded by a lesser hand than hers. Such a harsh reminder that she was no longer in this world but removed from it, and by more than one simple degree of separation. What she wouldn't give to truly feel the air she called as the wind whirled around her, or the water in the storm clouds that intensified overhead. There were so many things she wanted to experience again. Her ties to the elements would, at least temporarily, feed that void in her, even if only a little bit.

She'd take what was offered and be grateful for it.

The first thing she did was cast a protective circle around her. It would have been better to carve it into the earth with her hands, but that wasn't an option. The circle would serve its purpose as created and keep wandering and malicious magick outside her sphere of power. That was all she needed to accomplish.

Once beginning met end, Isibéal blessed the circle with the most powerful prayer she recalled. A flash of blue light raced around the ring. Nothing would get in and cause her harm so long as she remained in the unbroken circle.

Excitement coursed through her as her heart and mind recalled the magick she tapped into. Arms over her head and palms to the sky, she let that magick loose, the Latin returning to her with far greater ease than she'd expected. *"Ignis terraeque marisque, iubeo singulas respondere mihi. Non recedet nisi in eo Regno animo praecipio tibi me totum. Manum ad ignem aut pedem mare ventis quidem elementa tria. Quarta est terra, et legari potest, non mihi ego faciam terram occupat. Nunc ibo ad Lugh lore, praesidium—"* Fire and earth and air

*and sea, I bid you each answer me. I depart this realm
as naught but a soul, and hereby command you keep
me whole. One hand to fire, one foot to sea, one hand
to wind, elements three. Earth is fourth, her powers be-
queathed, she will ground me should I be seized. I go
now to Lugh of lore, my protection—*

"Stop," a man shouted, thundering over the turf.
"Stop it, Isibéal!"

Magick surged, the electric sting zipping over her as
if her form was tangible. She felt *alive*, and resented anyone who would steal that from her. Whipping around,
she was stunned to see Rowan standing only a few feet
away from her and, thirty yards behind him, Ethan closing in. The former was within arm's reach while the
latter raced toward her, arms and legs pumping as he
continued to bellow at her to stop.

Her heart surged, crested and then, as confusion settled over her, drifted to rest somewhere near the pit of her
stomach. Why would Ethan come after her with such insistence when he couldn't see her? She glanced between
the men. Neither man could have heard her summoning
the elements, although the visual would have sufficed.
Only Rowan had the gift of sight into the spirit realm.
That meant Ethan wasn't running toward her but was,
instead, reacting to Rowan, following Rowan, waiting on
Rowan to tell him what was happening. Until she could
gain a voice again, she and Ethan would be dependent
on others to interpret for her.

That wasn't acceptable.

Her frustration must have translated in some way, because Rowan dropped the satchel he carried and stepped
closer to her. "Don't do it, witch."

She stared at him, unwilling to let go of the thread of
power she controlled.

Magick spun around her, called to her, its siren song leaving her lethargic, her mind foggy, her limbs heavy. She lifted her face to the moon, fisted her hands and punched them into the night sky as she finished the spell. "Anchored in the elements, four."

Wind rushed at and then around her. A second, taller blue flame raced around the circle she'd cast. Lightning illuminated the pregnant storm clouds. Terra firma disappeared. She hung there, suspended in a void. And then the chains that had subtly bound her powers fell away.

Chaos ruled.

Isibéal screamed as the magick she'd thought to harness suddenly shattered, ripping her out of the mortal plane. Skin stretched until it could stretch no more. Then it split. Inhuman sound roared around her and drowned out every thought until her mind was naught but an infernal rush of white noise. Immense pressure threatened to crumple her chest cavity. Bones ached until they gave way with audible creaks and snaps. Every fracture was seasoned with despair before being cataloged with a spike in terror. The spell had been well within her capabilities, but never had accessing her magick cost her so much. Pain had never dictated her behaviors, save the single time she'd touched Ethan. That had been different, excruciating, the misery itself a sentient thing that sought to destroy Isibéal for her impertinence, death seeking to cleave to life. But this? This was a different beasty altogether.

She ground her teeth together until her molars cracked.

Darkness swallowed the light.

Isibéal closed her eyes, unable to focus on anything more than holding herself together, not allowing the aether to pull her into its bottomless abyss and consume her one cell at a time.

She sought the strength to scream, opened her mouth and then...nothing. Everything stopped. No sound assaulted her, though if she could have bled, her ears would have. Skin tears burned even as they began to weave together. Pressure on her physical frame relaxed. The land beneath her feet that had fallen away seconds—minutes? Weeks? Months?—ago now rushed up to greet her, and she landed with a solid *whump*.

Her knees buckled and she collapsed.

Isibéal tried to catalog her injuries, but there were too many. None seemed the type that would steal her existence, though. Probably. She hoped.

A shout of sheer agony followed by a second voice and rumbling laughter stole her attention, and she glanced around.

Sparse, monochromatic gray landscape held no visible life. Leafless, lifeless shrubs were little more than uncollected kindling. Soulless petrified trees were frozen in macabre interpretive patterns, their branches appearing to beseech the heavens to reconsider their eternal damnation.

The gods were silent.

An arctic wind pummeled her back with invisible fists, knocking her forward several steps before screeching across the plain. She turned slowly and, hunched against the cold, took in the mountain range that rose behind her. An anomaly of deep fissures and caves and cracks, it formed an obsidian monstrosity that was nearly impenetrable.

"The Mountains of Rhazi."

It would seem her magick had worked, and well.

She'd made it to the heart of the underworld, the Shadow Realm.

The Mountains of Rhazi housed the Shadow Realm's most egregious offenders from every dimension. She'd hoped like mad to avoid this place, not land on its doorstep. Literally. At the base and nearest her, two massive iron doors were closed, giant skeleton key locks mounted in the center of each door. Each key had to be enormous, and that meant whatever creature handled said keys had to be equal to the task.

Isibéal shuddered.

The one time she'd visited Lugh, the god was confined to a room with black walls that seemed to absorb light and create its own shadows. That she'd never considered he'd been incarcerated inside Rhazi made her feel rather thick.

"No use bemoaning your stupidity, then," she muttered to herself. "Get inside and obtain your next stone so you can prepare Ethan for Lugh's return."

Hyperaware, she strode toward the castle, stopping several feet from the doors. Set to the right of the doorway was a simple and morbidly deceptive well house. The iron bucket hung from a chain, encouraging passersby to scoop up a cool glass of water before carrying on. If rumor held true, the last thing she'd do was set her cast for water here. One sip would suck her into the Well of Souls. There was no known return.

Eyeing the well as if it would spit at her, she approached the doors. A handprint covered the lock and pulsed with a faint purple light. She laid a hand over the lock and spread it as wide as she could to cover as much of the palm print as possible. *"Apertus."* Open.

Nothing happened.

Stretching her hand impossibly wide, she curled her

fingers around the lock's razor-sharp profile, tightening her grip until metal cut into her tender skin. *"Apertus,"* she repeated with more force. *Open.*

The lock clicked, the sound soft, a millisecond before a manacle clapped shut over her wrist. Isibéal bit her cheek and fought not to struggle but instead, to remain silent as the lock clicked again and again, the manacle tightening and pulling her wrist down. Then ominous silence. Isibéal waited. A hard shudder rattled the door, and everything stilled. The entire realm seemed to hold its breath. Then something sharp stabbed deep into the meaty base of the heel of her thumb.

Isibéal gasped. Hand spasming, she yanked violently against the iron cuff.

Nothing.

Beneath her hand, the lock began to vibrate, fine tremors at first that quickly evolved into teeth-clacking abuse.

"Release…me…" she commanded with as much authority as she could muster.

"To-o-o-o-lllllll," something—the door?—groaned. *Toll. It demands recompense for my passage.*

Gritting her teeth, she pressed harder against the spike buried in her hand. "I've no blood to offer as payment. Toll," she amended.

"Bllleeeeeeed," came the same ominous voice.

The pin slipped from Isibéal's hand, and warmth spread down the underside of her forearm to drip off her elbow. A steady *plop-plop-plop* sounded as wet met hard-packed earth.

She *bled*.

The manacle released, slipping into the door, where it was once again invisible.

The doors swung open with a metal-on-metal groan, and she stepped inside.

She had a god to confront.

Chapter 9

Ethan barely suppressed a pained shout when he hit the hard-packed dirt. This sure as hell wasn't Ireland. Not that he'd expected it to be, but as he lay on his back and stared up at the three suns moving across the sky, the implications of what he'd done set in.

He'd followed Isibéal to the Shadow Realm.

Draping one arm over his forehead and resting his other hand on his stomach, Ethan focused on slowing his breathing. "'Go after her,' Rowan said. 'Save her,' Rowan said. And what do I do?" He scrubbed his hands over his face and shouted into his palms, "I jump on that dinghy like it's the freaking Love Boat and say, 'Okay, *mate*!' Like I'm some led-by-the-nose-card-hustler-on-a-busy-New-York-corner and not a respectable warlock!"

A shadow moved over him and he lowered his hands, squinting at…what was that? Far above, something dark coasted across the face of the smallest sun. He blinked and then counted again. There were definitely three pale suns, but damn if they emitted an ounce of warmth. It was colder than a witch's tit. In February. During La Niña. In Canada. If said witch was naked.

He regretted not getting the weather forecast before he left the mortal realm.

The dark thing in the sky dipped its wings left and then right before it passed him by.

Ethan let out a breath he hadn't realized he'd been holding.

Then the thing spread both big-ass wings…and circled back.

Descended.

Was close enough that Ethan saw it cock its head with considered intent.

Slowed before it opened its giant maw of a beak and screeched.

Ethan slapped his hands over his ears and sat up, spine tight, nerves firing. He performed a quick systems evaluation. *Heart's beating?* Check. *Breathing?* Check. *Bruises?* He flexed his muscle groups. *Ow-damn-it-ow.* Check and double check. *Broken bones?* He bent knees and elbows and didn't discover anything concerning. Wasn't that a miracle, given the stop-drop-roll…and roll…and roll landing he'd pulled moments before?

He took a deep breath and groaned. *Wind knocked out of me?* Check.

With the precision and grace of a geriatric gerbil who'd spent too many years running and getting nowhere on that sadistic wheel, Ethan stood, back hunched and hands planted on his knees.

Above him, the unidentified being squawked again, closer this time.

Ethan considered his odds as he started toward the

mountain at a rapid walk. Between him and his goal lay a marginally populated petrified forest, the tall trees a shade of gray he'd never seen on anything but a corpse. From thick trunks came gnarled branches that spread out and up like thorn-covered tentacles intent on spearing the sky. A wide path cleaved the forest down the middle and would deposit a traveler at the base of the giant doors that led into the mountain. Ethan thought he could make it if he ran straight out, but if his sky stalker proved to be a carnivorous predator? Ethan became prey, a meal that might not be fast enough to get away. Then there was the matter of the doors themselves. He'd have to open them. Otherwise, the adrenaline he'd expend getting there was little more than meat tenderizer.

His other option was to go slower, winding his way through the wide-set maze of trees standing between him and the mountain's entrance. If that *thing*—part raptor, part pterodactyl, part demon…raptodactylmon?— wanted a piece, or all, of him, it would be hard-pressed to snatch him out of the petrified forest without impaling itself on those thorny branches. No, the thing would have to land and come after him on foot. And given that it had the body of a rhino supported by the spindly legs of a chicken, Ethan's odds would go up if that thing came down. But in the open? The raptodactylmon had the advantage.

Wrapped up in gauging the distance into the Forest of Dead Things, Ethan didn't consciously process the whistling rush of air closing in on him. Thank the gods for his hindbrain. It registered the sound as "screw fight, take flight" and kicked his body into overdrive without a backward glance.

He sprinted for the maze of trees, arms and legs pumping. Wings flapped behind him. A massive backwash of air slammed into Ethan's back and propelled him forward so hard he stumbled. His knees hit the ground first, hands second. He kept moving, scrambling forward like a scuttling ape, ducking behind the first large stump he reached.

Shrieks of rage stirred up a small dust storm. Trees cracked and fell, one landing a foot to his left and breaking. Any piece of that trunk was heavy enough to have turned him into a pancake. He hadn't considered what the risk of falling trees might mean for him if he was caught up in what could become a domino effect. His survivability would be no better than that of a snow globe on a hockey rink during Cup playoffs. Sweat broke out along his upper lip, cold and clammy, winding around to dot the nape of his neck. Whatever had chased him to this point wasn't interested in a cuddle and clearly had no intent of relinquishing its claim to his meaty parts.

"Fee-fi-fo-fum," he whispered. "I'm a giant drumstick on the run."

The winged beast moved left and then right, presumably looking for a way into the forest. A susurrous sound, like its wings dragging the dirt, made the hair on Ethan's body stand up. Then that thing issued another deafening protest, its fetid breath washing over Ethan and choking him.

"Tic Tacs. They're a thing," he said softly, his humor, as always, his sanity's anchor. Peering around the edge of his shelter, he saw the *thing* and wished like hell he hadn't looked.

The demonic, batlike creature—all twenty feet of black, leathery body, beak full of razor-sharp teeth and wicked claws that made Jurassic Park's primary velociraptor look like she'd just received a socialite's Pom-Pom

Pretty Pink stubby manicure—paced the forest's edge. It scented Ethan and called its displeasure to the sky.

The sound shifted to something like a bark, and its pacing grew agitated as it bobbed its head and spread its wings low, posturing.

Ethan glanced at the sky, blinked, shook his head and then blinked again. "No. No, no, no. This is *not* happening."

On the horizon, two more of these M. Night Shyamalan nightmares were fast approaching.

Cupping his hands in front of him, he began to chant, calling on the power held in the Earth's ley lines to co-alesce in his palms. He was going to stun the shit out of this thing and get on his way.

But nothing happened.

That was when it hit him. His element was Earth. As in…*Earth*. And Earth this wasn't.

Ethan was powerless in a realm of raptodactylmons and more. Much worse.

That decided it.

He was going to retrieve his wife and haul nine kinds of ass. Final destination? The human realm. He cringed. Maybe "Final Destination" was—definitely—the wrong way to approach this. Land of the living? Not much better. He'd settle with arguing with her about her travel choices when they survived this cross-breeding-that-defied-common-sense, made-for-HBO-After-Dark-horror-fest of a realm.

Yep. That worked.

Grabbing a decent chunk of wood, he hurled it to-ward a dark mark on a tree trunk roughly twenty yards away. The piece rattled through dead limbs before it hit its intended target with a decided *thwack* and fell to the ground.

The raptodactylmon jerked around at the noise and then vulture-hopped toward it, issuing a clicking sound as it went. The demonic animal—demonimal?—shoved its scaly head into the thicket and chuffed, turning this way and that as it sought out the source of the sound.

He kept low, backing away several paces. Then he spun on the balls of his feet to dart through the trees. "When I get back, I am *so* getting a T-shirt that says 'Cornhole Saved My Life.'"

The forest ended abruptly. Ethan stopped, looked back and realized the raptodactylmon had found where he'd been and was sniffing like some demonic blood-hound, trying to pick up its prey's scent. No way was he waiting until *that* happened to make his break for the doors.

Heart pounding out a heavy-metal beat, he kicked off, refusing to look back as he ran across the open expanse as hard as he could, his focus on those giant metal doors.

The raptodactylmon barked once more, but this time its pack—herd? flock? gaggle?—was close enough to respond in kind.

Ethan's heart jackhammered against his sternum as visions of being ripped apart filled his head. Glancing over his shoulder, he realized the possibility had obtained probability. The three creatures were all on the ground and doing the shuffle-hop toward him.

A quick look left and right confirmed he was out of options. It was get through the doors or make Isibéal a widow. He slammed his hand down on the faint, palm-shaped outline. A manacle appeared, clasped his wrist and tightened with brutal force. The bones in his wrist ground together. His vision wavered as an unsolicited memory surged forward, dragging with this horrifying emotional refuse he wasn't at all prepared to confront, let alone own.

But it was his.

Lachlan stood over Isibéal, considering her fine form. She'd dressed, or her maids had dressed her, in the blue gown. His favorite. It suited the woman if not the event. The color was too light, that of spring skies that promised a new season of growth and inherent hope.

He hated it, that particular color blue, and would ban fabrics bearing that color from being used in any project commissioned within the keep or the village forevermore.

A hand rested on his elbow. He jerked away. "You take your life in your hands. Do not touch me."

"Yes, Assassin." *The man stepped away, creating space.* "The villagers are here as well as many who traveled far on the news..." *He swallowed loudly enough Lachlan heard him.* "We open the doors soon, my lord."

Footsteps sounded as his secretary left the room.

Lachlan waited for some soft comment from Isibéal, some remark regarding the pomp displayed for such a morbid occasion.

Silence ruled, heavy and oppressive, stealing his ability to draw a fair breath.

He took her hand and laced their fingers together, her fine, pale skin so markedly different than the coarse callousness of his own. Releasing her, he stepped back, drew his dagger and sliced his palm deep enough the wound bled freely. Lachlan dropped to one knee and bowed his head. "I would swear this to you, mo shíorghrá, *for my eternal love you are. There is naught that will come between us, be it circumstance or distance, nay, even time. You are* a thaisce, *my true treasure. Aye, I know you've more than once protested you're more pence than pound, but I would argue to the end of all days. You are more precious than all the gold and silver, gemstones and pearls. There is no price sufficient."* He stood, stepped forward and rested his bloody hand over her heart. *"And so I make this vow. There is no place in all the realms where he, the coward who wrought this upon us, can hide. My word is my covenant, my sword my vengeance. This is not over, will* never *be over, so long as he draws a breath."*

Chest heaving, Lachlan forced himself to break contact with Isibéal. Then he turned to the men manning the doors of the Great Hall, those stalwart men of the Arcanum who had served him for more than a century and grieved with him now. *"Open the doors."*

Before they could execute his order, Lachlan strode from the room and left his life, his heart and the bloody mark of a promise made there on the funeral pyre that would, per custom, be lit come nightfall.

He would not bear witness to it, would not be here, for he had a promise to keep. He would ride this night to kill the individual responsible for this, see the coward's head on a pike and his heart ripped from his chest for what he'd cost Lachlan. And even that wouldn't be enough. Nothing would be enough. For there was no returning to him that which had been stolen.

His heart.

His humanity.

His purpose.

Lachlan made it to the courtyard before grief overtook him, driving him to his knees. He fought it no more, instead throwing back his head as agony consumed him on a keening wail.

His wife, Isibéal Cannavan, was dead.

A spike pierced deep into the fleshy part of Ethan's

hand. He didn't register the pain. Couldn't. For what he felt now was nothing compared to what he'd experienced then when he lost his reason for being—the day Lugh made him a widower.

The doors to the mountain swung open and he staggered inside, all thoughts of the creatures behind him gone. With a vicious groan, the doors closed and darkness, blessed and appropriate darkness, consumed him.

Isibéal crossed her arms over her chest and stared down at what could only be madness. "I'm *not* lying with you, Lugh."

"I've an ache all about me, Lady Isibéal." He peeked under his arm. "Won't you offer me ease?"

"What I'm here to offer is help, and not of the physical kind, you letch." She only crossed her arms over her chest when Lugh sprang to his feet and dusted himself off.

He considered her before dropping his glamour, his true appearance flashing back and forth over his face and body. "You don't flinch at what must be a mightily offensive sight."

She shrugged. "You are what you are." Pushing herself off the wall, she moved closer. "Now, I'm here to negotiate. If you intend nothing more but wasting my time with egregious flirtations, I'll see myself out."

Dull eyes sparked and then went flat. "And just where would you go, lass?"

"To the mortal realm." Posing it as a statement rather than a question proved harder than anticipated. "Where else?"

"And how would you get there?" Lugh began pacing back and forth across the tiny room.

"I'd…go." Her brow furrowed. "Cast the spell to return myself."

Lugh paused and turned his focus on her. "And if I told you that what few magicks you possessed, no matter that they were indeed returning to you against all odds, were useless to you here?"

I didn't consider… She raised her hands, centered herself and called on the energy seated in her soul. Called again and again until her fingertips turned an even paler shade. There was no response, no awareness of anything but the empty space her magick had always resided. *Oh, gods. What have I done?*

"You have no anchor for your magick, Isibéal. You aren't grounded." The cast-off god cocked his head and narrowed his eyes, a grim smile spreading over his face. "And now there's no one to call you back to the human realm."

"What do you mean, 'and now'?" She rubbed her brow. Headaches. She'd never appreciated the fact that she ceased to suffer from headaches when… "Why do I… *How* is it possible I have a headache?" she demanded.

Lugh shifted his gaze to hers and grinned with wicked satisfaction. "Three…two…one…"

The handle-free door to Lugh's small cell crashed in, and a flurry of fists erupted. Isibéal couldn't make out what was happening, only knew that the sounds of fists striking flesh and the occasional pained grunt assured her this was very real. Inching away from the fight, she started for the door only to stop when Lugh hit the floor. Time took on a comically slow pace as several things registered at once.

Fight.

Blood.

Rage.

Ethan.

Lugh rolled out from under Ethan and lurched to his feet. "Back off, warlock."

"I'm going to kill you, you son of a bitch," Ethan said, spitting at the god's feet.

"You would dare talk this way to the one man who can provide you with your greatest desire?" Lugh's taunt was lost to his hiss of pain as his bleeding lip split wider. A dark bruise bloomed along his jaw.

"You killed my wife," Ethan said, low and slow, his control absolute. "Seeing as you robbed us of a lifetime together, I'd say that makes you the purveyor of our problems, not the fairy godmother to bop in and start granting wishes. Unless you can somehow manage to undo her death and give her back to me? Screw. You." He charged Lugh again in a flurry of fists.

Lugh took the first hit and shoved his palm against Ethan's sternum. *"Fugite!"* *Fly.*

Ethan was thrown across the room, his back slamming into the opposite wall.

"Habere!" Lugh snarled. *Hold.*

Ethan's arms and legs stretched wide and to the point of visible pain, splayed out, as immobile as if he'd been pinned at both wrists and ankles. "Still a coward, Lugh, God of..." Ethan's eyes narrowed as he panted, though whether it was with pain or exertion or both, Isibéal wasn't sure. His lips curled into a vicious snarl. "Nothing. Daghda stripped you of your godhood. That makes you the God of Nothing."

"I thought you said magick didn't work in this realm," Isibéal snapped.

"I said it was *your* magick that wouldn't work in this realm, darling. Mine works just fine."

"She's not...your darling," Ethan ground out, struggling against the invisible ties that bound him.

Lugh spared the man a brief glance before focusing on Isibéal once more. "Jealousy isn't a good look for him. I suppose the puce color could also be lack of oxygen. Hanging that way is a real trial for the lungs."

Isibéal stormed up to Lugh and shoved the god hard enough to send him stumbling away. "Release him," she commanded.

Lugh dragged his forearm over his mouth as he watched her through glittering eyes. "I won't." When she opened her mouth to protest, his attention shifted from the suspended warlock to her. "I. *Won't*," he repeated with vehemence. "You, I believe, will hear me out. He?" Lugh tipped his head absently toward Ethan though his eyes never left her. "He is as bloodthirsty and driven by vengeance as he ever was. For anyone to receive the gift of reincarnation is to be given a second chance, to have the opportunity to transcend your past and evolve into a better person."

Then he did look at the warlock, eyes conveying a temper barely held in check. "At least it's *supposed* to be. The Druid here has yet to believe that he, like all others who have come before him and will come after him, is subject to Gwynfid. He must accept that he will die and be reborn until he achieves enlightenment, sheds the confines of the physical world and can enter the afterlife as an enlightened soul. Until then, the cycle of life and death and rebirth will repeat until the soul either achieves its grace or is damned for its darkness." He shook his head and huffed out a derogatory sound. "The idea of you as enlightened, Cannavan— or Kemp, I suppose—makes my head spin as if I've been in the mead."

Isibéal stepped between the two men and drew Lugh's attention. There were hundreds of things she wanted to know, but one question topped them all. "What did you mean you could provide Ethan with his greatest desire?"

Lugh shrugged, the movement short, sharp. "It matters not. I won't be attacked with fists and dishonored by a thoughtless mouth when both are operated by the same brain, no matter how small." He snorted and then winced, laying a finger along each side of his nose. "You broke my nose, warlock."

"You broke my heart, broke *me*," he rasped in return, his shoulders curled forward so every breath was labored. "You killed the man who dishonored you and your wife. Tell me how what I did is any different when you *killed* my *wife*." When Lugh didn't respond, Ethan lifted his chin, forced his shoulders back and shouted, "Tell me!"

"I did not kill Isibéal."

Ethan's chin and shoulders had fallen forward again, so his response was a harsh rasp. "I saw you—saw what you did."

"You saw what you were meant to see, and you did not question it at all, did not even attempt to seek the truth. You failed in your responsibility to ensure that justice was delivered. You judged me guilty and took my life, damning me to this immortal hell. For that alone, I'll have your head."

Isibéal watched as her hand tightened into a fist and struck out of its own volition, connecting with the fallen god's already bruised jaw with a dull but solid *whump*. "You do not disrespect his intelligence any more than you downplay the fact that you cost me my life. Whether you swung the blade or not, I am beyond certain that you were the reason this came to pass."

Lugh slowly wiggled his jaw back and forth. "This

all began when my wife was unfaithful to me with the demigod Cermait. You believe that I am somehow accountable for her actions?"

"Did you not hold Cermait accountable for the exact same thing—your wife's choices?" she countered.

"No," Lugh said, his tone bitter enough to taint the air and as close to a death warrant as she ever wanted to hear. "I held *him* accountable for *his* actions. She paid for hers before I faced Cermait."

Isibéal considered Lugh warily. "How?"

"Do you know her name? Recall her place in our written records?"

"No." She paled as the blood left her face in a rush. "You struck her from history."

"I cursed her to ne'er be remembered, neither her good deeds nor bad. Only her infidelity."

"But you spared her from being named in the history books," Isibéal countered. "Why not name her as you did Cermait?"

He shrugged. "I loved her."

Ethan wheezed. "A...little help...Iz."

She stepped closer to Lugh. "Let him down. I have suffered without him for centuries, existed in silence, been forced to listen to the sounds of an everyday life that was forever out of reach. And for what? Faithfulness? Loyalty? Love? Surely if you saw fit to cause this strife over your wife's betrayal, you'd now see fit to end it in the name of loyalty. For what is loyalty if not the actions of a wife who loved her husband enough to die in his place?"

Lugh's jaw locked, muscles and tendons in his neck standing out. "Your petition is heartfelt and sound. However, I find I'm indifferent where he's concerned. I would be just as well served if I left him to hang and rot and called him art."

Her mind spun and came to rest on the only option she considered might be reasonably attractive to Lugh. She couldn't help hesitating, though. Last time she'd attempted to bargain with the gods, she and her husband both met a violent end. Would bargaining with a fallen god be the height of stupidity? Would it cost her—or them—more than it had last time? Or would it be the wisest approach to the seemingly impossible problem of a love divided—life on one side, death on the other and a bottomless chasm of hopelessness separating the two? The sound of Ethan's wheezing grew more labored. *Decision made.* "You previously asked for my help. I will hear you out and, provided your request does not harm me or mine, I will give you what I am able. I will even give you what it is you ask of me in aid, if—"

"Don't," Ethan ground out.

She waved him off, carrying on as if he hadn't spoken. "—*If* you will vow to me one thing."

Lugh didn't breathe. "Name it."

"You will grant me something of equal or greater value than that which you seek for yourself." Her heart threw itself against her breastbone like a trapped animal. "And you will ensure that I'm provided that boon immediately."

"And if you fail to provide me what I want, witch? What then? What if your best attempts to render me aid do not bear fruit?"

Isibéal stepped away from Lugh then, but her gaze remained trapped within his. "The choice is yours. You can operate on faith, or you can stay here and suffer until eternity's end."

"Eternity has no end, woman," he said, eyes narrowing.

"I know." Adrenaline rushed through her veins. "That's why I'll encourage you to garner my best efforts by ensuring that your gift is something I would deem invaluable."

"Name your prize."

Had she done it? Had she struck a bargain that redeemed her centuries-old mistake? There was only one way to know with any certainty. "I want him." She jerked her chin over her shoulder. "All of him."

Without warning, he crossed the room, laid a hand on Ethan's forehead and murmured something below his breath. Ethan's arms and legs fell away from the wall just before his body followed. He landed in a gasping pile on the floor.

"Get up," Lugh commanded.

Ethan flopped over on his back. "Busy breathing."

"If you want your wife back, then get. Up."

Isibéal's heart stopped, and it was then she realized it had been beating. She rushed to Ethan's side. She reached for his arm, only to hesitate. Twisting to face the fallen god, she did her best to not let her voice convey the emotional strain Ethan's nearness placed on her. "Want me back?"

"With the proper 'support,'" Lugh said with ridiculous air quotes, "I intend to give you what you both seem to most want."

Beside her, Ethan stilled.

Isibéal opened and closed her mouth, too scared to think that large, too scared to hope.

"I offer you the greatest gift I have to offer, Isibéal Cannavan." He clasped his hands behind his back and spread his feet, a superior look settling over his coutenance. "The gift of—"

"Reincarnation," she breathed.

Chapter 10

Ethan knew he was pulling a Who-Framed-Roger-Rabbit-ah-OOO-gah moment, his eyes nearly bugging out of his head. Damn if he could help himself, though. What had been laid at his feet with near-casual indifference warranted every bit of his "Want... Iz... Real... How... *Reincarnation*?"

Lugh arched an eyebrow, the singular movement saturated with disdain. "You do realize you would be more likely to find yourself associated with modern man versus the much older biped known as the Neanderthal if you would see fit to reduce your nonsensical grunting. Speaking in complete sentences wouldn't hurt, either. Of course, if you *were* a Neanderthal, it would explain much."

Ethan wanted so badly to give the fallen god the one-fingered-hey-how-are-ya, but he couldn't. Not when the guy stood there cloaked in the undisguised certainty that his powers would be sufficient to do exactly what he said they'd do. Namely, bring Isibéal back to life. If he could? He could give Ethan everything he wanted. Or thought he wanted. Because, really? If Lugh could give Isibéal another chance, give *them* another chance...

Ethan wasn't sure if he shook his head or if he simply shook.

What would it mean for him if Isibéal were returned to life? What would it mean to *her*? Did she even want to try? How would Lugh garner enough power to bring Isibéal back when he, Ethan, couldn't even pull the proverbial rabbit from the hat in this realm? And what could Ethan do to ensure that the jackass didn't renege, do things halfway or hand over a generic attempt at bringing his wife back only to demand whatever it was he would have of her in order to see the reincarnation through?

Then there was the magick to be invoked. Ethan didn't suffer false modesty. He knew he was a badass in his own right, able to perform complex magicks well beyond almost anyone but the Druids. But his power was element, based on life. What Lugh would invoke was tantamount to death magick. It was unfamiliar. Unwelcome. *Dark*. There were too many things that could go wrong that Ethan couldn't interfere with, let alone stop. How could he ensure that Isibéal wouldn't be hurt? Or worse?

He glanced between his wife and the fallen god.

Truth? He couldn't, and he knew it. Whatever Lugh set in motion, Lugh would be required to stop. That meant Ethan and Isibéal would both have to trust the guy to do what he said. The irony wasn't lost on Ethan that he and Iz were bargaining for her existence with the very man who had taken her life.

"Ethan?"

He whipped his chin up and looked at the beauty he had only just recognized as his woman. She was the very image of everything he thought he'd known of love and then some. Like, a lot of *some*.

Isibéal stepped closer to him, but not close enough. She always kept a fair distance between them, never allowing them to touch. Like their hands on the window earlier just after he'd lost sight of her. They'd been close, no more than a hairbreadth apart he was sure. Something akin to raw desperation had dictated to his most fundamental self that he touch her, establish a connection between them, feel her under his hands. He'd inched toward her.

She'd inched away.

And he'd respected that.

Still, her reserve drove Ethan nuts. After all, he had the memories to know they hadn't been chaste partners even before their vows were spoken. He knew what she looked like in moonlight. He recalled the way her silky hair slipped through his work-roughened hands. He was confident that the spot just in front of her hipbone would be an erogenous zone. So much he recalled. So much more he ached to reaffirm.

He wanted to touch her now. Hold her here. Taste her tonight. He needed to know if her skin was truly as smooth as the alabaster it resembled. He wanted to know if the faint flush on those full lips tasted of the same color they bore—nearly ripe strawberries—or if it was coincidence the colors were the same. He craved the weight of her breasts in his palms, curious if that flesh would fill his hands. He knew the answers, of course, but he wanted fresh memories with which to overlay the old ones.

Ethan reached for her and she started, jumping out of reach so fast she stumbled. Instinct shouted to spare her the fall, and he obeyed, lunging forward and grabbing her arm. She was soft but toned, skin cool. But still it heated his blood.

She stiffened in his grasp, her breathing growing choppy, almost panting, before halting even as her face contorted.

Confused, he eased his hold and she yanked away from him. "Isibéal?"

Lugh stepped forward, something suspiciously akin to compassion filling his eyes. "It seems she's suffered a hard lesson."

"What did you do to her?" Ethan demanded, stepping in front of his wife and halting the god's approach.

"Nothing." Lugh met Ethan's flat stare with one of his own. "You forget that death cannot touch life without considerable consequence." He sighed then and reached out to caress Isibéal's pale cheek.

Ethan reached out, faster than a snake's strike, and gripped the other man by the wrist. "Don't touch her, not without her permission. No. You know what? Don't touch her at all. Ever. Understand?"

Isibéal opened her eyes and gasped, drawing Ethan's attention. Her slender, delicate hands, so capable in so many ways, shook wildly. She gripped the excess fabric of her skirt and wadded it up, released it and wadded it up again. Stepping back from both men, shaking her head as if to clear it, she bit her bottom lip even as her gaze darted back and forth. "I cannot touch the living, Ethan. The pain…" She tried, and failed, to stifle the sob that rose from deep in her chest. "You can't imagine the pain."

He rounded on Lugh. "Fix this," he demanded. "As part of her reward for helping you, fix this."

"I already have." Lugh looked askance and cleared his throat. "For the setting and rising of Searbh Liath, the smallest of this realm's three suns, I shall bear the burden of your death, Isibéal. You may touch him and he you without consequence, provided you stay in this room. Leave and you will return to your incorporeal form the moment you step through that doorway. You will have use of your physical body until Searbh Liath breaks the horizon tomorrow morning. I will return then and see you restored to the mortal realm, where you will bear fruit for me in return, as promised. The bargain has been struck."

Life seemed to infuse her, animate her, as she stepped toward Lugh. "Wait. What do you want from me? What will you ask me to do on your behalf?"

"It's irrelevant. I've met your terms, granted you a prize greater than that which I shall ask of you in return. You'll honor the bargain, witch." He spun away and started across the room, pausing when he reached the door. "I suggest you make the most of this time together and determine if reincarnation is the reward you each seem to believe it would be."

"And why wouldn't it be?" Ethan demanded.

Lugh glanced over his shoulder, his smile grim. "Not every marriage was meant to be, warlock. Was yours?"

Ethan's head snapped back, the words striking him harder and with more violence than a physical blow would have. "Why wouldn't it have been meant?"

Lugh's grim smile spread before he opened the door and stepped into the hallway with a surreptitious glance left and then right. "That's not for me to answer."

The door closed behind him, and Lugh was gone,

leaving Ethan and Isibéal alone for the first time in over half a millennium.

She gasped, and he whipped around to face her.

A small, inarticulate sound escaped from deep in his chest as he took her in—hair, skin, eyes, form.

Physical form. Lugh had kept his word. The moment he'd shut the door, she became corporeal. There was no more gazing through her. No more "almost there" about her. Her hair moved with a susurrous sound as she turned to face him. Her feet made small taps of contact on the stone floor, and the air was disturbed as she moved toward him. She was as solid as the floor beneath him.

She was radiant.

And Ethan had never been so grateful for anything in this life or the last.

Butterflies with razor-tipped wings sliced through his belly, every flutter a nauseating cut. Never one to react much to adrenaline-inducing events, Ethan was surprised to find the urge to puke tangled up with the need to close his eyes and gather his wits about him. Electing to forgo the physical reaction, he took a second to try and find his center, that familiar ground that was his and his alone where he could just take a second and regroup. It confused him that he was almost…bashful. Shy. Out of sorts. None of this fell in line with his modus operandi. Ethan had always been the suave one, the smooth operator, the guy his friends always joked they wanted to *be*. But with Isibéal standing in the fringe of his peripheral vision, her hands still clenched in her skirt fabric and her eyes as wide as she was silent, he couldn't figure out what to say or do. Humor didn't feel right, and that was his standby. Serious conversation? She'd just been granted a body. Touch? He wasn't sure she'd welcome it just yet. Didn't they need to—he mentally cast about—get to know each other or something? Better, anyway? In this incarnation?

Those butterflies took up kamikaze maneuvers, dive-bombing his self-confidence until it hung in tatters.

Here he stood across from the woman who had followed him across centuries, a woman he'd returned for, and he couldn't find the words or actions sufficient for the moment.

Taking a deep breath, he envisioned working the air through his system, pushing it into his lungs, saturating his bloodstream and infiltrating his muscles. He repeated the process several times before he began to relax.

"You used to do that very thing, you know."

Her smooth voice jolted him out of the meditative moment, his eyes slamming shut as his muscles knotted and his blood heated. *That lilting, suggestive voice.* He wanted her to say something ridiculous in a hundred different ways—something like circumlocution—just so he could listen to her.

"Ethan?"

He forced himself to control every muscle, every movement, as he faced her. Visually, she was a feast he wanted to gorge on, but how did he say that without making an ass of himself?

Instead, he cleared his throat and latched on to her comment. "I used to do what?" His voice dropped at least two octaves, and the irreverent thought that they could make a killing narrating super sexy audio books crossed his mind. A small laugh escaped him, dragging with it the tension that had threatened to coalesce in his shoulders. Lacing his hands behind his head, he met Iz's gaze. "Why is this so difficult, do you think?"

The hint of a smile pulled at the corners of her mouth. "We're out of practice?"

"Could be." Dropping his hands abruptly, he shoved one in his pocket while tugging at the unraveling hem of his shirt with the other, all while he considered her. "What do you want, Isibéal?" He swept a hand out, showgirl-style, around the room. "Out of all this, I mean." When she only looked at him, he sighed. "Probably a more accurate question would be what do you want, or expect, of me?"

Fierce pink stained her cheeks, the blush burning through him like fresh accelerant lit by a flint strike. He could only imagine where her mind had gone. The predictable hope was that it had followed his straight into the gutter. But Ethan made it a point to aim for more than predictable. Always.

He closed the distance between them, shaking his head when she tried to move out of reach. "We need to know if he lied, if touching you will hurt me."

"It won't hurt you."

"How can you be sure?" He lifted his hand, hesitated when she flinched and let the same hand drop back to his side.

Her eyes tightened. "It hasn't ever hurt you before."

"You've touched me." A statement, not a question. "When?"

This time her grin was wide and undeniably sardonic. "I'm dead, not daft. It took me only the one time to determine that having my soul shredded while I was conscious would never be my sport of choice."

"Ouch." He laughed, pained as the sound was. "Did it really hurt that bad?"

"Worse."

Ethan winced. "I'd hoped Lugh had exaggerated."

"Unfortunately, he told the unadulterated truth." She closed the distance between them by half.

Ethan's breath caught, fluttering tight in his throat, tickling until he coughed again out of necessity. And nerves.

She lifted her chin, that stubborn set so hauntingly familiar and yet new. "That doesn't change the fact that we need to know, you and I."

"I don't know if it's a good—"

"Morning approaches with every tick of the clock, Ethan," she said softly, guileless eyes that flashed from gold to hazel and back in a blink so full of sensual hunger he stopped breathing. "We need...*I* need...to know."

Ethan searched the face he knew now he'd never again forget. There was so much he wanted to say, so many reassurances he needed to offer, yet only one line from all of film and literature and life seemed relevant. He smiled and laid at her feet an offering she wouldn't understand. "As you wish."

Isibéal took Ethan in, curious about the mischievous smile that played around the corners of his mouth as his eyes wrinkled with unchecked humor. Oh, this man. Centuries she had loved him, centuries she had wanted him, and now here he stood. Accessible. Willing. Waiting. But she couldn't force herself to move. To act. To seize the moment with unabashed intent and take what he freely offered. The cost of her touch would, for him, be nil. Probably. Every reassurance she had hinged on a damned god's word. How trustworthy was Lugh when it came to Ethan's well-being? The reassurance lessened with that single question. If Lugh had lied... She would die a hundred deaths before putting Ethan through the type of pain her touch could bring, a pain that defied description. It had scrambled her more thoroughly than a basket of tossed eggs. Never had she been forced to fight to simply coalesce and hold her form. What had always been instinctive, second nature since death, had, without warning, become a battle to maintain. She'd never felt so insubstantial, not just in form but in fact, as if it wasn't only her body that had ceased to be but her consciousness, as well. Any soul collector could have lifted her out of the plain then, and she would have been helpless, indefensible. She would never allow herself to be placed in that position again. As for Ethan? She wouldn't see him slog through that same battle, potentially losing himself, for the sake of a touch.

Not even *her* touch.

Rubbing her fingers together, she couldn't help focusing on the thing she wanted most, the thing that had been denied her so long. *Human touch. His touch.* She remembered the way he felt, though the specifics had faded with time. Years ago Isibéal had sworn she would never forget the heat of his skin or the shift of his hair through her fingers, but time had proven itself a sly and persistent thief, stealing away the smallest details first, then larger bits and pieces of memories until only the framework remained. Now she found it impossible to recall the location of calluses on his work-roughened hands, but not the shape of the hands themselves. She could recall the sensitive spot on the inside of one wrist, but time had stolen the detail that specified whether the spot was on his left or right side. To reclaim details like these and more, to fill in the emptiness she'd craved for so long, what *wouldn't* she risk?

To touch and be touched.

Oh, to have that singular point of contact that would form a connection between them, to feel the slide of his skin against hers, unimpeded by current circumstance or cosmic fate. *Just once more*, she'd always promised herself. *One more touch and I'll count myself satisfied.*

Never had she lied to herself with such ease.

A million touches, even more, would never satisfy her need to touch this man, only this man—her heart, her reason for being, her happiness manifest.

She couldn't deny she wanted that touch more than anything, wanted to know his warmth again. Wanted to feel the way the small whiskers on his chin, the stubble that even now caught the light if he turned his head just so, would scrape her softest skin. Wanted to hear the catch of his breath in her ear when she stroked him just so. Wanted to let his fingers trace her form and linger as they would, where they would. She wanted to *experience* him. To carry with her the warmth that materially infused his skin as if he'd spent the day under the summer sun. He'd always been like that, felt like that. On the coldest winter morns she'd turned to him, wiggling beneath the massive mound of bedding to draw close and curl into his side. He would jump, make a small sound of protest and then growl as he pulled her close with a muttered "Woman." Each time. Every time.

"You're smiling."

His observation drew her out of the reverie that had commandeered her attention, but her smile hung on as she shook her head with a self-deprecating laugh. "Memories. Nothing more."

He stared down at her, those eyes of otherworldly blue locked on hers.

So close after so long.

"Memories."

She nodded, her smile teasing wider.

"Of what?" he pressed.

"You. Us," she answered without hesitation. No, Ethan might not be Lachlan in every sense. Each individual reincarnation bore small differences, after all. But the man who stood before her carried the majority of Lachlan's memories. To Isibéal, this warlock, this warrior, this assassin was, for all intents, the man to whom she'd pledged her life.

"What about us?"

Ethan stood so close now that she felt the tenor of his voice, the very rumble of his words, through her worn wool gown and stiff kirtle. Her hand went to her breast of its own accord as if to catch the sensation and hold it close.

"Iz?"

She shook her head. "You used to…" Looking up through her lashes, she felt her confidence shored up by the singular intensity of his gaze. "You would call me 'woman' with such playful aggravation—"

"When you put your cold feet on my legs," he finished for her. His eyes widened. "I remember." Then, without warning, he threw his head back and laughed, the booming sound so incompatible with their surroundings. No way would she ask him to refrain, though. Let their environment morph to suit the man's mood, not the other way around. That particular defense wouldn't protect him from the teasing that came to her like second nature.

"What do you find so entertaining?" she demanded with mock irritation.

Laughter quieting, he faced her and, once more, raised his hand to her cheek. Yet he didn't touch her. Instead, with naught more than a whisper's distance between them, he traced the outline of her face, its very contours, without the skin-to-skin contact she craved. Air moved, the faintest disturbance that followed in the wake of his fingertips. Gods, what she wouldn't give to be touched by him after all this time. Only by him. Her eyes fluttered shut.

Over and over her face he went, never touching. So close. Not close enough. The pads of his fingers emanated the warmth of the living, murmured promises of salvation and called to her to breathe him in. She parted her lips and tilted her face to his.

"Isibéal."

Never had her name been issued with such reverence.

She hesitated even as his fingertips lingered in one spot. With desire born of hundreds of years of waiting, she took a slow, deep breath and opened her eyes.

Ethan stared down at her, a bastion of emotion in his gaze. "This is who I am now," he said, voice rough. "I'm not Lachlan. Not here, not in this time or in this place. Not in the mortal realm. Never again. This body, this mind, this magick—it's who I am *now*, and not centuries past. And just as I am similar but different, so is the opportunity before us. A choice to be made, to claim joy as our north star, to declare that fear and pain have no stronghold here, between us. To touch and be touched, to hold and be held." His fingers moved, further closing the finite distance between them. "To know and be known—" he slowly reached for her with his free hand "—all without the burdens of the grave separating us." He hesitated. "I would take every hurt you have ever suffered." His fingers splayed wider. "I would bear every ounce of pain you have ever known." Air whispered over her skin. "For this."

He settled a hand at her waist at the same moment his fingertips came to rest against her jaw.

Under his touch, Isibéal came alive. She reached for his hand at her waist, first clutching it wildly before twining their fingers together. Blessed heat spread through the connection and raced over her skin. Not only did her heart beat for the first time in centuries; it also beat with surety, every breath necessary.

Her very soul trembled as she stepped into his embrace. And when he wrapped his arms around her?

Isibéal simply let go.

Her knees collapsed.

Her hope surged.

Her tears fell.

Her heart soared.

And then he kissed her.

Chapter 11

Tentative at first, Ethan skimmed his lips over hers, considering his every touch, calculating her every response. Growing bolder with each small noise she made, he caressed her jaw even as he sipped from her mouth like she was the finest single-barrel whiskey, one to be appreciated for its complexity and nuance, never to be downed like a two-dollar shot in a smoky dive bar. He wanted to savor her, this woman.

She moved against him, running a hand up the back of his neck, her fingers tunneling through his hair. Short, blunt nails scraped against his scalp, and he couldn't stop his hiss of pleasure, a wordless affirmation that she should *definitely* do it again.

She did.

The way she responded fueled something in him, setting fire to emotional kindling that time and loneliness had stacked around his feet and ankles with neither his awareness nor his blessing. That kindling crackled.

Caught. Roared. Need for her built with inferno-like intensity. Flames licked under his skin and set small flash fires wherever her fingers landed.

He pulled her closer, their bodies fitting together as well as two laser-cut puzzle pieces. The way she molded herself along his front, the way her slim leg settled between his, the way her full breasts pressed against his chest, the way the slight dip of her lower back deepened as he leaned her into his embrace, chasing her lips down—it was intense. Perfect. Meant. He craved the familiarity that came with the feel of her lips against his, the sound of her breathing whispering in his ears, the way she moved against him with wanton desperation reserved for him and him alone.

It was everything.

And it wasn't enough.

He wanted more, wanted to relearn everything about her in full. Needed to renew her taste on his lips again and again so that he might never forget her no matter what life, or death, threw at them.

Driven by near madness, Ethan nipped her bottom lip.

Isibéal gasped.

With her lips parted, the opportunity presented itself, and Ethan didn't hesitate. He delved inside. His eyes slammed shut on a near-desperate groan. She tasted like warmth and comfort, promises made…and kept. Passion and desire collided in him with brutal, unchecked need and rendered him completely blind to the intricacies and nuance of both seduction and finesse. This thing between them could be nothing more and nothing less than brutal honesty, raw in its delivery. It was emotion unchecked. It was lifetimes of love that had been buried and now unearthed. Exposed. It was the first of what he could only hope were an infinite number of chances to make right the wrongs they'd suffered.

She had been his end, ripping his heart out when she left him.

Now she had come back. She would forever be his beginning, his do-over in a life cycle that didn't offer do-overs. He'd take this one and run.

Wild with the need to physically see her, terrified she'd be snatched away from him again, that he'd lose her and have no idea where to begin to look to get her back, he broke the kiss and leaned away so he could see her. His gaze roamed over every inch of her face as his hands explored over her every dip and curve with a certain brand of innocence. "Isibéal." Her name was little more than a throaty rasp.

She looked up at him through unfocused eyes. "Lachlan."

"No," he said, low and fierce. "Not Lachlan." He gripped her shoulders and stared down at her. "He was, but I *am*."

She raised a shaking hand to his face and traced her thumb along his cheek. "You were as much my past as you are my present and everything good about my future."

"Say my name."

"I know who you are." Eyes serious as a smile fluttered at the corners of her bee-stung lips, she cupped his face. "Ethan."

He swooped in and claimed her mouth with a savagery that demanded she never forget him, never be content to let him go, would never willingly leave him again. The emotionally saturated kiss laid at her feet everything he'd held back.

She not only took his offerings, she also made one of her own.

Each of her responses was colored with a wildness that was barely reined in.

He wanted that. Craved it. Wanted to take her to the point she dropped all semblance of control and spurred his hunger on, racing to that flash point where it threatened to consume them both.

Gods save him, but he was already close and their clothes were still firmly on.

He could change that. Now. And he would.

Ethan nipped and licked and praised everything about her that crossed his mind, clutching her to him with one hand and stroking the length of her neck with the other. The thunder of her heartbeat against his thumb thrilled him, and he reveled in his ability to affect her. It was only fair, seeing as she did the same, *more*, to him. His heart hammered against his chest, his pulse frenzied.

She was his past, his present and his future. His everything. The thundering of her heart beneath his touch said she was as affected as he, that she could no more deny this impossible thing between them than the shore could turn away the sea's approach. This proverbial emotional tide would rush in, undoubtedly stir up some issues and reshape the face of their relationship before receding and leaving them to determine where best to build their future. Wherever it was, it would be together.

"Pay attention, warlock." Blunt-edged teeth sank into his lower lip and held on as she suckled the sting.

"*Unh*," he said, not at all sure what the guttural sound meant. Probably something like "More, you witchy woman. Claim my mind for conversation, my body a hundred different ways and my heart for always. Once you're done, I'll take it from there." Awful lot of responsibility for a wordless noise.

The need to be closer, to stretch out on top of his woman and pin her with his weight, made Ethan's mind blitz out. He glanced around the room, irritated to find nothing but four walls, a ceiling and a floor. Surfaces were smooth and solid, the interior corners rounded so that they blended seamlessly one to another and gave the impression he'd been stuffed inside a toddler's soft-edged building block.

If the block was in hell.

No matter. The time he'd been granted with Iz was here and now, and he had no intention of wasting a single moment.

Setting her away long enough to yank his shirt off, he spread it over the floor. The gesture was pitiful for all it was sincere. "You deserve to be laid on nothing less than silks beneath the bluest sky, your skin touched by nothing but the sun's rays and the Earth's breath. That's not what I give you, though. Oh, no. I offer you a premium stone floor, lighting that would make the gods' own children look vampiric and a worn, one hundred percent cotton slip of nothing on which to lay your head." He planted his fists on his hips, dropped his chin and shook his head. "I'm pretty sure this is the worst attempt at seduction ever."

A heated, trembling hand came to rest over his heart.

Ethan's chin slowly rose until he was able to meet Isibéal's wide-eyed gaze. "You deserve more." He swallowed hard, his Adam's apple bobbing. "So much more."

"I see nothing but you." She ran a thumb over his bottom lip. "Want nothing but you."

"Always knew you were a brilliant lass," he said, ignoring the faint Irish accent that wasn't his and never would be. "Let me give you what you want, Isibéal."

She smiled up at him, the anticipation banked in her eyes blazing to life with untempered intensity that ensnared him all over again. That she wanted him so much was like the first note of a siren's song. Count him enchanted, ensnared, ensorcelled, en-whatever. He was good with any of it. "Say yes, Iz."

"Yes."

Easing her to the floor, he followed her down.

Isibéal arched under Ethan's tender touches. He was gentle with her, stretching out beside her and settling in, watching her for minutes before laying his hands to her exposed skin.

"I…" His voice broke, forcing him to clear his throat.

She struggled not to smile. "I remember when that cracking voice was the norm."

The blush that stained his cheeks charmed her. "Always the bane of a man's existence, that cracking voice. It seems to wait to show itself until right before a man makes his opening move on the woman he's had his eye on. Then?" He made a warbling sound. "Buh-bye, sexy times. Hello, humiliation."

She laughed. "My poor, poor man."

"Have mercy, lady."

"We'll see," she teased. "Depends on how strong your opening move is."

"Oh, it's strong."

"Go on, then, warlock," she murmured, letting her desire for him show in her eyes. "Move me." When his hand drifted along the column of her neck, she sighed. He didn't stop there, though, continuing down the slope of her shoulder and on farther until his fingers teased the outer swell of one breast. She shivered under the promise held in that touch. "You're on the right track."

He ran his hand up, over her skin and wound his fingers through her mane. Canting her head back, he studied her face, seeming to commit every detail to memory. Just when she could stand no more, he whispered, "You ain't seen nothin' yet."

Then he lowered his head and claimed her mouth with authority. He gave her no quarter and sought none in return. His mouth commanded hers and demanded she acquiesce to his attention, this male settling in to take what he wanted and claim it as his own. The tip of his tongue traced the seam of her lips with silent insistence that she open to him now even as his free hand cupped her jaw, tilting her head back to make opening more difficult. Still, she would do as he asked because for all he'd taken control, every touch, every taste, every caress was a request. Beyond that, it was *he* who asked. She'd waited centuries for this moment, never knowing if it would present itself.

Finally. Finally, I am in his arms again.

Her heart beat heavily against her breastbone, every blow registering with a rapid percussion.

And she loved it.

She opened to him on a gasped single word. "More."

Ethan sealed his mouth over hers, swallowing the last of her plea. He tightened his grip on her hair, easing up just short of discomfort, threading the needle between pain and pleasure, request and demand, partnership and dominance as only he could.

Her body grew more taut than a drawn bow. "Ethan," she begged.

Hesitation and concern sprang up, their presence unwelcome as they alternated to carve deep runnels in his forehead. "I ache to push you further, but at the same time, I don't want to hurt you, Iz."

"You've never hurt my body. Not once, Ethan."

"*Lachlan* never hurt you," he corrected, some of passion's wildfire fading from his blue eyes. "I may remember much of life as your husband, Isibéal, but I—*Ethan*—have never touched you." He loosened his grip on her hair and rolled onto his back, bare skin to stone floor. Frustration leaked from him in palpable waves. "I won't screw this up. I *won't*."

"Then don't stop," she murmured.

Hooking a leg over his hip, she flipped him in a single, swift move.

He made a small sound, something like "Oomph!" as he gripped her hips. "Like that, is it?"

"If my man won't engage me as I wish, I'll simply change the terms of engagement." She kissed a finger and then laid it over his lips when he sputtered toward argument. "Hush, man. You never used to talk so much when I was intent on getting in your trews."

He gulped down a laugh even as the fire returned to his eyes. "Lachlan was clearly wiser."

"It's you I want, Ethan Kemp. None other will ever do."

Resting a hand on each shoulder, she rained butterfly kisses over his face until, with a near growl, he leaned up and seized her mouth in a searing kiss. Their tongues danced to that ageless rhythm, mimicking the steps their bodies would take, the forward thrust and retreat, the careful touch followed by wordless demands. It was everything she remembered between them and yet somehow more. So much more.

Long, tapered fingers fumbled with the unfamiliar lacings and ties on her kirtle until, with a foul curse,

Ethan set her aside and surged to his knees. Scowling at the lacings, he looked as fierce as an injured boar. "I'll have you out of these clothes, Isibéal. Now." Then he grinned. "Throw a drowning man a rope and show me to the nearest exit?"

Already ahead of him, she'd begun unfastening the lower lacings but paused. "The nearest exit?"

He waved her off. "Means show me how to get you *out* of these clothes. Pronto." He grinned wider. "Which means 'fast.' As in 'now.'"

She dipped her chin to hide her blush. Or grin. Both. With a deft move, she loosened the lacings and she took her first deep breath in centuries. Nothing was so grand as the reprieve from an unbearably tight corset.

Ethan's hands rested on her shoulders, and she wasn't sure just then who vibrated with greater need. Ultimately, it didn't matter. Nothing did beyond the fact that she wanted this, wanted *him*, more than anything she could imagine.

"Turn around," he said, soft and gruff.

She gave him her back.

He further loosened her laces and, with infinite care, eased the fabric down her arms, pausing at her wrists.

Isibéal couldn't stifle the small, desperate sound that escaped her when warm lips pressed against the ever-sensitive skin at the juncture of neck and shoulder. Disengaging her hands from her sleeves, she reached up and wove her fingers through Ethan's hair, pulling him closer as she leaned into him.

He abandoned his efforts to see her disrobed and, instead, ran his hands up her bare arms. When he pressed his hips to hers, the length of his arousal settled against her, both heavy and insistent.

She had no idea who gave in to whom. It mattered

little and, in the end, not at all. With her standing there, breasts exposed to the cool air and her nipples pearled with arousal, all she could think about was her hunger for the man at her back.

He drew a deep breath and, exhaling, lowered her arms.

She spun toward him, planting her hands against his bare chest. Going up on her toes, she met his stare with her own. "At some point you'll stop bloody 'seducing' me and simply follow through, yeah?"

He grinned. "Yeah." In one swift move, he hooked a foot behind her knee and took her to the floor. "Remind me to thank Dylan for that." Then his mouth was on her breast and she couldn't think, couldn't speak, could only pray to the gods he was done messing about.

Pent-up frustrations mixed with the tick of the clock, fueling an almost desperate sense that they had now and only now. Hands fumbled clothes as mouths tried so very much to never stop, to always stay in skin-to-skin contact. There was hunger and longing and the knowledge that finally satisfaction was in reach. Then he was above her, her wild-eyed lover, poised to return to her after so long.

One long, slow push.

A gasp.

His.

Hers.

And the years melted away.

They were who they'd been meant to be from the beginning. Each other's.

Ethan moved in her with care, watching her as closely as she watched him. Conversations were completed. Endearments exchanged. Promises forged in renewed flames. And never a word was spoken.

He moved faster, encouraging her to race toward that precipice she'd longed for. Reaching between them, his gaze boring into hers, he manipulated her sex, and that was it. Her back arched as she took him to the hilt with a shout and flew over the edge into the brilliance of release, calling his name as she went.

"Lachlan!"

Chapter 12

The boundaries set by the grave, the boundaries between the living and the dead, would once again be in force—the same boundaries she could not believe Lugh would be strong enough to conquer in the end.

Boundaries she was not sure could, in fact, be broken at all. Isibéal watched Lachlan—no, Ethan—as he lay beside her on the cold stone floor. It seemed a shame to wake him, but even in this dark, windowless place she felt the pull as Searbh Liath rose toward the horizon. Where now Ethan's—it pained her to think of him as such, but she must adapt to the odd new reality— body pressed against hers, she knew when the little sun rose she would be once again reduced to a spirit. Every place her skin drank his warmth would be replaced with naught but pain. She took a moment to drink him in. A healer. What a wonder to think of master assassin Lachlan Cannavan now a man of medicine. A man of medicine so advanced and wondrous it seemed to her like more magick. Would there be time in the future for her to learn of it? Would there be a future at all?

The solemn thought pushed her from her reverie, and she lowered her face to Ethan's. Her lips brushed his full ones, and a sense of magickal completeness flooded her. Centuries she'd been waiting for him. Whatever happened, she vowed, this night with him made all her torment and suffering worthwhile. His memory was all that had kept her from going mad trapped with only her mind as a companion.

Her touch brought his eyes fluttering open, and he reciprocated, parting his lips for her. The familiar kiss was a balm to her aching heart. *Whatever it took.* She wouldn't lose him again.

"Time marches on, pulling closer even as it interjects itself between us," she whispered.

Ethan sat up and rubbed his eyes. His hair was mussed, eyes still bearing the vestiges of sleep, and she found that it wasn't so difficult to reconcile the sleepy man before her with the assassin she'd loved lifetimes ago.

She watched Ethan become more aware of her attention, watched as he searched for something to say. What he offered was so unexpected that it stole her breath.

"I'm sorry I didn't remember."

The bare honesty of his apology came to rest between them, hers to accept or reject. But truly? Rejection was no option. "How could you?"

"I feel like—you read about love, you hear about love, and I, well, I should have remembered something of who I once was. I should have experienced some sort of awareness or understanding that you were important."

Were. Past tense.

She wanted to ask him to alter his statement, to deem her just as important to him now. Maybe even more so. Instead, she shook her head, curls obscuring her vision as effectively as they kept him from witnessing the longing she knew she failed to disguise. "You weren't aware of your previous life. Or lives. Nor of me." She stood, distinctly aware of her nakedness, and longed for the time to come where she wouldn't yearn to cover herself but could again move freely. Ethan was just so...different. Lachlan, but not. The man she'd loved for lifetimes, but not. Her husband by rights. But not.

She took a deep breath before offering him a hand and helping him to his feet. "We haven't time to consider how we should have handled this or what might have been done differently."

Ethan glanced at the pile of fabric that represented all that remained of her dress. Its impromptu use as a pallet during their lovemaking had destroyed the garment. "I'd apologize, but I'm not sure I could do it without lying."

She chuffed out a laugh. "Be you Lachlan or Ethan, you're much the same in more ways than one. Never sorry how, or where, we found our pleasure." She grinned up at him. "Neither am I." Holding out her hand, she wiggled her fingers. "My only option is your shirt. It will be far easier for you to do without it than me."

The shirt was halfway over her head when she felt Searbh Liath top the horizon. It was as though her body dropped into a vat of ice-cold water, all the warmth sucked from her at once. She couldn't feel herself anymore, and not even the sudden vanishing of her headache could make the loss of herself any better. Instinctively she took a step back from Ethan. He reached for her, but she maneuvered herself out of his grasp.

"Morning has come," she said.

Ethan's face went blank. "No." Expression rushed back, hardening his jaw and making his cheekbones stand out in harsh relief. "No! Lugh!"

The door opened, and the god stepped in. "Rarely do I answer when summoned with such irreverence."

"Like I give a damn," Ethan spat. "Make this right."

Lugh's glamour was back, and Isibéal understood Ethan saw him the way he wanted to be seen…muscular body, lush hair, the very image of virility. All that Lugh wanted to be and wasn't.

"I struck a binding agreement with you, Isibéal. All you need do is accept the conditions." The god let Ethan stew as he considered her and her alone. "Your choice?"

"I accept." She moved between the two men, careful not to touch either.

Lugh's eyes narrowed. "You realize that the moment you're returned to your body, you will be subject to true death, not only in this realm but every other as well. Should you die here, your soul will be bound to the Shadow Realm for eternity. I do not possess the power to release your soul should that occur."

Ethan looked confused.

"I was well aware of the risks—all of them—when we negotiated the terms agreed upon." She squared her shoulders and lifted her chin, refusing to look at Ethan. For the chance to feel him again, she would suffer a thousand times what was to come. "That said, let's not dally, hmm?"

Ethan shook his head. "I don't like this, Iz. There's got to be another way."

Lugh stepped into Ethan's personal space, bending forward until their noses nearly touched. "I, *I*, am the God of Reincarnation. No one has the power necessary to return your woman to her body but me. Had it been a recent death, you might have managed to coerce one of my high-ranking brethren to perform a ceremony that would return to her something comparable to the life she had. But it has been centuries, warlock. *Centuries.*" He snarled the last word, spittle flying. "I am the only god in existence who can create a body and fuse it to her spirit. *I* am your option. *Me.* Do not think to back out on our agreement now, or you will suffer in ways mankind has long forgotten exist."

"A moment, please," Isibéal said softly as she leaned in to gain Lugh's attention. Eyes blazing, he spun and stalked across the small room. Isibéal lowered her voice even more as she addressed Ethan. "Look at me." When he didn't, she spoke just as soft but with an edge to her words that had been lacking seconds before. "Look at me, Ethan." He did, and she felt a thread of tension snap. "There is no other way. I bargained with Lugh, we reached an agreement, and that agreement stands. He'll do as he's promised, Ethan. And so will I."

"But—"

"No." The sharp denial left no room for discussion. "No." More gently this time. "I want this done. Dragging it out is unfair to me."

Shifting to place herself between the two men, Isibéal moved into the center of the room. "I'm ready."

Without flourish, Lugh produced a great broadsword and reached for Ethan.

The warlock recoiled and visibly prepared to defend himself.

"Be at ease, warlock. It is but a gift. You'll need this as you fight your way to the portal out of the Shadow Realm." With a flick of the wrist, Lugh spun it, and offered it to Ethan, helm first.

Isibéal stepped out of the way as the weapon was

transferred from one man to the other, and listened as the dark god described their way to the portal.

Lugh faced her then. "Isibéal, for this to work, you must come to me of your own accord."

Fear coated her tongue, the acerbic taste one she would never forget. That mind-numbing fear wasn't enough to stop her, though.

She began to step forward.

Her foot hadn't yet made contact with the ground when Lugh reached out and pressed a fingertip to her forehead. She had the briefest thought that the power in his eyes wasn't normal, that it was beyond otherworldly, before the tempest of change struck and Isibéal understood what it was to suffer. Every sense was brutalized. Her nerves melted as her bones went up in flames. What had been her skin turned to ash. Sheer agony stole through her, the little bit of air she might have possessed in her lungs only fueling the inferno.

The first convulsion struck as Isibéal threw her head back and screamed.

Ethan watched as Lugh, using nothing more than a finger pressed to Isibéal's forehead, levitated her thrashing body. It took every ounce of willpower Ethan possessed to keep from surging forward and seizing Isibéal. He'd understood that reincarnation wasn't a walk in the park, but this? No. This was beyond tolerable. Nothing was worth what she clearly suffered.

She shook as if being electrocuted, her eyes rolled back in her head and her lips peeled away from her teeth. Skin that had been touchable, even healthy less than an hour ago, developed fissures that looked like thin black thread. Those filaments raced across her skin, weaving a random but dense pattern that left her with the appearance of tempered glass.

The woman who comprised a large part of his past and somehow would be part of his future, a part he wasn't willing to look at too closely, was literally coming apart in the god's arms.

Ethan stepped closer, unaware he'd raised the sword he'd been given until Lugh's voice echoed through his head.

"Stand. Down."

The undisguised strain in the command registered with Ethan on a visceral level, and he had a moment of clarity where he recognized what the god was doing and the undiluted power it required. Truth struck Ethan a nearly physical blow, and he dropped the sword, the metal blade striking the stone floor with a sharp, ringing twang.

Isibéal's scream stopped, cut off as effectively as if her voice had never been.

Raw energy filled the room and made Ethan's every hair stand on end.

Lugh's spine arched, twisting his body into an unnatural shape. Tendons in his neck stood out as he strained against the magick he sought to harness. He remained frozen in the position as the seconds passed with agonizing lethargy. Without warning, the god's head fell back and a scream rose from deep in his chest. Head tipping forward, Lugh's eyes appeared milky white, his physical body no longer disfigured. An unnatural wind gusted through the room.

Ethan's heart pounded in his ears. Never had he witnessed anything so fiercely primal, and he shook with the weight of what had passed.

Because at Lugh's feet lay Isibéal, her body lax and

pale as death. Her chest was still, failing to rise and fall with breath.

Grief welled in him unchecked, but he couldn't force himself to go to her. He didn't want to touch her if she was actually gone. He wanted to remember her warmth, the feel of her supple skin as she moved over him, the way her cheeks lifted and her eyes crinkled when she smiled. Gods, he wanted to—

Lugh's voice interrupted Ethan's mental wish making. "She'll live or she'll die. Should she live, you'll both need to make your way out of the Shadow Realm as discussed. This is not a place for the living. If she dies?" He made his way to the door and paused, coughing hard enough that something in his chest rattled. "You're on your own." Then he was gone.

Ethan looked at Isibéal and found himself praying for the first time in far too long. "Let her live." A simple prayer but no less heartfelt for its brevity.

A fine tremor passed over her skin, so faint he wondered if he'd imagined it. Her first deep breath was affirmation enough that he hadn't, her first gasp was music to him.

She bolted upright, eyes wild.

"Isibéal?" he asked quietly.

Rounding on him, Isibéal's lips moved in silent conversation as thoughts raced across her face.

He stepped closer. "Iz? Honey, talk to me."

"Honey?"

Relief swept through Ethan like a spring wind. "I could call you any number of pet names."

A brief nod sent her stumbling. "My balance…"

He reached out and grabbed her arm to steady her. "It'll come back."

She winced...and then her face went lax. "You're touching me. Ethan? You're touching me!" she shouted.

And promptly threw herself into his open arms.

He held her close, reveling in the beat of her heart against his chest. There was absolutely nothing he wouldn't have given to hold her there, just like that, for days. Perhaps weeks. But they had to get out of the Shadow Realm, and sooner rather than later.

After all, Lugh had held up his end of the bargain.

Chapter 13

Isibéal hesitated at the mountain's massive doors. Opposite the protection of these doors lay the Forest of the Forlorn. The petrified trees created an eerie landscape and almost no shelter at all from the predators—humanoids to true beasts—that inhabited the realm. Once she opened the doors and stepped through with Ethan, it would be a mad dash to the portal.

Laying one hand against the preternaturally warm metal, she waited. Nothing happened. Not that she'd truly expected anything of significance, but her time here had been far from ordinary. So much so that it made sense to wait a few moments and feel the situation out. Call it foresight or premonition or woman's intuition. All Isibéal knew for certain was that the trip across the Shadow Realm as a mortal, magickal null would be unlike any challenge she'd taken on before.

She curled her fingertips against the doors and pressed.

They pressed back.

Isibéal jerked her hand away.

Ethan moved in close, eyes scanning for any threat. "Iz?"

"I don't want to do this." The admission escaped her before she could mind her words. Foolish to let her fears bleed into her partner, no matter that partner was Lachlan. "Ethan," she corrected herself, low and fierce.

"What?"

"Nothing."

He laid a hand at the small of her back. "You said my name."

"So I did." She forced herself to smile over her shoulder. "Nerves. It helps to know you're here."

"Always."

His fervent and immediate answer slathered her with guilt, as thick and cloying as too much jam on fresh bread. She shouldn't resent him for who he wasn't but should love him for who he was. And she did.

Mostly.

Nerves jangling, she tucked her hands into the ends of the long sleeves of Ethan's shirt. "Search as I might, I cannot come up with a legitimate cause to delay."

He shifted around her and placed himself between her and the doors. "It's the Band-Aid effect."

"Pardon?"

"The Band-Aid effect. You rip it off fast so it's over… Band-Aid bandages. You wouldn't be familiar with those."

The "either" hung between them as loud as if it had been unspoken.

"You'll get used to things," he added with swift assurance. "Give it time."

Isibéal nodded and swallowed around the anxiety

wedged in her throat. Speaking, even trying to, was pointless.

Ethan grabbed the main door handle, only to glance over his shoulder. His pupils looked like new moons in the dim light, so dark they swallowed all but the slim ring of his irises. "There's a...*thing* out there. Okay, three things. Maybe...probably...waiting. For me." He rolled his chin back and forth. "Us." Whipping his chin to one side, he cracked his neck. "Whatever it is, it's hungry."

"Wh-what?" she stammered. "What is it, then?"

With a loose wrist, he swung the sword Lugh had provided in a lazy circle. "No clue."

A scream broke nearby.

Isibéal lunged forward, landing in Ethan's arms like a damned damsel in distress. Furious with her reaction, she forced herself to straighten and square her shoulders. "Sure, and if it's waiting, we'll deal with it."

"We've no magick, Iz. Only the one sword."

"And two capable minds." Reaching behind her head, she spun her hair into a twist and knotted it at her nape. She glanced between Ethan and the door, biting her bottom lip as she summoned the courage to lay herself bare. "The longer we stand here predicting just how horrible it will be, the more terrified I become. I want to be done with it."

A smile ghosted around the corners of his mouth. "Hors d'oeuvres or bust?"

"Pardon?" She shook her head and waved his answer off. "I seem to be asking that far too often. I'll manage."

Ethan gently pinched her chin between his thumb and forefinger. "Nothing gets to you without going through me."

Drawing a deep breath, she held it to the count of

five and then let it out with slow control, never breaking his solemn stare. "Valiant as that sentiment is, I'm not keen on the image. I believe I'd rather nothing gets to either of us."

He held her steady as he lowered his lips and kissed her, a quick buss, then faced the door. "There really should be some sort of speech, something powerful and striking." He shook his head and gripped the handle. "But I've got nothin'."

And he yanked the doors open.

Dry, stagnant air devoid of the smells of damp earth or vegetation—living *or* dead—rolled over her. Sand scraped her skin. Tall trees disappeared into a low gray sky, their trunks stretching so high that Isibéal had to crane her neck to make out the few tops the brewing dust storm didn't obscure. Nothing moved beyond the doors save the wind.

Isibéal's shoulders sagged.

It would suit her fine if they'd perhaps caught their first break.

Ethan slipped outside, sword tip low, his narrowed eyes shrewd and calculating. "Stay close. If I tell you to run, you run and don't look back."

"Not without you," she said under her breath, sure he couldn't hear her. Rolling her borrowed shirtsleeves up with swift efficiency, she managed to cling to his pale shadow as he darted across the open expanse of ground between the mountain's doors and forest's edge.

Ethan pressed his spine against a sallow tree trunk and pulled Iz to his side. Their every collective breath was labored. The silt-laden air all but guaranteed she would spit mud if she had enough saliva to spit at all.

She didn't.

Licking her gritty lips, Iz peered around the tree

trunk at the same time Ethan gestured with his chin toward a rolling landscape pockmarked by dead shrubs and sand dunes.

"Lugh said we head straight away from the mountain."

Something continued to nag Isibéal. Was it something Lugh had said, or was it the expediency with which he helped them both last night and this morning? Whatever the reason, the sensation that she'd missed something significant wouldn't let her go.

In the distance, a sharp *chirrup* sound carried across the breeze.

"Damn it," Ethan said on a rushed exhalation.

"Damn it what?" Isibéal scanned the horizon.

"It's the thing I dubbed the raptodactylmon." He rolled his shoulders. "Same thing Lugh called an animorge. It feeds on souls. As in, wholly consumes them and leaves a deflated skin suit behind."

Isibéal shuddered. "Lovely image, that."

"You didn't see them when you came across the forest yesterday?"

A small shake of her head was her only answer.

"Count yourself lucky." He peered at the sky. "I don't know anything about them beyond the fact that they seemed anxious to pull a Men in Black on me. I wouldn't look good in an Edgar suit."

Once again, the conversation and contemporary cultural references stumped her, driving her mad. Would she never find her footing in the modern world and its myriad references and off-the-wall humor? Would she never fit in with any sense of comfort or belonging? Would she never have that comfortable common ground with Ethan? She'd always shared that familiarity and common background with Lachlan. A chill settled in her veins. Perhaps Lugh's intimation that they should examine their situation closely held more merit than she'd initially assigned it. What if... Her stomach clenched and rolled. She forced herself to slow down and articulate the dark thought. What if Lugh had been right and this passion between her and Ethan was nothing more than the dregs of a love long gone to its grave? Hadn't the fallen god warned of that very thing when he told them that not every love was meant to be?

Too many questions and too few answers had a scream barreling up her throat. Fists clenched, she forced herself to swallow the sound down and suppress it there in the heart of her being. She had loved Lachlan beyond reason, cherishing him above all else. Even her life. What of Ethan? Had she superimposed her feelings for Lachlan over the man he'd been reborn as? Because if time had taught her anything, it was that the heart was a predictable beast, loving who it loved without apology or, often, reason.

The *chirruping* sound resonated through the petrified forest, forcing her back into the moment. What the heart wanted meant little if it ended up as whatever this "Edgar suit" was that Ethan referenced. She chanced a look around, but the demon still hadn't come into sight. Given the reduced visibility and the realm's unknown aspects, that meant little. The animorge could be obscured only feet away or it could be miles.

Ethan shifted the sword to his other hand and reached for her, speaking as if he'd read her mind. "I'm going to hazard a guess and say that it would be best to get moving while we can't see the beasty and, just maybe, the beasty can't see us."

She took his proffered hand. The reassurance in his grip settled her frazzled mind a bit. It was enough, and she found herself grateful for the comfort she found in him.

Winding their way through the forest, they moved as silent as wraiths. Only their rapid breathing gave away their presence. Isibéal had forgotten how a pair of lungs could burn when taxed, how a stitch in one's side could ache like a fresh wound and the way sweat stung sensitive eyes. She'd forgotten how tender bare feet seemed to find every object with a point or an edge. Above all, she'd forgotten how much effort it took to keep up with a male in his prime. It was maddening and, in a twisted way, exhilarating. Many a time she'd fought beside Lachlan, sometimes with strategy, sometimes magicks and, on the rarest occasion, swords. Every fight had been memorable and had taught her something. This conflict would be no different. First and foremost? She'd reinforced what she already knew: haring off into realms unknown in search of answers was better approached with finesse than fists. And though her heart had gotten in the way of her head a wee bit in this case, she couldn't bring herself to regret anything. She was embodied now, could sort out the differences between the man Lachlan had been versus who he was now, and she'd emerge better off for having seen the difference between them.

And if you find you love Lachlan more than you can bring yourself to care for Ethan? her subconscious whispered.

I'll love each man for who he was and who he is, she answered. *That I have the chance to love the man Lachlan has become is a blessing. I'll not see it as anything other.*

Her subconscious remained silent, and Isibéal had a

fleeting moment of panic. *What if my mind recognizes something my heart is too enamored to see?*

What if indeed.

Ethan knew he basically dragged Isibéal along both harder and faster than she was comfortable going, but the sense of foreboding in him was growing exponentially with every tick of the countdown clock's minute hand. He had no idea what was coming, only that it was. And when it got here? All hell was going to break loose. No pun intended.

The terrain began to change shape and appearance as the forest abruptly ended and left him and Isibéal exposed. Nothing grew here, not even the occasional shrub or scrap of weed. The earth was charred here and there. It looked as if chunks of burning *something* had fallen from the sky and hit the hard-packed dirt at random intervals, leaving behind black starburst patterns that pockmarked the ground. There was nowhere to hide, nothing to duck behind and very little opportunity to do anything besides dash for the rolling hills ahead.

He hated the feeling that this was little more than a test, a chance for him to fail on an epic level and lose Iz after having just gained her. Regained her. Whatever. It mattered that they didn't end up separated by life *or* death, and the best way to see that through was to get her to the other side and into the Arcanum's protective care. The men might not know exactly what to do to keep her safe, but they'd manage. At least until Ethan could figure out what it meant for them—him and Iz—too. He was admittedly flying blind here, not sure what to do to keep this woman and her newfound mortality safe in an unpredictable immortal world of threats and things that went boo in the night.

They were halfway across the barren ground when Isibéal yanked her hand free and stopped.

Momentum had Ethan stumbling as he turned and backtracked with the grace of a cow recovering from general anesthesia. "What's wrong?"

She stared at a burned spot on the ground, eyes wide.

"Iz?" he pressed.

Pointing at the sooty mark, she asked in a horrified voice, "What *does* that?"

He glanced at the dark blotch and did a double take. He'd thought the blemishes were charred spots, but looking at them now? Not even close. The inky, ashy area wasn't the black of soot but rather a black*ish* color. Edges were defined, not fuzzy. The marks were also spread out farther apart than he'd originally thought, and they were…wet? No, not wet. Damp. In a viscous way. Then the breeze shifted and the smell forced him back a full step. *Blood. Old* and *new*. "Iz, we need to move."

A fine vibration ran through the ground and up through the soles of his feet.

Isibéal went to the balls of her feet and stepped sideways. "What was that?"

"I have no idea." The vibration hit again, and he couldn't help reaching for her and pulling her close. "But I don't think it's anything we should stick around and see for prosperity's sake."

She took a step toward the hilly terrain they'd been headed for and froze when the vibrations beneath the surface intensified.

"Stand still," Ethan said so quietly the wind nearly carried his words away.

Isibéal looked over her shoulder at him. It was the only reason she didn't see the ground fracture and that… that…*thing* emerge. Thin, albino-pale skin stretched taut over a blue-veined neck. The thing had no eyes and no truly definable face, only a gaping hole about two feet across filled with rotting teeth and a prehensile tongue that looked sharp enough to slice a human body in half if the thing felt so compelled.

"Isibéal, don't move." Hell, he wanted to tell her to not breathe, but that would eventually make her fine muscles shake, and any attention from this earthworm from—literally—hell would be unwelcome.

"It's behind me, isn't it?"

He dipped his chin.

"What is it?"

"Not sure."

"How bad is it?"

He didn't want to answer that, but if it helped prepare her for the reality she would have to face, answer he would. "I'll need to change my shorts when we get home."

"Good thing I'm..." Her brow creased.

"Commando." Breathing through his mouth to try to avoid as much of the thing's stench as possible, he said very quietly, "Remember when the basilisk-lindworm hybrid threatened the village of—"

"Ballinknock." One eyebrow rose. "Pale, no eyes, several antennae on top of its head, thick body, serrated teeth?"

He gave a short nod as the creature rose another foot from the sand. "Short front legs with shiny black claws that look like they could eviscerate a cow in one swipe?"

"Durand."

"How deep is the shit pile we're standing in, Iz?"

She worried her bottom lip. "I wouldn't breathe through my mouth."

His balls drew up so tight to his body they probably

resembled those teeny, tiny crafting pompoms. *Freaking fabulous.* If ever he needed testosterone production, that sense of male invincibility combined with the urge to protect what was his, it was now. He needed the boost that would hit his system like nitrogen and drive him to move with aggressive abandon. He *needed* the help, the confidence booster, because there was no getting out of this without it.

As for Isibéal? His mind raced over what seemed like a thousand examples of her bravery during his former lifetime. She would hold up, keep up in a fight. She always had done so. In truth, she had always been the catalyst that kept him ahead of trouble and out of death's reach over the years they partnered together. This time was a little different, though, and circumstances? Far, far different.

No matter.

They'd make it out of this because the alternative was no alternative at all.

The durand's antennae flexed and twitched. That was all the warning it gave before it lunged for Isibéal, its body fully emerging from the sand, its claws clacking and its gaping mouth raining saliva like a rabid animal. It whipped its antennae like weapons, each one clearly capable of causing damage, but it was the thing's waxy gray tongue, impossibly long and forked, that lashed out with obvious intent to do more than simply wound its prey.

Isibéal.

"Run!" he shouted, reaching for her.

The monster's tongue caught Isibéal across the shoulder blade, and she screamed in pain even as she arched her back and threw herself toward Ethan's outstretched hand.

Yanking her behind him, Ethan forgot everything

he knew about finesse with a sword and relied on brute strength and rage. To hell with maiming the son of a bitch. He swung with the intent to kill.

Contact.

The sword tip bit into the durand's flesh below its yawning mouth. Deep blue blood arced in a wide spray that stained the ground.

Tail thrashing, the monster squealed with furious protest and yanked its head out of reach of the blade, its sinewy body twisting over itself repeatedly as it coiled.

The ground vibrated and Isibéal shouted at him, "Incoming!"

Ethan stepped into the swing this time. The durand snapped its jaw. Steel met muscle. Head separated from neck, the creature's body flopping to the ground, where it roiled as if in angry protest to its unforeseen death.

Isibéal grabbed Ethan's hand and yanked him away from his first kill. Not that he would have gone all Davy Crockett and skinned it and made a hat or anything, but damn, he'd kept them alive. That was worth momentary reflection.

Until he followed the line of her pointed finger and saw the undulating ground. "How many?" he asked as they sprinted toward the hills.

"One is one too many." She ran in front of him, the shirt she wore gashed open over her damaged shoulder. "Two and you've got yourself a mob as far as I'm concerned."

Ethan kicked harder to catch up, doing his best to get a look at the place the durand had struck her. The ripped shirt finally gaped and revealed ragged edges along the wound, the cut deep. A flash of bone showed as she pumped her arms. Sweat and blood intermingled and wicked into organic fabric, the shirt sticking to her back everywhere the fabric touched her.

She didn't make a sound as they ran.

As she began to slow.

As the arm belonging to the wounded shoulder hung at an odd angle.

As the skin began to weep poison.

As blood began to flow more freely.

As, right before his eyes, Isibéal began to die.

Chapter 14

There was cold, and there was *cold*. This kind of cold was unbearable, leaching through Isibéal's bloodstream and chilling her to her very marrow. This was the cold that froze tissue, rendered a sufferer a victim. And as her blood cooled and began to crystallize, a bitter, achingly familiar feeling stole over her, cascading from the crown of her head to the arches of her feet and stealing the color from her toes. The tenor of the threat that approached was familiar. She knew it. Recognized it. Possessed a nauseating certainty regarding what it would feel like in many ways. Wondered morbidly how it would be different for others. Less than two degrees of separation stood between the horror of uncontrolled pain and the reality of imminent death.

Isibéal knew what it was to face death's call and be unable to refuse.

Damn if she would go through that again.

Behind her, Ethan cursed. He was closer than he'd been since they took off, almost hovering.

She didn't mind. Having him right there was a reassurance. If she stumbled—

The ground erupted before her, a massive durand blowing through the packed topsoil with enough force that dirt flew in every direction. Vibrations beneath her bare feet said more followed. It wouldn't matter how many showed up if she didn't survive *this* one, though.

"Ethan!" She reached for the sword with her good hand.

Her husband eased up behind her. "On three, you dart to the left. I'll go right." The durand clacked its claws and teeth, spittle flying, and Ethan shouted, "Three!" and shoved her.

The demon whipped its head around to follow her as she fell, then caught Ethan's movement and started to turn for him, but the thing was too late.

Ethan swung wide and sliced the creature's tongue off before plunging his sword hilt-deep into its unnatural skin. Blood sprayed. The thing screamed. Ethan bellowed, retrieving his blade to swing again and again, beating the giant monster until it fell. Death took it quickly and with little more than a final twitch.

Isibéal made it to her hands and knees, the resonance in the ground beneath her increasing. "Ethan? I can't…"

The flash of steel made her squint in the faint sunlight as Ethan drove the blade into the ground beside her. "We have to move, Iz."

On her hands and knees, she studied the ground in front of her. She had so little left to offer, so little time left. "Run, Ethan. Get to the portal as fast as you can. Leave me the sword and I'll hold them off as long as possible."

He laid a hand on her neck, fingers twitching at the icy cold. "What did that thing do to you?"

"Poison," she said around her tongue gone thick. "Go. Now. While you can."

"The hell I will," he snarled.

Strong arms scooped her up as if she weighed no more than a lamb and, with infinite care, shifted her so she hung over his shoulder. With one arm wrapped around the backs of her thighs, he held her close. With the other, he retrieved the sword.

Her bad arm and shoulder screamed in protest, demanding the same of her. She obliged.

"Shh, baby. Just…hold on." He took off, running in a low, smooth gait. The sword often served as an alternative to a walking stick, helping him maintain his balance as he traversed the growing cracks in the soil. Some were little more than hairline fractures in the expansive dry crust of land, while others were wide enough he was forced to jump over them.

Isibéal had the best view of those, seeing as she stared down Ethan's back. The deep, dark chasms yawned beneath her every time he pushed himself to cross one. She only thought she'd been terrified until he crossed an expanse at the same time a durand burrowed beneath them…and she saw it at the same time it saw her. Shifting course, it tried to throw itself out of the mini-canyon, but Ethan had crossed it and moved on before it broke the surface.

Isibéal watched it sink back into the depths and the more radical vibration took up again, passing through Ethan and into the tender part of her abdomen, as the demon resumed its pursuit.

"Ethan," she wheezed. "Beneath us."

"I know."

He pushed harder, his legs pumping. Every jarring step repeatedly drove his shoulder into the soft fullness of her belly until she couldn't breathe. Bracing her good hand on his lower back, she pressed up, desperate for relief. What she saw was a durand blow through the soil's crust, half slithering and half dragging its body toward them at an impossible rate of speed.

"Go, go, go!" she managed on a strangled cry. Ethan dropped the sword, swung her into his arms...and jumped.

There was a moment of suspended weightlessness when everything seemed possible—flight, escape, survival. And then they began to fall.

You jumped, *Kemp? Mission Impossible much?*
Above him, the durand roared.
Too close. Why is it so close?
He looked up and clutched Isibéal tighter. The damned demon had followed him over the edge and now tumbled ass over teakettle, gaining on them in its free fall. Below, the river he'd seen and heard—broad as a twelve-lane interstate and black as pitch—raced along, tumbling over rocks and spilling over short falls. There was no way to know how deep it was, but his choice had been to chance a horrendous fall or be eaten alive.

Yeah...no.

He'd risk a hell of a lot before he'd offer up his thigh as some nightmare's drumstick.

What he wouldn't give for control of his magicks right about now. Gods, he'd taken them for granted. For years they'd been his constant, his go-to, the first thing he reached for when a problem arose. It didn't matter if that problem was a difficult delivery in the hospital where he'd worked in the States or a temperamental ghost who'd haunted him incessantly. Magick had been available, so magick he'd used. Liberally.

Now, faced with the inability to conjure a rabbit out of a hat, he had to resort to what he knew as a healer and what he'd learned among the Druids' Arcanum.

First rule of thumb: Survive.

The distance between him and the river dissolved like gelatin in hot water. There and then gone. He smelled the foul stench of the durand as it shot past him. Ethan twisted away, guarding his woman with his body.

She's too cold.

The durand screeched its fury at being denied the meal it had pursued. Then the stupid creature seemed to realize that impact was imminent, and none of its temper tantrum would matter in three…two…one…

It hit a rock and came apart in spectacular fashion, bits and pieces being carried away in the river's rapids.

Ethan issued a short prayer, asking for deep water. "Hold your breath," he said into Iz's ear.

They hit with bone-jarring force. Something in his left ankle flexed and then snapped. He shouted involuntarily and took on mouthful after mouthful of rancid water. Choking and sputtering, he fought his way toward first the surface and then the shore. A small eddy caught him and Iz and spun them like aquatic tops, bouncing them off smooth-faced boulders before jettisoning them down a small straightaway and right over the face of a short waterfall.

Through it all, he held on to her. The water was cold. She was colder. And it was scaring the ever-loving snot out of him. She was mortal now. Her skin shouldn't feel like ice. She shouldn't feel as limp and boneless as an anesthetized surgical patient. But she did. She hadn't answered him since she told him to "Go!"

Panic proved an incredible motivator. It pushed Ethan past the excruciating pain in his left foot and forced him to fight his way to the shallows. On his knees, he carried Isibéal ashore.

When she was laid out before him, panic stepped aside and fear moved in. She was pale. Not the traditional pale of an Irishwoman, but pale as in her-ghost-had-possessed-better-skin-tone. He turned her gently and blanched at the durand wound's appearance. When he'd first looked at the injury, a very small area of bone was exposed. Now? There was a solid three square inches of white bone glaring back at him. The tissue had begun to look necrotic, sloughing off in small pieces as it died.

Was the durand that poisonous? It didn't even bite *her. It tongue-lashed her.*

He racked his brain trying to think about what he knew of the demon, the river shallows in which they hovered and treating injuries with naturally available field supplies in the Shadow Realm. The results were, in general, the equivalent of a "404 Page Not Found" internet search.

Awesome.

"When we're back at the keep, I'm doing a crash course in alternative realms. And demonology. And all the other scary crap. Anything that might get thrown my way. Or, you know, that might *kill me*. I'm going to figure out how to survive every damned bit of it. Screw the rest of the world's—and the Arcanum's—guaranteed mockery."

She didn't answer his mini-rant but instead lay there silent and slowly bleeding.

That scared him more than anything.

"You stay with me, Iz. I didn't just find you only to

have you be taken from me by some gods-be-damned carnivorous earthworm."

He pulled his pants off and emptied the pockets. A small pack of unopened stick gum, a paper clip, $0.76 in change, two rubber bands, a soaking wet Band-Aid and ChapStick. Dropping his chin, he let fear take hold for a split second. His heartbeat ran wild, his pulse hammering. Whatever had broken in his ankle was threatening a full-on revolt of consciousness. Black spots danced across his vision.

Studying the flotsam in his palm, he snorted. "If I was MacGyver, I could take this shit and make a two-person hot-air balloon that would cross the realms and get us home. Instead? I bet I can't even get the Band-Aid to stick to your skin, honey."

"Who's MacGyver?"

He dropped everything and reached for Iz. "Total chump. Now talk to me. What hurts? Clinical assessment and five-dollar words, Iz."

"Everything hurts." She shivered so hard her teeth clacked together with enough force that Ethan winced in sympathy. "Did you actually *jump*? And did the durand really follow us over the edge?"

Ethan looked around. "Yes and yes."

"Where is it?"

He gestured toward the rock it had initially hit. "Part of it's still there." He pointed across the river. "Part of it's over there." And he waved downriver. "Most of it's down there somewhere, but not all in the same place." Leaning over her, he stroked the wet curls from her face. "Talk to me, Iz. I'm serious."

She swallowed and gasped. "Durand poison crystallizes the victim's blood. Slows the system down until the blood thickens and the heart can't pump it. The durand prefers carrion, so it waits for its victim to die and then… then…" She looked away, swallowing repeatedly until she simply couldn't anymore. With a shove, she rolled over and heaved out the meager contents of her stomach.

It would feed. That was what she'd been unable to say—that the durand would then feed on its kill. All those black spots on the ground weren't burn marks. They were places where the demons' victims had bled out and then been consumed.

Ethan stroked her hair off her face and murmured nonsense until she rolled onto her back again. "What do I have to do to purge the poison?"

"You can't."

He gripped her shoulders, albeit with gentleness. "Hear me, Iz. I *will*."

"My blood has already begun to thicken, Ethan, and I'm…" She rolled her head to the side so she looked away. "I can't."

"You'll survive this, Isibéal Cannavan, because I won't settle for anything less. Now *think*. What cures a durand's bite?" Something danced around the fringes of his mind, just out of reach. "For every curse, there's a counter-curse. For every light spell, there's a dark. For every poison, there's an antidote. Nothing exists in this, or any, world without balance. *You* taught me that."

Mild shaking had set in, a palsy-like reaction to her system shutting down. He wanted to scream at her to think and to do it faster. She'd been the wise woman, the ultimate healer. He'd been the strategist and the gods' sword arm in the mortal realm. He needed her now, needed her to do what she did best.

And want? Oh, he wanted. With a vengeance. He wanted to demand she hold on and not give in to death here, in the Shadow Realm, where her soul would be trapped. Tortured. Even consumed.

"Mint," she breathed. "Infusion."

"Mint? I need a mint infusion? Into the wound? A poultice? Topical?"

"I think…" Her eyelids fluttered.

"I'm in *hell*. Where am I supposed to find mint?" He stood to pace—or stomp—and immediately ended up on his knees again when his wrecked foot gave out. It felt like he'd broken the cuboid and at least two metatarsals. Not just damaged. *Broken*. "Mint," he said over and over, tunneling his hands through his hair. "Where do I get mint?"

Gripping handfuls of hair, he lifted his face to the sky and closed his eyes. He was unraveling at the seams. If he didn't gain control of himself, he was going to come apart completely.

"I smelled…" she said so softly he instinctively leaned toward her. "MacGyver."

He sat back, more confused than ever. "What exactly does smelling MacGyver have to do with finding mint for an infusion?" Understanding hit so hard he sat up as if shoved. He almost dislocated two fingers trying to dig the junk out of his pockets again. Change, rubber bands, wet Band-Aid and gum. *Mint* gum.

To create an infusion, he needed water. The river raced along in front of him. Yeah, that wasn't an option. At all. Whatever else might be under the surface that gave the water its unique color and repulsive smell, the durand's body parts had been added to the mix. Not even boiling the stuff would be sufficient to rid it of the nasties it harbored. And as for hunting down another source? There wasn't time. He'd have to make this one work on the fly.

"Improvisation is the hallmark of genius. Or something." Unwrapping the little pack of gum as fast as his fumbling fingers would go, he shoved piece after piece in his mouth until he was chewing a wad of the stuff and drooling like mad at the pungent, nasal-clearing taste.

With anxiety driving him like a show pony in a carting parade, Ethan rolled Iz over, trying not to despair at her lack of response or the way her body moved—boneless but not with fluid control. She was too cold.

Pulling the gum from his mouth, he grimaced. "W-W-M-D?"

What would MacGyver do, indeed.

Chapter 15

Isibéal jerked away from the searing touch to her back and scrabbled for purchase with her fingers and bare feet as she searched for any avenue to escape the excruciating burn in her back.

Can't.

Cold.

So cold.

Died.

Resurrected.

Heat.

Too much heat.

Gods, the pain.

Can't.

Of course, this wasn't nearly as bad as the soul-shattering experience of resurrection, but neither was it pleasant. Heat spread through her, relentlessly seeking the source of her cold and annihilating it one hellish lick at a time. For what seemed like hours, days, weeks, she lay on the hard ground and suffered, alternating between shivering and sweating. When warmth slowly returned, it manifested first in her shoulders before washing up her neck and down her spine with lazy insouciance. She didn't know whether to groan and plead for more of that blessed warmth or remain silent so the ministration wouldn't stop. In the end, silence won out. She found her focus reveling in the sound of her heartbeat and the aching of her joints and muscles.

Evidence she had survived.

Proof she was alive.

Poison.

Her eyes snapped open and her body, relaxed only seconds before, went as rigid as a ship's main mast. No flexing. No wavering. No forgiveness. She'd faced death yet again. If what her wavering vision translated proved true, she'd beaten death before it could claim her with any permanence.

Behind her, Ethan muttered with unapologetic vehemence.

"You listen to me, woman. You don't return to me and then screw around with death as if it holds no consequence. You get your ass back here. I've things to say to you that won't be nearly as effective if uttered to a corpse. In fact, it might be illegal. And the Arcanum will think I've lost my mind. I might have. Lost my mind, that is. I don't need that kind of trouble. If I get harassed or arrested, it will be your fault. In fact, I'll have that inscribed on your headstone. 'Here lay a lovely wife, who caused her man nothing but strife. She courted death like an unrequited lover, and when she was a ghost she did nothing but hover.'"

"I certainly did more than hover," Isibéal insisted. "I haunted you properly."

Pressed to her back one moment, Ethan's hands were gone the next. The man himself scrambled around her on his hands and right knee, his left leg held off the ground so his foot touched nothing. "Oh, thank the gods." He pulled her into his arms with tender care and held her close for a single heartbeat before he leaned away and let his gaze rove over her face. It was as if he searched for irrefutable proof she was indeed with him. Whatever he found satisfied him. He tightened his hold and pressed her cheek against his bare chest. "You stay with me, Isibéal. You stay."

She smiled, her mouth and cheek twisting oddly against his skin since he refused to relax his hold. "It's not as if I intended to wander off."

"But you did," he said, shifting so he whispered into her hair. "You took years off my life."

"Can't have that."

Chapped lips pressed to one temple and then the other before moving on to deposit tender kisses all over her face, neck and bare shoulders. "You stay."

"Not here," she amended.

Ethan glanced first at the sky and then at her. "The suns are setting. We have to find shelter. No way do I want to spend the night out here, exposed."

"The day has finally come when you're not comfortable exposing yourself?" She let out a mock gasp. "Ladies, let your daughters loose. The day has finally come that Lach…Ethan is no longer comfortable exposing himself."

He pinched her butt. "Very funny."

Leaning back, Isibéal propped herself on one hand and considered their surroundings. "Lugh said if we ran into the River of Harrow, we'd veered off course. I don't imagine there are many rivers in the Shadow Realm, let alone more than one we might run into as we followed his general directions. Just how lost are we?"

Ethan settled her and stood, favoring the ankle that had swollen to the size of a small melon and planting his hands on his hips for all the worlds like a conquering Viking. "We were headed in the right direction until that thing herded us to the cliff."

Isibéal's chin snapped up. She ignored the sharp pain in her neck. "Say that again."

Ethan's brow furrowed and he looked down at her. "Which part?"

"The part about being herded." She held out a hand and, when he hesitated, bade him hurry with a wave of her hand. Though she was a wee bit wobbly on her feet, she managed. "The durand herded us to the cliff's edge."

"It seemed like it, yes. There were three, total, that we dealt with, and each of them was intent on driving us to the cliffs."

"And away from their killing grounds. Why, Ethan? What sense does that make? They kill—and consume— where the first one confronted us." She crossed her arms over her chest, the cooling evening air beginning to seep into her skin and settle in her joints. Reaching back, she touched the wound, and her fingers sank into something dense and sticky. She pulled her hand away, rubbing it against what was left of her borrowed shirt. "I'd like to know where you managed to obtain mint."

"Gum."

"What is 'gum'?"

"It's this stuff you chew."

"Why?"

His eyebrows winged down. "Why what?"

"Why do you chew it?"

He opened his mouth to answer and shut it. This happened twice more before he shrugged and simply said, "Because you want to?"

"Is it food?"

"No."

"Is it used medicinally, then?"

He grinned. "Not exactly."

"Then what do you use it for?"

"Nothing. Honest. It's a pleasurable thing for some people. Others might use it to fend off a strong oniony or garlicky lunch. But really? It's a sweet. A candy."

"You saved my life with a type of sticky sweet." She shook her head. "I may never truly find where I fit in this time or place."

He crossed to her and cradled her face in his hands. "Never say that. You'll fit because you're meant to fit."

Her heart had hoped to hear him call her his own, but again he neglected to claim her.

She gave a single dip of the chin and turned away. *Focus on the now. Survival first. Sentiment second.* "You're right in that we'll need shelter this eve."

"Where there's water, there's often natural shelter."

She looked around again. "I would hazard it's safe to say there's nothing 'natural' about this place."

"Let's hope the general standard of shelter near a natural water source holds true across the realms." Ethan hobbled around to move in behind her and began peeling the gum away from her wound with extreme care. "How did you know to use mint?"

"My mother taught me much about the healing arts."

"I remember her, but the memories are dim." He tossed the gum aside and kicked sand over it, partially burying it. "Did we get on, then?"

"You adored and respected each other." She glanced over her shoulder. "She was so pleased when the Elder's Council appointed you as the Assassin. She also privately feared for your life but was far too proud to say so." Isibéal couldn't stop the soft laugh that rose at the memory. "Mum was so afraid someone would think her fear for you equated to a lack of faith in your ability to run the Arcanum and protect the Druidic race with the necessary brutality. I do believe she would have cursed anyone she overheard speaking ill of you had I not solicited her solemn promise to do no such thing."

"I dig around for memories all the time. Sometimes I come up with small nuggets of the past, but most of the time I'm left beyond frustrated at the giant void in my personal timeline." He settled his chin on her head. "I wish I remembered more."

"Time heals much." She reached up and trailed a finger along the short stubble that decorated his jaw. "And for those wounds that fail to heal cleanly, time diminishes the pain to a dull ache that the heart and mind can live with."

"Did time heal your wounds?"

The question elicited a sharp response, her body jerking as if shocked. Dropping her hand to her side, she intentionally broke that fragile connection, that point of touch. "It's not the same, and well you know it. I was dead but not gone, an incorporeal soul trapped in a cursed grave. I heard everything and could do nothing."

"Iz, I..." He sighed and pulled her tighter. "I'm sorry. It's just, I don't know that time will be able to heal this for me. Not on any level."

She twisted around in the shelter of his arms, intent on seeing his face when he answered. So much could be hidden in a light and deceptive tone, but the eyes inevitably gave away the secrets a man sought to disguise. "Why?"

Ethan's mouth twisted into a hard grimace. "How can it? 'Time' would have to return to me the very things it *took* from me, and that's impossible. So…what? I'm just supposed to settle for what it might offer me now and count myself lucky?" He shook his head. "No, Isibéal. I'm due more than a token gesture of goodwill from time, the universe, karma, the gods—whatever source you want to lay the blame on. I don't care. I'm due a little more than a trip to the Shadow Realm and a handout gesture from a dark god."

"A 'handout' is one thing, certainly," Isibéal croaked, shoving out of his embrace. "But a…" She tunneled her hands through her hair and spun away from him. "A… *token gesture of goodwill.* Do you even hear yourself, Ethan?" The last was called over her shoulder as she stalked away. *Token.* That singular word struck her a near physical blow. He had been so adamant that she consider the consequences of her reincarnation, had insisted he didn't want her to go through the pain if she wasn't certain the outcome would be worth it. Maybe the truth was far more complicated. Or it could be that the truth was much simpler. Perhaps…perhaps he hadn't wanted *her* but had been too guilt-ridden or even too caught up in the moment to admit he hadn't been ready for the obligations inherent to marriage. He clearly thought that her reincarnation held little of value for him—considered it a pittance and not an immeasurable boon, an offering so insignificant in scope that he refused to assign it value.

Circumstance had withered away any objectivity and practical sense he'd retained, had left him so angry, not about what *they* had lost but what *he* had lost. He couldn't see beyond that anger. Couldn't see the single opportunity standing in front of him, the opportunity that represented the heart of what had been taken from him without recourse.

Anger and hurt and a sense of injustice had blinded him until he couldn't see *her*.

If he continued to embrace this narrow viewpoint, he'd miss his chance to reclaim what might have been, and that? That was his recompense—the very same one most people were never afforded. He had loved and been loved, and he stood there prepared to throw it all away over unresolved anger.

His words had hurt her like none before, not in this existence or her previous lifetime. They cut deep, and she'd lost her emotional heart's blood. Never had she wanted to strike someone for uttering such an idiotic, hurtful sentiment.

Walking along the river's alternately rocky and then sandy bank, Isibéal put some distance between herself and Ethan. She needed to think. An unnatural cold emanated from the river, the running water pushing the gelid air toward Isibéal, where it twined around her as if she were a familiar and beloved totem. Physically and emotionally numbed by both the chill and the hurt, she tried to feel nothing, think nothing and, above all else, hear nothing.

The breeze grew stronger. It whispered against her skin as if the breeze itself was a sentient thing, its paper-thin voice depositing doubts layer after layer until she was drowning in it. She tried to turn back to Ethan, to reach for him and have him reach back. He could ground her. But her feet wouldn't obey, wouldn't turn to carry her to where she'd left him standing. Alone. The whispering morphed from a single voice to a cacophony of voices that echoed through her head, some lobbing questions at her while others planted the seeds of self-doubt and nurtured them.

Did you cause this? Did you push Ethan into accepting your reincarnation because it's what you wanted? He doesn't want you. Not like this. Not like you are now. Cursed. Did you fail to see what he really wanted? Did you consider his needs at all? No. You didn't. You're too selfish and self-serving in your desire. He can't possibly love you. And what proof do you have that you truly love him? You don't know *him. Not as he is now. He's smarter. Smarter than you'll ever be. He's received years of formal education and training, the kinds you can't fathom. He knows things, understands things, so far beyond your capacity for learning that you look like nothing but a fraud. A deceiver. A pretender in a world of authentic physicians. He's a licensed healer who is surrounded by men...and women...all of whom are his true equals in all things. What do you know? Why did you ever believe he could accept you as a simple,* rural *healer who works with herbs and magicks that require you to draw from the earth? Even your magick isn't your own.* Borrowed. *Ethan can go into the human body and effect healing with his hands in a way you never could. Or* will. *He delivers infants to those who were told they could not have children. He uses his strengths to save the mothers who, under your care, would be lost to death's cold grasp. You aren't even a proper midwife. You are no healer but a charlatan who sells her services like a common doxy. You are, at least, smart enough to see that you cannot possibly fit here. Not now. Not ever. You were not then and are not now made for this time, this place or this man. He will never give up what or who he is in order to remain near you. Fool! He will return to his former life and his career and likely a casual lover, and he'll never look back. You realize all this, right? You died and remained stagnant while he was born again, born to do more, to be more, than you ever will.*

Isibéal went to her knees, hands pressed over her ears as she rocked and cried. She couldn't do this. She was no match for all the intricacies of modern life or the way he fit so seamlessly into the Arcanum's daily routine. This and so much more—it was all she needed to affirm what she had begun to suspect.

She tightened her arms around her waist and held on. The self-comforting gesture was a poorly concealed effort to hold herself together as the cruel voices grew louder, each one clamoring for the right to feast on the misery and darkness of being buried in the innermost reaches of her soul. Those voices had done what no one, either individual or group, had ever accomplished before, though there had certainly been attempts to bring her down. She, the strongest witch in all of Ireland. But these voices had managed, laying undiluted pity at her feet like a dark offering.

Isibéal found she didn't care for their brand of gifting. At all.

Ethan watched Isibéal stalk away, her hips swaying seductively despite her ramrod-straight spine. And, gods deliver him, he knew she had a spine on her that could go rigid in 2.7 seconds flat when she was pissed off. Not if, but certainly *when*. The woman was a spitfire. With her temper brewing, he probably should have been a little more concerned than he was, but he couldn't bring himself to get too upset. He'd expected they'd each garner some emotional bumps and ego bruises as they sorted out what this thing between them was now and, very possibly, would become. They had plenty of time to explore their options now that she had a corporeal body, though. There was no rush, even though every future he imagined had her square in the middle of it while the thought of any kind of life without her was becoming harder and harder to fathom.

The very idea of her not being the heart of his every day made his stomach pitch and roll without warning, the feeling much like that of a ship sitting dead on the water in the heart of a storm-tossed sea.

He rubbed his belly, brow furrowing. *What's that about? And why isn't she stopping?*

"Isibéal?" He took a wobbly step, then two after her, and before he could stop himself, he was following her, his progression more run-hop-skip than anything resembling a jog. "Don't go far, okay? I don't know what lives in the river."

Without warning, she fell to her knees and slapped her hands over her ears before she curled in on herself and began rocking.

He didn't hesitate, mostly because he didn't—*couldn't*—think. He simply broke into the running version of his awkward gait. Whether he was charging after her, to her or because of her? It didn't matter. All Ethan knew was that he had to get to her. Now.

His lungs burned with every deep draw of insufficient air even as his foot threatened to turn to ash with every searing step. Gods, he hated this realm. He longed to take Isibéal back to the peace and quiet the Nest, and Ireland, generally afforded. Sure, the castle was drafty and Ireland's weather almost required inhabitants to possess professional ark-building skills, but the beauty of both home and country had become so critical to his sense of well-being. He wasn't a coward, but in a place where rivers either ran cold or burned the skin from your bones? Where skies had three suns, all of them bleak? Where scary-assed, half dinosaur, half raptor and wholly terrifying creatures lived and no one thought it was remotely odd? And, above all, where cranked-out dark gods with bad attitudes hung out and granted wishes that weren't exactly wishes but could become wishes? None of this shit equaled his cuppa, but put them all together? He wanted out of hell's tea parlor. Yesterday.

Going to his knees, he skidded to Isibéal's side. "What happened?"

She jerked at his touch.

He ignored her response and the way it pierced his heart like a narrow hatpin. Ethan ran his hands over every inch of her he could reach, some areas twice. Result? He found absolutely nothing wrong.

Sitting back on his heels, he dug his fingers into his denim-clad thighs until the weave of the fabric imprinted on his fingertips. "What just happened?"

"Nothing."

Her coarse, whispered response could have been shouted for all that it rattled him. Ethan forced his hands to relax, stretching his fingers out and turning his hands over to rest them palms up on his thighs. He needed to remember that this couldn't be easy on her, either. That he had to make a conscious effort to keep that fact at the forefront of his mind shamed him. It wasn't that he didn't care about her. He did. In fact, he'd even go so far as to say he cared for her a lot. What bugged him was that his emotional investment in her had gotten carried away, and he'd let his feelings for her dictate his actions, even when it hadn't been in his best interest. *Their* best interests. Of course that was what he'd meant.

Beside him, Isibéal stopped rocking. She uncurled her

body and, balanced on her heels, lifted her chin toward the setting suns. "You were right. We'll need shelter."

"Yeah." He ran a hand behind his neck and pulled. "Shelter." She was discussing shelter after falling to the ground? Behaving like this was normal? Nothing about *any* of this could be filed under the heading of normal.

As if to punctuate the necessity that he take action, a shadow passed overhead.

Ethan jerked as if shocked. "Shit, shit, shit. I bet it's the raptodactylmon."

She shielded her eyes with a hand as she searched the sky. "The what?"

He pointed toward the creature cruising the skies, riding thermals and searching the ground. Apparently it hadn't seen them yet. It would.

"Raptodactylmon. I didn't know what it was actually called, so I bastardized a hybrid name that made sense. Okay, it made sense at the time," he amended at her sharp look. He reached over and settled his shirt more solidly over her shoulders. "I don't know much about it except that, like everything else in this cursed realm, it's a carnivore that feeds on whatever it can catch. If it sees us?" The muscle at the back of his jaw worked as he scanned the sky before looking over at her. "We'll become the blue plate special on today's menu."

"I have no idea what a 'blue plate special' is."

"It's tasty, but it really means we need to go."

Something large splashed downstream. Ethan glared at the heavens. "Right. Because we don't have enough working against us." Holding out his hand, he wiggled his fingers. "Let's put some distance between us and the splash and a ceiling between us and my old friend up there."

Iz grabbed his hand, and, balanced on his good foot,

he helped her stand before pulling her in close. The gesture would have been tender in almost any other situation, but right now, Ethan needed the physical support. They followed the twisting riverbank, the going slow as they picked their way around huge rocks, fallen trees and the occasional skeletal remains of creatures Ethan refused to consider too closely. The uncanny feeling they were being watched had him glancing over his shoulder repeatedly, but nothing was there.

The next time he looked back, Isibéal followed his line of sight. "Do you think it saw us?"

"No idea." Ethan shivered and rubbed his arms. "Man, this realm sucks. Seriously sucks." He glanced at her. "Hard truth? I can't watch Shark Week without suffering nightmares, and vacations at the beach? No, thanks. But this realm? This is a new personal high on the terror scale. This little vacay is going to land my ass in therapy for the rest of my life."

Like every other time he made a pop culture reference, her brow furrowed. This time, though, she didn't ask for clarification. Didn't utter her predictable "Pardon?" that he'd grown so accustomed to. Probably because the sentiment was clear: soulless creatures that were stronger, faster and hungrier than they were hunted them. Actively.

The need to protect his woman rose in him, to see her to safety and claim her body as a reminder that she was his.

Before he had the pleasure of visualizing the latter, his long-established bachelorhood rose with a fierce howl of indignance and beat against his skull in violent protest. That piece of his psyche had been simmering, dropping comments—some subtle, others not so much—since Rowan first declared Ethan's ghost to be his wife. Rife with denials, that little voice had grown sharp, clawed and vicious. Like now. The part of him that revered his independence, that same part that rebelled at the idea of commitment and relationships that lasted through more than a lunar cycle, was opposed to the idea he could simply be saddled with a wife because he'd taken vows in a previous life. He'd chosen her hundreds of years ago as a different person. He hadn't chosen her *now*, in *this* life. How could the man he'd been then realistically be the responsibility of who he was today? They were two different men, he and Lachlan. And as Ethan, he hadn't wanted a wife. Not in this life, anyway. If he had, he'd have married.

Not that he didn't like Isibéal. He'd even go so far as to admit he had feelings for her. But Ethan had spent his adult life protecting his independence with near-rabid ferocity. No way would a sane person expect that the vows of marriage would, first, carry across the boundaries of time or, second, hold the same—or even similar—levels of obligation and responsibility as they had when originally repeated.

Ethan shook his head.

A screech ripped across the air, rolling forward and over his shoulders. Instinct made his muscles contract as the fight-or-flight instinct surfed the waves of adrenaline that flooded his system. Damn if he'd race blindly down the riverbank. He'd run once today already. The result? He'd been forced even farther from the portal that would get him and Iz safely home. Running was out. That didn't mean he'd stroll along until death snatched him up.

"Ethan?" Her voice had risen an octave or five. "It's coming."

He glanced over his shoulder at the same time he

tightened his grip on Isibéal's hand. "We're going to make it."

"Going to make it *where*?" she demanded, squeezing his hand in return so hard his bones ground together.

"It's going to work out," he muttered, eyes darting left and right as he sought a cave, a rocky overhang, a thick bush—anything that would give them protection from an overhead assault. He wished desperately for the sword he'd dropped on the plains above and figured it wouldn't be the last time he longed for a weapon before they found their way out of here.

"Was that for my benefit or yours?" she asked, moving ahead as she broke into a swift jog and dragged his broken self along.

Looked like he'd be running after all.

The need to protect Iz grew stronger as the raptodactylmon closed in. Having her in front and pulling him meant he was between her and the creature in pursuit. If anyone was going to be Hell's hors d'oeuvre, it would be him. That soothed in the most disturbing way.

She yanked on his hand and made him step up the pace. "Seriously," she called back between hard breaths, "was that for my benefit? Are you trying to distract me from the fact that we've become a...what was it? Tasty menu special?"

Close enough. "Does it matter?"

"Not really." She looked again, her hand spasming in his. "If you have a plan, it would be good to, you know, put it in motion. Soon-ish. Preferably in the next, oh, thirty seconds."

"I'm open to suggestions."

She didn't answer, just went from a jog to an all-out sprint. "Keep up!"

He did his damnedest.

The familiar beat of air against his back forecast the raptodactylmon's rush to grab Ethan. Survival instinct took over, and every thought he had centered on getting Iz to safety and defending his position once *safety* became a defined place. Running as hard as he was, he nearly missed the small fissure between rock and earth, but the depth of the shadow snagged his attention. Leaping forward with serendipitous timing, he tackled Iz to the ground with a hard *oompf* as the raptodactylmon swept over them, claws outstretched to make the grab for its prey. For Ethan. But because Ethan hit the dirt, only one talon raked over his shoulder. He couldn't stop the shout of outrage that ripped through him like that claw had his flesh. Then the pain hit. Hard. Fast. Deep. If he hadn't already been down, the pain would have felled him.

Blood flowed down his left arm and left the limb essentially useless. That didn't stop him from doing the three-limbed shuffle-and-hop as he grabbed Iz and spun her around then let her go in order to point at the small opening. "There!"

She helped him to his feet and, with knees bent and shoulders low while doing his best to ignore the screaming pain in ankle *and* shoulder, they raced the few yards back to the fissure he'd seen. The opening was just as small as he'd feared, and that meant one thing.

Isibéal was going to be safe because she'd be able to get inside. Hide. Defend herself.

Ethan wouldn't.

Chapter 16

Isibéal scrambled through the narrow fissure, surprised to find a dark, dry, low-ceilinged but fairly good-size room on the other side. She crab-walked in a few feet and turned back. "It's clear."

The raptodactylmon's screech resonated, muted but nearby.

"Don't dally, Ethan," she called, fear sharpening her words.

The doorway didn't darken.

"Ethan?" When he didn't answer, she scrambled to the entrance and began wiggling through.

"Stay put."

The rasped command lacked the heat she would have expected. When her shoulders cleared the opening, she saw why.

Ethan half sat, half lay against the rock face. He had been wounded and bled profusely from shoulder to hand.

Blood dripped from his fingertips. With nothing to bandage the wound, he wouldn't be able to stanch the bleeding. He was in trouble.

"You'll not tell me to hold when you need help." She continued to press through.

"I won't fit, Iz, and the thing is on its way back." He waved absently in the direction the self-named raptodactylmon had gone. "No reason to offer it dessert after the main course. Namely, me."

She popped out of the crawl space and scanned the area. The sky was clear, but she had no doubt the thing would be back to claim its kill. "Get up," she said, grabbing Ethan's good hand and pulling.

He grunted in either protest or pain.

She wasn't sure and didn't really care. All she knew was that he *would* fit if she had to shove him in amid grumbles and protests. So she pulled, demanding he come with her.

Ethan made it to his knees.

Isibéal could work with that. "Come on, Druid."

"I'm not a Druid."

"Fine. If we're going with what you unquestionably are at the moment, come with me, you arrogant," *tug*, "overbearing," *pull*, "fatalistic," *push*, "obstinate," *shove*, "thickheaded," *yank*, "gobshite with a death wish!"

He looked down at her and wiped a bead of sweat from her brow. "That was impressive."

"You've no idea seeing as it hardly tapped into my rage. Now move." She pushed him even harder.

"I won't fit."

"Try!" The half-shouted command was laced with a wholehearted plea. "I don't want to lose you, Lachlan…" His blank stare heated with anger, but before he could rebuke her for calling him by the wrong name, she blurted out, "Just try, Ethan. Please."

"I'll never be Lachlan."

"Not. Now." She shoved her hair out of her face. "Fight with me inside."

Eyebrows winging down, he turned his attention to the opening barely big enough for her narrow frame. "It's too narrow, Iz. My shoulders will never fit."

"Then you bloody well best begin digging with your good hand, because 'never' isn't an option." She dropped to the ground and did that very thing, flinging sand like a madwoman.

He joined her without further comment, digging one-handed.

A shadow passed overhead, followed by an unquestionable squawk of rage.

"In," he shouted. "Now! My word that I'll follow," he added at her outraged look.

She scrambled through the widened opening much faster than before. Twisting, she reached for Ethan, gripped his good wrist as he gripped hers and held on.

He shoved and pushed every bit as hard as she pulled and tugged. The frantic look on his face drove her mad. Sand slipped beneath her as she dug her feet in, searching to gain purchase. A large rock scraped her heel raw. *Yes!* She didn't care about the shallow hurt. The rock equaled leverage, and she needed it. At this point, she would use, borrow or bargain for what she needed, she'd steal what couldn't be otherwise gained and she'd sleep well tonight and every night hereafter if it meant Ethan was safe.

A muffled *whump* vibrated through every part of her that touched the earth.

"Iz," Ethan said, her name on his lips a warning. "Pull harder."

So she did. Bracing herself, she put everything she had into hauling him through the opening. His shoulders made it past the narrowest spot, scraping his skin and stealing a shout of pain from him. The rest of him tumbled through without any trouble. He was through.

The opening to their little cave was now large enough they could see the raptodactylmon rush the entrance. Beak snapping and sounds of denial reverberating through the enclosed space, they watched—hands over their ears—as it scraped at the dirt. When that didn't work, the thing tried to push the rock aside.

Dirt sprinkled their shoulders as the giant rock slab shifted.

"Seriously?" Ethan asked, slightly dazed. "I went from the hors d'oeuvre tray to a veritable soup bowl?"

Isibéal hadn't considered that possibility. She held her breath and prayed that the gods of light could hear her from the Shadow Realm. "Lady, let it hold."

And it did.

Nothing the creature tried gained it any ground, and she finally started to relax. She shifted on her knees and found Ethan leaned up against a near wall, his gaze locked on the thing trying to get to them.

"We need to dress your wound," Isibéal said softly.

He didn't look at her when he answered, "It'll wait. Don't turn your back on that thing."

"I don't think it can get in."

"Just…" He lifted one shoulder in a rough shrug. "I'd feel better if we were a little more sure."

She didn't comment, simply moved in beside him to wait. Her heart quieted a bit when he took her hand in his and laced their fingers together.

Comfort given.

Comfort taken.

The voluntary gesture encouraged her to revisit the source of her ire. More accurately, her hurt. They needed to talk about this thing between them. Nothing had played out like she had dreamed it would, and the reality that they were different people—he more so than she—stung. It embarrassed her that she found she needed reassurances from him, reassurances that after they made their way from here there would be something waiting on the other side. Something that would give her some, any, hope that he wanted her as she wanted him. Some clue that he wanted a future with her—the very future they'd been denied. Nothing could be right between them and no future could possibly exist until her reincarnation was secured. That meant she had to obtain Ethan's word that he wouldn't impede her in her execution of the oath she'd made to Lugh. That Ethan wouldn't stop her from delivering her brother-in-law, his brother, Sean, to Lugh. That was the only way to avenge her murder, Lachlan's death and to settle whatever blood debt existed between the dark warlock and Lugh.

Still, she hesitated to broach this particular conversation. So much could be lost if he squashed her hope for more between them, if he denied he had feelings even similar to what they'd shared when their past lives crossed. If he told her he wanted his freedom more than he wanted her, a part of her would die. There would be no reason to solidify the reincarnation. Yet stalling would gain her nothing but a nervous stomach. *Into the breach, then.*

That was when he spoke. "Seems our friendly carnivore has given up."

She whipped her chin up and listened. Just as he'd

said, the beast seemed to have moved on. "That's a relief." Releasing his hand, she repositioned herself so she rested on her knees and faced him. That was when she realized his wound still seeped, the laceration much deeper than she'd realized. "I'm guessing we'll rest here tonight?"

"Would make the most sense." He looked at her and then away. "I'm not keen on leaving our dirt camp until the suns are up. It won't change the fact that we're still prey, but at least we'll be able to see what's coming for us."

"True." She considered his shoulder. "I'd tend that if you'd let me."

"We don't have a field kit."

She wasn't sure what a *field kit* would contain, so she didn't feel its loss as clearly as he did. "I'll work with what we have, namely your shirt." Shrugging out of the dingy garment, she ripped the sleeves away first then tore the rest of it into strips.

"Uh…" Ethan's pupils grew wider, the black eating up the colour of his irises. He shifted where he sat, adjusting the denim covering his groin.

Hiding her smile became a priority. It soothed a very feminine part of her to know he couldn't deny his attraction to her. Of course, he was a man and she'd just stripped. Perhaps it wasn't her so much as proximity to any naked female. The idea deflated her reaction and wiped the humor from her face.

"You're, um…" He gestured toward her, head to toe, with his good hand. *"Naked."*

"Problem?" The subdued tenor of her question couldn't be disguised, nor did she care. Let him know he treaded through her emotions.

"I don't know what to do with this."

This time, humor won. Hands down. Gazes locked, she blinked slowly. "I beg to differ. You proved just last night that you were well versed in 'what to do with this.' Certainly you've not forgotten."

A faint flush stole over his cheeks, chasing the pallor away.

Laughter bubbled up from deep in her chest, and she sank to rest on her heels. "You don't honestly believe I'd accost you while you're wounded." She crossed her arms under her breasts. "I assure you I can control my basest needs, sir."

"Not sure I can," he muttered, his stare locking on her bare breasts for several moments before he ripped it away. Closing his eyes, he let his head rest against the dirt wall behind him.

Hope had stirred until he looked away. Now? There was no way to interpret what he meant. She busied herself laying the strips across her thighs, the cleanest of the bunch topping the small pile. "You've seen me such hundreds of times. What would be so different now?"

He shook his head slowly, rolling it back and forth. Dust and debris drifted down to land on his shoulders.

"Stop," she admonished. "You're only getting the wound dirtier."

"You keep calling me Lachlan."

The admission caught her off guard and she fumbled the sleeve she'd rolled up as packing for the wound. Snatching it off the ground, she shook it out. "You've had this lifetime to be Ethan Kemp. I've had centuries in which I've known you as Lachlan Cannavan. Surely you can afford me a few mistakes as I adjust?"

"I'm not Lachlan."

She swallowed around the inexplicable lump in her throat. "I know."

"Do you?" He opened his eyes and looked at her with undiluted intensity.

She truly felt bare before him in a way she hadn't before. Physical nudity was easy. The way his eyes stripped her down and exposed her emotionally? Not so much. "I see the differences in the man you were and the man you are. But there are times when the two intersect and you say or do something that is so familiar... I slip, Ethan." She leaned forward and placed the packing against the wound, hoping against hope he didn't notice the way her hands shook.

"That's exactly what I'm talking about. You look at me and see him, hear him. I look at you and see *you*. Who you were doesn't dominate my perception of who you are." He closed his eyes again and let his head fall back, pain stealing what little color had returned to his face. "I need to know it's me, Ethan Kemp, you're attracted to, that it's me you turn to in the middle of the night. That you're not so desperate for what you had with Lachlan that you're willing to settle with this version of him that isn't him. I'm me." He tilted his chin back. "Gods save me, I'm rambling."

But he wasn't.

In a moment of clarity, the kind that strips away layers and leaves the truth exposed in its most fundamental form, Isibéal realized she'd done to him the very same thing she'd been angry at him for doing when he asserted that this chance was no more than a token opportunity. In failing to assure him she cared for him, in repeatedly calling him Lachlan—no matter that it was by habit and simple error, she'd made him, Ethan, a token she settled for in place of the husband she'd once loved.

With that shock came the intimate understanding of his motivation in withholding the last of himself from her. *Fear.* Fear that would stop him from allowing himself to feel for her the residual love Lachlan's spirit carried for the wife he'd lost. Her. Ethan couldn't reconcile that he was, at least in part, Lachlan Cannavan. No more than she'd been able to wholly reconcile that the man in front of her was, first and foremost, Ethan Kemp. Until they could reconcile this within and between themselves, they would forever be at odds. Always wondering. Never sure that what was between them was truly theirs and not shadows of what had belonged to the people they once were.

Isibéal worked on in silence. She thought she'd been prepared to fight her way out of the Shadow Realm. She thought she'd understood that they faced nearly impossible odds. The picture was much clearer now.

The battle in the Shadow Realm was a perilous one, but the subtle battle she and Ethan fought had far higher consequences. Lose a battle in the Shadow Realm and she'd lose her life. Lose the battle with Ethan and she'd lose her best chance at happiness in hundreds of years. She knew what that happiness felt like. To lose it now, when half of it rested in her palms and waited to be paired with its other half—the half Ethan possessed?

She forced herself to subdue the shudder that threatened to tear her apart.

She'd had happiness ripped from her grasp once before. Death would be a kinder fate.

The only option was to first win this battle and then focus on winning the entire war. Nothing else mattered. The choices they each made now would direct the path they would each take and the subsequent decisions they would make, by choice as well as necessity. That much she knew. But how could she approach this and ensure that, no matter the words exchanged or the looks shared or the touches both given and taken, she gained Ethan's personal investment? Should she be direct or more roundabout in her communication? Bold or passive in sharing her feelings? Provocative in her need for him or... No. She would never be less than direct with him. She would never be passive in speaking her needs. And she would never be accused of using sex to manipulate or, worse, as a weapon. She would be who she was. If she failed in her authenticity, she had failed long before the final battle.

Settled on her personal approach, she realized she was truly no better off in her plan to handle this strategically. All she wanted was to find the best method to encourage him to be bold in his choices where she was concerned, to find the words that would turn him toward her and then carry out the actions that would garner his loyalty. Only then would they have a chance, a real chance, at nurturing what was between them. No matter that the seeds of opportunity had been planted in the past. The love she had for Lachlan would nurture what she felt for Ethan now. It must be so. And she had to show him that what had once been between them now created the potential of what could be, a relationship built on a foundation of trust and fidelity and, above all, a foundation from which a new love could grow. That battle, if won, would afford her a chance at happiness. Should she have to make concessions to win, she would. Nothing was too great a sacrifice. But to win not only the battle but also the war, she would have to convince Ethan to let go of his anger and choose love over bitterness, and new opportunity over a history he could never change.

The problem?

Isibéal was no more a strategist than she was a commanding general, and the first shots had already been fired.

* * *

Ethan watched Isibéal through slitted eyes as she bandaged his arm. Sure, he watched her naked body, too. Who could blame him? No one who had a pulse, that much was certain. Being emotionally confused did not an eunuch make.

She hit a tender spot on his arm and he winced.

"Sorry."

The whispered apology didn't sit well with him, particularly seeing as it was all she'd said in the last fifteen minutes. Before that she'd been talking to him about the way she saw him. They'd been making progress. Then he'd apparently stuck his foot in it because she'd shut down. Oh, she hadn't stopped her side of the conversation. She'd just taken it inside. All of it. The way thoughts raced across her face—eyes tightening at the corners, her mouth curling down or feathering up, where she let her gaze rest, how aggressively she worried her bottom lip—told him that she'd carried on in her head, effectively shutting him out of something in which he held critical stakes, as well. Watching her now, he saw that her fingers no longer trembled as she touched him. She'd clearly turned some corner. What he didn't know was whether or not he was still along for the ride or if she'd kicked him to the curb and motored on.

The idea that she would move on without him having his say made his skin feel too small for his large frame.

Rolling his good shoulder first, he stretched his arm out from neck to shoulder, elbow to hand. He flexed his fingers, splaying them wide. Good for so much and yet helpless here without his magicks. He was little good to the woman he sought to protect.

His mind wrestled with the need he had to keep her safe and the desire he had to hold himself apart. Preserving his bachelorhood was…such a crock. That wasn't what was tying him up in knots, though. No, that particular acrobatic feat stemmed from their sexual escapade in Lugh's little love shack. Isibéal had cried Ethan's name at the height of passion, but his wasn't the name she'd unthinkingly whispered when they both came down and he held her close, stroking her bare skin as she drifted to sleep. That spot belonged to Lachlan. In her mind it was Lachlan's arms she'd been sheltered in. It was Lachlan she'd responded to, Lachlan she'd given herself to, Lachlan she'd loved. Not him. Not Ethan Kemp. And that chafed.

Badly.

But more than that, it hurt.

Horribly.

And it shouldn't have. Not this much. Not unless Ethan cared for her on a far deeper level than he was prepared to not only acknowledge but also deal with. No dealing. Not right now.

Soft fingertips trailed down his injured arm. "The bindings aren't too tight?"

Breath banged around in his chest as if it were a solid thing, ricocheting through his lungs before rattling its way up his chest and out his parted lips in short, rapid bursts. How? How did her touch turn him into a nonverbal, chest-beating, grunt-happy Neanderthal? He was a freaking warlock, for the gods' sake. And nurse practitioner. Sidekick to the Assassin's Arcanum. He had the respective cloak, scalpel and sword skills to prove he was who he claimed to be.

Lachlan.

The name settled at the forefront of his mind, seeming to have been laid there by a power far greater than his.

"Not dealing with this right now," he ground out.

"Tight bindings?" Concern colored her question with its sincerity. "If they're too tight, I'll redo whatever—"

He didn't think, just gripped the back of Isibéal's neck and pulled her in for a fierce kiss. She was form to his fracture, light to his dark, hope to his despair, certainty to his indecision.

Everything he needed.

Everything he most feared.

"Stop thinking," she murmured against his lips. "Feel me." She picked up his good hand and laid it over her fluttering heart. "Just me. Only ever me..." She pulled back and met his gaze. "Ethan."

Oh, hell, that was low...and exactly what he needed to hear.

He swooped in, claiming her mouth with something much larger than run-of-the-mill sexual hunger. This was huge. Enormous. So big it dwarfed his hesitation and cast his trepidation in deep shadow. He would have had to dig for those excuses and fears to find them, and the firebrand in his arms would have none of it. She gave him no quarter, demanding his entire focus. Like the first time he'd kissed her, she was alive in a way that defied description. And when he closed his eyes? All he smelled was *her*. Tasted was *her*. Felt was *her*. Heard was *her*. Saw in his mind's eye was *her*. All of his senses were overloaded with everything that was *her*.

Their tongues touched and repeated, shallow and then deep, slow and then with furious demand, the parody of sex so perfect he groaned. She gave as well as she got, fearless in her desire to give herself up to this thing blazing between them even as she took from him everything he offered her.

Gripping her hair at the nape of her neck, he angled

her head to drive the kiss harder, to take her where they'd never gone.

She went without question, and understanding nearly felled him.

This is what faith looks like.

Not since he'd delivered his first baby in an emergency situation had he been so humbled. Similar feelings swept through him like a chinook wind, warming his superficially cold parts while starting to thaw his deep-frozen pieces. He breathed her in like sunshine and let himself simply experience what it was to be with her without barriers, with nothing held in reserve.

She began to shake a little, and he forced his bad arm to come to heel, settling his hand on her hip. Extracting his good hand from her thick mane, he cupped her jaw and traced the smooth skin of her cheek with his thumb. He never expected to find her face painted in tears.

He forced himself to slow down and then break away, to look down at her and use his words like any good higher thinker. "Iz?"

Brilliant.

She shook her head and moved in to reclaim his mouth.

"What's wrong?" he demanded. "Talk to me. Please."

Yet more articulated brilliance.

She took a deep breath and held it.

Peaked dusky nipples rose like twin temptations born for him alone.

Thumb wet with her tears, he circled the nearest areola before gently pinching the nipple.

She gasped and arched into his touch, her breast filling his palm.

"Please, Iz," he repeated, softer this time.

She lifted her gaze to his face, her eyes full and bright

with unshed tears, fuller still with unspoken emotion. "It's you."

That doesn't sound good. "Me."

A tremulous smile spread over her face, and a tear fell with her nod. "You."

He shook his head, words abandoning him. Likely for their mutual benefit.

"You're *here*," she said with surprising passion that bordered on vehemence. Pressing her palms to his cheeks, she pulled him closer, and he let her. He didn't anticipate her pause a split second before their lips touched. "You're here, Ethan. With me. All of you is with all of me. Finally."

If he thought understanding had been epiphanic earlier, it only emphasized how sorely ill prepared he was for the real thing. Her words sank into him like a hypodermic needle full of truth and understanding balanced with compassion and something akin to possibility. Something far too close to raw hope than he could handle. Like looking at the sun, it left his vision spotty and his eyes burning with the need for relief. It was easier to look away than force himself to see the very thing he needed to see, so he did. Small steps.

But they were steps forward.

This thing between them was gaining momentum.

Ethan could only pray the gods would keep this emotional train on the track, because if it came off?

There would be casualties.

Chapter 17

Isibéal had a body and a pulse, but she truly came alive under Ethan's touch. He demanded her response, driving her higher without comment or apology, stroking her body and stoking the fires of her passion until the former writhed and the onslaught of the latter's inferno burned out of control. Whispered suggestions painted pictures in her smoke-hazed mind, fueling the flames like dry tinder shoved into the fire's heart.

Her heart.

She burned for this Druid, this nonconformist, this warlock—all that he had been, was and would be. This man who owned her heart and ruled her very soul.

The way he worked her body, mastered it, left her crying out for more. Nothing would sate her but the pinnacle, the moment when he took her apart with absolute skill, shattered her, cast her to the aether and then brought her back together in the circle of his arms. She hungered for every second of the experience, every hot breath, every scrape of teeth on skin, every intimate touch.

Ethan worked his way down her neck, pressing his lips to the hollow of her throat. "Say my name, Iz."

"Ethan."

He dipped lower, seized a nipple and flicked it with his tongue before blowing over the damp skin. "My whole name."

"Ethan Kemp," she said on a gasp, arching her back and offering herself up to him.

"You neglected my middle name." He nipped the underside of the other breast before giving that nipple the same tender treatment he had given the other. "I want to hear my full name cross your lips."

"I don't know your middle name."

More teeth followed by more tender kisses elicited more pleasured gasps. "Guess."

She couldn't think and said so.

"Guess or I'll quit."

"Quit what?"

He raised his head from her breasts. "Everything."

Isibéal tunneled her fingers through his hair, pushing it off his face and then gripping handfuls. "Mark."

His eyes lit with amusement. "Mark?"

"Your mouth." She gently tugged his face toward her bare chest. "My skin."

Grinning, he complied. "Not Mark." He began kissing his way down her abdomen.

"Colm."

He pressed his lips on the narrow space between her belly button and the top of her pubic bone. "Mm-mm." Then he dipped lower and lower still until his breath teased her sex.

Again she tugged on his hair, but this time she added the wiggle of her hips. "Braden."

"Nope." Exaggerating the "p" sound sent a strong puff of air against her heated core.

"Gods preserve me," she said in a rush.

"Not." He moved in. "A." Closer. "Name." And he traced his tongue up her feminine valley.

Fine dots winked across her vision as her hips came off the ground. All she could think was that there was nothing she wouldn't do to ensure that he didn't stop this heavenly torture. He wanted names? She'd give him names. "Michael, Finian, Allen, Hagan, Flinn, Torin, Liam, Giarárd, Alexander—sweet Lady!" she nearly shouted as he pulled her clitoris between his lips.

Then he suckled.

Her sensibilities dissolved like sugar in boiling water.

Pleasure coursed through her. It turned her muscles soft, her bones softer. One hand left his hair and she slapped it to the ground, curling her fingers into the soft dirt in a futile effort to ground herself. The effort proved pointless.

He suckled harder and slipped a single finger inside her sheath. That simple act proved more than she could bear, her orgasm smashing into her like a summer wave tackling a sandcastle on the beach.

Breathing became impossible for several seconds as she opened her mouth in a wordless scream. Back arched, she pulled one hand from Ethan's hair and slapped her palm to the dirt, her fingers curling into the soft earth as she sought purchase, attempting to ground herself to no avail. Then her lungs screamed for air. It took concerted effort to comply with their demand. Even then, the best she could manage were short, random gasps.

The ability to hear anything beyond the rapid

drumming of her heart abandoned her, and that beat pounded through her in time with the pulsing orgasm that wouldn't cease.

Small pinpoints of light flashed behind her eyelids and decorated the darkness like an artificial night sky. She crested and that night sky blurred and then faded to dark as she drifted back into herself. Her body seemed heavier than before and pleasantly languorous in the afterglow of such intense pleasure. A soft sigh escaped her parched throat. What she wouldn't give for a glass of cold, clear water and, as she wished, a feather bed made up with the finest Irish linen, a fire in the hearth, soft rain pattering the window and candles lit throughout the room. *Their* room. For it would mean little to enjoy such luxury alone. Moments that made memories were meant to be shared. Always.

Ethan prowled up her body with sensual grace for all that he had a wounded, ineffective arm. It clearly didn't slow his approach or derail his clear intent. He didn't stop until his face hovered over hers. Knees between her thighs, he lowered his groin to hers and waggled his eyebrows at her purred approval.

That wasn't what gave her pause, though. The look in his eyes—that look that straddled a fine line between morbid curiosity and open demand—confused her. She rested a hand over his heart, reveling in the way it pummeled his rib cage in a rhythm that matched her own. But she couldn't look away, couldn't break from his gaze that held her captive with its undisguised conflict. "Ethan?"

He lowered his face to hers until she thought he would kiss her instead of answer. At the last second, with a hairbreadth between their lips, he stopped. His eyes searched hers. "How did you know?"

She let her fingers wander over and through the dips

and valleys that created his chest's topography as she met his open stare with her own. "Know what?"

Pulling back, he blew out a short, sharp breath but tempered the frustrated sound with a small smile. "My middle name, Isibéal."

"I didn't. I threw names out willy-nilly and…" Her fingers spasmed against his abdomen, tips curling into muscle that tightened in response. It amused her that she could react so after such an intimate act. His words suddenly registered, and she cocked her head. "I spoke your middle name so quickly?"

He dipped his chin once in answer.

"Which was it?"

"Guess."

"I already did." She hooked a leg behind his thighs and pulled him tighter to her heated core. "What might my prize be this time if I speak your whole name?"

He rolled his hips, the ridge of his erection sliding over her slick sex.

"Men always think their manhood's a prize," she teased.

This time his grin spread wide and fast. "Mine is."

"Aye," she said. "It is." The smoky timbre of her voice earned her another roll of her lover's hips, the pressure well placed and exquisite.

Ethan rose to settle on his knees and rest his good hand on her knee, hiking it up and draping her leg over his good shoulder. "My middle name, Iz."

She watched him watching her and grew anxious when the answer settled over her with absolute certainty. "Alexander. Your name is Ethan Alexander Kemp."

"How did you know?" This time the question was almost inaudible, barely stirring the air.

"It was a guess." *Lord and Lady, convince him it was naught but luck.*

"Of the thousands upon thousands of names to choose from, you picked mine with roughly half a dozen tries?" He shook his head. "No one's that lucky, Iz."

Apparently the gods weren't of a mind to honor her request. It was moments like this that made Isibéal wonder why she was loyal to her faith, to her patrons, to the ethics handed down to her with her magicks. They certainly hadn't proven as loyal in return. Not remotely.

Ethan pulled his hand away from her bare skin and settled it on his thigh, palm up. The move was telling, the twitch in his fingers even more so.

Gods, she didn't want to do this, but she saw no way out without answering him, no way forward without practicing the truth. Always. She swallowed hard before forcing herself to respond, voice steadier than her jangling nerves. "It was an educated guess." At his silence, she pressed on, offering the damning truth despite her myriad fears.

"Alexander was Lachlan's middle name, too."

Of course it was.

Ethan's heart stuttered and stumbled, his desire snuffed out faster than a newly lit campfire exposed to a torrential downpour. His cock followed right behind.

Of course it did.

Scooting backward on his knees and extricating himself from between Isibéal's thighs proved tricky with only one good hand for added support. He managed. There was no other choice. If he didn't gain some distance, if Lachlan didn't stop popping up along every path Ethan navigated… Every time he tried to forge ahead with the woman before him, he ended up sidetracked and his mind threatened to dump its contents at his feet. As it was, as of this very second, he was three clicks from sane and too close to losing his shit.

Never had he wanted a woman so much and yet been so insecure about her motives for wanting him in return. Sure, there were women who wanted him for the financial benefits and women who were forever shopping for their very own title of "Dr. & Mrs." Then there were the witches looking to align with a warlock of his standing in order to gain the power upgrade to their own magick. He knew how to play that game, knew how to handle the gold diggers and social climbers and power-hungry manipulators. None of those titles and none of those machinations applied to Isibéal. He doubted any of that would ever matter to her. What did matter was rediscovering the relationship she'd had with her husband—the man Ethan used to be. The man he *decidedly* was not.

He could accept that he'd been reincarnated. He could also see that he was an entirely different man than Lachlan had been. Why couldn't she do the same? Why couldn't she want Ethan for who he was now?

Clearly, it was too much to ask.

"Ethan, it was a name. More than that, it was a name I was familiar with related to an Irishman I knew…once."

The hesitation cost her, he knew, but she'd made the effort. For him. She'd admitted the name belonged to Lachlan of Ages Past, not Ethan of the Here and Now. Why couldn't he just accept that and move on? Why couldn't he laugh it off, lose his pants and finish what they'd started? Why did he feel like knowledge had become a noose, and with everything he learned regarding the similarities between him and Lachlan, that noose tightened? He'd never been one to attack the truth in an attempt to bludgeon it until it resembled something else or, if that wasn't an option, resembled nothing at all. But that was exactly what he was doing, every blind swing and shouted denial ratcheting the noose tighter. At some point he'd say or do something that would be the equivalent of the floor falling away and he'd emotionally hang himself. He knew it. *Knew it.* And yet he couldn't stop himself as he verbally lashed out at the very woman he wanted, the very woman he wanted to want him in return. To want *him*, the man he was versus the man she remembered him as. Ethan had been and still was many things, some good and some bad, but he wasn't some random memory. *Not the cloth I'm cut from.*

The small, distressed sound she made dragged him out of the pit of introspection he'd fallen into. Glancing over, he found her looking at him with something akin to hope. What would she hope for? His understanding that she'd pulled Lachlan back into the mix? That was the one thing he couldn't give her.

He struggled to stand on legs gone weak from the physical injury and weaker still from the emotional one. "You know, I should have guessed. It's always going to come back to Lachlan, isn't it?"

"Ethan, I simply retrieved a name I knew. I didn't think about it belonging to Lachlan. I didn't offer it as a possibility so that I might cause you distress." She followed suit and stood, dusting herself off with short, sharp movements. "You sound as if you believe I acted on a calculated attempt to put something from my memories of Lachlan in front of you. You asked me to see you, and I put my efforts there. No matter what you choose to believe, I do see you, Ethan." She stepped into the nearest shadow and offered him little more than a sliver of her profile, arranging herself as if she was trying to shield her nude body from him.

Considering his wounded arm and the fact that she'd given up his shirt and her modesty to tend him, he could at least afford her a modicum of civility. He focused on something opposite her in the small room. "I don't have anything to offer you in the way of a top."

"Whether you like it or not, Ethan, you're familiar with this body. What good would covering it up do?" She huffed and shook her head. Before he could summon a decent response, she rounded on him. Her words were smooth but sharp, like a high thread count, combed cotton sheet laid over a bed of nails, the points of which had been filed to make them weapons, not tools. "You obviously believe I am a singularly focused, manipulative woman."

"I—"

She didn't cede the floor but pressed on, talking over him. "I must admit I'm rather surprised you think even that much of me. No matter," she said smoothly, waving off his slack-jawed look.

He might have been building a good head of indignant steam, but she outshone him, glorious in the storm front of her building rage.

With her hands fisted at her sides, a fine tremor passed through her. She leaned forward then, voice low. "Do allow me to stroke your ego, darling, if only this once. Your sexual prowess ensured that I wasn't in a position to think much at all, let alone execute such a devious plan. Rest assured I'll never put myself in that situation again."

Something akin to panic wound through his chest with thick, invisible cords. He rubbed the valley between his pectoral muscles and cleared his throat. Frayed ends pulled tight, and he found himself struggling to catch his breath, to give substance and weight to his response.

"What do you want me to say?" he wheezed. "That I do it for all the ladies? That you're welcome?"

"No, Ethan." She swallowed so loud he heard it. "I had hoped to hear I was different. That I, above all others, mattered."

An impression of her, wavy hair spread over his pillow and burnished by the morning sun, blew through him with hurricane-force winds. He had no idea if it was a long-ago memory or a present-day wish. Honestly? He wasn't sure it even mattered when she opened her eyes and smiled up at him. Her undisguised faith in him cast aside any doubts about how she felt for him, and that? That knowledge? It made him feel like he was the most powerful man in the world. When she looked at him like that, he had no doubt that he possessed the power to slay armies, lay waste to darkness and command the light.

Ethan cursed a veritable blue streak, flexing his one good hand repeatedly until his knuckles ached. This was all Kennedy's fault. His best friend had gone and fallen for the one man she should have feared, not loved—the Druid's Assassin, Dylan O'Shea. And damn if the guy hadn't fallen just the same.

Ever since those two had beaten the odds—odds stacked against them so heavily that hope couldn't find a foothold with a compass and a seasoned guide—and ended up with the kind of love the old bards wrote about, Ethan had wanted the same for himself. He had begun to crave a true life partner, a woman who had her own purpose but found the missing piece in him, just as he would in her. He wanted a woman who filled the dark voids in him and let him do the same for her. This mystery woman would also want him with such unabashed hunger that anyone who saw them together would wonder if the couple would make it back to their bedroom or if a linen closet would end up as a sacrificial love nest. When he'd first seen Isibéal, when he'd *remembered*, hope flared, as powerful and brilliant as a supernova. Ethan had clung to that hope, truly believing she could be his chance.

At least until she'd repeatedly called him by another man's name.

Then she'd become corporeal. They'd touched. He had truly believed that she'd started to see him, *him*, as she tended him and made love to him with as much passion as he had shown her.

How could it have all been a lie?

Those invisible cords in his chest tightened with a sharp yank, squeezing his lungs until nausea nearly overwhelmed him with…guilt?

What the hell?

No. No way was he going to second-guess his thought process or let guilt worm its way into this discussion. What did he have to feel guilty about, anyway? Nothing, that was what.

He wasn't the one fixated on a dead man. If she wanted to get pissy with him over him calling her out on her obsession? Fine. That was her prerogative. Just as it was his not to apologize when he wasn't wrong. He was allowed to say that the absolute last thing he wanted out of life was to be some kind of surrogate walking, talking Lachlan doll she pulled out to fulfill her fantasies of what might have been with a man he no longer was. Not once had he presented himself as anything other than Ethan Kemp. The idea that he wasn't enough on his own, *as* Ethan, made him want to strike out, to excise his anger on an inanimate object that would take the beating and crumple appropriately under his fury. This little dirt cubby would work just fine. He could raze the little hideout and wipe it from the face of this gods-forsaken realm. While he was at it, he would eradicate the memories of what he'd allowed himself to hope for as he'd been sequestered here with Isibéal. And hope he had, proving himself all the more a fool.

Yeah. Total annihilation would stroke the part of him that needed to be nurtured just then.

Ethan's subconscious swam to the surface of his awareness without invitation and whispered, *That? Yeah, that part of you that you want "stroked"? That's your ego, you narrow-minded, emotionally stunted, undeniably self-centered prick.*

He reacted as if he'd been shocked…by a locomotive battery.

The silence must have worn on her, because Isibéal sighed and turned to face him. Her face was devoid of all emotional cues. Raw despair filled her gaze, though, and she didn't try to hide it. "This wasn't what I wanted. Ever. I didn't hold on all these years to end up here." She took a single step toward him. "I want to find my way to who you are, Ethan. Can we try? Just one more time."

She's obviously a manipulative woman hell-bent on your personal emotional destruction. Why, look at her! She is everything you ever—

"Wanted," Ethan whispered, so low he knew she couldn't have heard him.

Was it possible he'd been wrong? Had he let his ego feed his pride even as it starved his common sense?

"No," he nearly shouted, shaking his head in open denial of the allegations leveled by his subconscious. "Not possible."

Isibéal choked on a short sob before straightening.

Wait. She'd asked him… He'd said… *Shit.* "No."

"I believe you made that clear." She crossed her arms over her chest in an attempt to cover her breasts.

You have the social and observational skills of a box turtle.

"Isibéal." Uttering her name made those invisible cords tighten until he wondered that he didn't bleed out right there.

She held out her hand in a stop-motion gesture. "There's nothing else to say, really." Chin up, she gave a sharp nod. "I would appreciate your help reaching the portal. You shall not be forced to deal with my person any further once we're returned to the mortal realm. I assure you."

Those three words and the magnitude of the truth each one held struck Ethan like a closed-fist blow to the solar plexus.

He choked, and it wasn't lost on him that, for the first time, she didn't turn around. Didn't seek him out. Didn't express any interest in his well-being.

What sweet hell had he created for himself?

What hell, indeed.

Chapter 18

Isibéal's concentration should have been wholly invested in considering each step she took and double-checking each handhold as she climbed the steep hill. In a perfect world, *should* would translate to *do*. This wasn't a perfect world. Not even close. Still stuck in the Shadow Realm, land of demons and dark gods and failed magicks, she felt as if nothing ever went right here.

Forced to remain in Ethan's company in order to maximize her chances at survival, she continued to follow his very attractive, boxer-clad backside up the steep hillside. She tried not to look. Truly. She also did her conscious best to not openly admire his flexing thighs or toned calves or feet clad in fierce and oddly appealing shoes known as "Doc Martens." The broken ankle had been tied so tight he'd cried out in sheer agony, but without the stiff leather support, he hadn't been able to walk this morning.

Denim chafed her skin and she tried not to think uncharitable thoughts. Truly, she should be grateful Ethan had offered her his pants after she shredded his shirt, her only garment and borrowed at that, in order to dress his wound. When he'd insisted this morning that she take his pants, she jumped into an unnecessarily loud verbal battle with him for thinking she wanted in his pants at all.

Heated embarrassment stole across her cheeks at the memory. She would never admit to anyone that she'd protested loudly to disguise the path her mind had followed with unfettered enthusiasm. The very path that never considered she'd have a legitimate use for his pants. All she'd been able to think about was the superior body hidden by the proffered denim. The same body she craved. The body she had been denied the previous night.

The images that danced through her mind had prompted her to protest louder and argue at his continued insistence that she take his pants.

He'd then pointed out that, without his pants, she would have no alternative but to proceed to, and *through*, the portal in nothing but her skin. Then he'd cocked his head to one side, his eyes growing considering, shrewd. "I suppose you don't need to worry about the portal or crossing through." Shrugging, he settled the jeans over one shoulder and turned away. "If I were you, I'd be more concerned with the male species we're likely to encounter on the way."

She'd lunged forward and snatched the pants from him with a muttered "Thank you." Concentrated fury nearly choked her as she realized his generosity would leave her indebted to him. Further proof that this was, indeed, her own personal hell.

Thank you. Those two measly words had been the

last words they had exchanged, even as they worked together to fashion her current wardrobe.

Jean legs had been torn off before she slipped into the bottoms, cinching them tight around her waist. The legs had been tied together haphazardly and then wrapped around her upper chest to form a bandeau that covered her breasts as well as afforded her a modicum of modesty. Not uncomfortable for all that she'd been trussed up in men's dismantled trews.

There had been nothing available that could be repurposed in order to spare her bare feet, though, and they'd suffered for that. Bruised and bleeding, she ached for the chance to get off them, maybe sit and rest for an hour... or three. She hadn't been too worried when they left the little cave this morning, but the trip out of what had proven to be a small canyon turned out to be far more brutal than she had anticipated and, as it stood, looked to get worse before it got better. Complaining wasn't an option, though. Not with Ethan suffering as he was with his broken ankle and badly wounded shoulder.

Gravel skittered down the steep incline, and she looked up. Dust coated her skin. Grit filmed over her eyes and coated her tongue. Her eyes and mouth were gritty with the fallout. She paused to look up and found herself appreciating the scenery despite it all. *Ethan*.

Ahead of her, his bare back flexed as he navigated the last of the steep climb. She opened her mouth to say something, suddenly desperate for anything that would break the awful tension between them. She racked her mind for any conversational thread that might hold up under duress. The silence stretched on as she realized that nothing she said, no olive branch she offered, would be sufficient. Not after their interaction followed by their confrontation and harsh exchange last night. All those callous words that lay between them…

Despite that, she was privately ashamed she hadn't made a stronger effort to summon more authentic gratitude to offer him, seeing as the gesture he'd made—giving up his jeans—had been truly kind. She couldn't get past the words and allegations he'd thrown at her. Both had wounded her deeply. Whether or not she would recover remained to be seen. She would have to be able to find a way to move beyond the hurt and shut down the unsolicited mental replays her mind randomly dragged to the forefront of her consciousness.

How long before the memories fade? Surely time will dull the pain so it isn't so raw.

She wished she knew. Lachlan had never spoken to her, hurt her, in such a manner, so she had nothing with which to compare. The best she could do was tend every wound as it reopened and pray to the goddess that the wounds didn't cause her to emotionally bleed out.

Thoughts turned inward, she failed to realize Ethan had stopped. She bumped into him and they both slid down the hill several feet. Ethan's eyes, wide and wild in equal parts, found hers at the same time he reached for her.

And she reached back.

Skilled but calloused hands closed over her smaller, smoother ones. His hold proved tight, stronger than the pull of chaos that would have sent them careening down the slope and, likely, left them bloodied and bruised, if not worse.

Isibéal gripped his hands and held them tight. Had he not reached for her, she would have tumbled down the steep incline. She was grateful for him, tried to convey the depth of that gratitude in her gaze.

He watched her with quiet intensity, his eyes narrowing. Recognition dawned bright and clear, but it proved a weighted moment when his hand spasmed around hers. The way he withdrew—a solid, volatile yank—made her wince.

Isibéal rubbed her hand and fingers over the sliver of denim that covered her hip. "I—"

"Mind your step," he interrupted. Lips that had been irrefutably kissable thinned into a hard line. Dropping her hand, he restarted the climb, this time with jerkier, more aggressive movements.

She couldn't help wondering if he'd been warning her to mind her physical steps or her emotional ones. Neither felt stable. Both struck her as out of control.

Loose dirt and rock made resuming the climb all the more challenging. Her wandering mind made it even worse. Fingertips raw from scrabbling to find—and hold on to—the random, well-seated rock, sufficiently exposed root or strong branch, Isibéal fought her way up the unsteady face of the hill-cum-ever-taller-mountain.

What she wouldn't have given to maintain even a small bit of physical contact with the man in front of her. It mattered little whether it was his fingers threaded through hers, his hand around her waist or any of a thousand simple but willing offered touches that would center her. She longed for the normalcy of her hand in his or his eternal warmth against her grave-chilled skin. Yet neither of them had willingly given themselves over to such casual affections. It had all been done within the boundaries of physical intimacy or not at all.

Fiercely bothered, she frowned.

As the Fates would have it, Ethan chose that moment to look over his shoulder, lips parted as if his intention had been to speak. He stopped and turned more fully to face her. "What?" he demanded.

"Nothing." Her one-word, emotion-saturated response rolled across the short distance between them and seemed to plow into Ethan.

His shoulders hunched and he chuffed out a short breath. "Sure." A short nod. "If that's what you're selling."

"Selling?"

He exhaled, the sigh short and sharp. "Just a turn of phrase."

"So you've said." Layer upon layer of frustration began to unravel. One hand clutching the nearest thick root, her other had balled into a solid fist she now beat against her thigh. "The problem is that, for all I know, you could have just called me a goat's teat in current vernacular, and I'm none the wiser. Do you have any idea how frustrating that is? To constantly hover on the fringes of every conversation?" A tight smile. "Of course you don't, Ethan. You're of this time and place. It belongs to you as much as you belong to it. But I?" She forced the fingers of her free hand to unfurl and pressed her palm over her heart. "I am an outsider. Always."

He started to speak, only to stop himself and stare at her.

Silence ruled the moment with a heavy, dictatorial hand, carving the chasm of their personal differences wider and wider still with each second that passed until she could stand it no longer. "Tell me one thing, Ethan. One truth of my choosing." When he didn't respond, she flayed herself, laying open the deepest part of herself and exposing her heart's lifeblood. Revealing the part from which her every need sprang—the need that had lifted incorporeal hope from its grave, that drove that same hope to eschew danger, that bade her enter the Shadow Realm to seize her single chance to physically manifest, that part of her that claimed him as her heart's mate.

That part she had all but sacrificed with love's blade on faith's altar.

Her soul.

She watched him, gauging his every response, from her first word to her last. "If you could have me, claim me as your own—of your own free will, mind you—what would your choice be?"

"I'm not sure…" He licked his lips.

"Do you regret that I came back for you? Do you regret that I followed you, rose after you did, and followed you into this time?"

"What, exactly, are you asking me?"

Her stomach shook, each tremor as sharp as it was violent. "Given the choice, would you have brought me back from beyond the Veil, Ethan?"

"I'm not sure I understand what you're asking me."

If ever a man had hedged with such transparent mendacity…

Her heart screamed its denial even as her head's practicality demanded she afford herself a final chance. Here. Now. There was no way she would risk a misunderstanding. "Disregard both past and present as well as all probabilities and possibilities. Approach the question from its most fundamentally simple form. Yes or no. Would you have moved the heavens or laid waste to the darkest reaches of the Shadow Realm to bring me back had I not come on my own?"

He didn't answer her. Not verbally. But then, he didn't need to. The way his throat worked, his breaths coming faster, all color bleeding away and, above all, his damnable silence said it all. Like the sun rising on the horizon when the first shades of dawn appeared, a person understood that the hint of color was just that: a hint. What inevitably followed would paint the sky a hundred different hues, those brilliantly concentrated streaks of color bleeding one into another. So his silence and non-verbal responses did much the same, layering one over the other again and again, building an answer that held myriad emotions and colors. It was that, beyond even his unwillingness to articulate either affirmation or denial, which decided her.

"Okay."

"What's okay?" he wheezed. "I didn't say anything."

You don't have to, love. Your silence is more damning, more deadly, than the report of an executioner's rifle, your aim just as true.

Her voice had been crushed by truth's incredible weight. Her lungs proved to be nothing but collateral damage and now wouldn't allow her to claim a deep breath. The bones that had been her chest's framework felt as if they'd been shattered and then driven into... nay, *through* her, the force such that naught but slivers remained, each one cutting her so that she bled quicker. Harder. Fiercer.

Instead of trying to force herself to speak around the detritus of her pierced and pulverized heart, she waved Ethan on even as she forced herself to search for her next handhold though eyes filled and her vision swam. "Climb, Ethan." The first tear slipped down her cheek. "Let's reach the portal as fast as possible so we might declare ourselves done."

"Why the sudden rush?" he asked, tone clipped. "And 'done' how?"

There were a hundred answers she could have given

him and a thousand lies she might have told. None of it mattered, though. This wasn't her place, her time, her home…or her man. That last fragment of truth ruled them with dictatorial brutality.

Obviously misinterpreting the look on her face as one of sincerity instead of severity, Ethan returned his attention to the climb. Reclaiming lost ground was swift and uneventful. The resulting distance his efforts gained them and the physical distance created between them provided a visual complement to Isibéal's internal turmoil.

What surprised her most was how effectively he caused additional hurt when he turned his back on her. That he could do so without flinching, that he could put such distance between them without apparent remorse?

A second tear slipped down her cheek and a third quickly followed.

"Fool," she said, openly condemning her unchecked emotions.

Images of what might have been began flipping through her mind. If they'd only made different decisions, pursued different paths forward with each other, treated the relationship with more care. She found herself fervently wishing things weren't so broken between them. Living life alone was so very different than living a lonely life. She recognized the difference, understood the often subtle nuances that made the former tolerable and the latter absolute torture. The centuries she'd spent loving Lachlan from the dark, silent prison of her grave had convinced her that, above all else, the chance to love and be loved should always be cherished. She'd promised herself that, if she was ever able to see Lachlan again—touch his face, feel his breath on her skin, experience the surety of his presence at her side—she would do whatever it took to cherish every moment she was given with him. Nothing would be wasted.

The sound of disgust that escaped her was small in volume yet immeasurably deep.

For so long she'd made vows to herself, yet here she was, Lachlan's current form within reach as Ethan Kemp, the very man she'd yearned for available to her, his heart free of current commitments, his memories of her strong enough to lay the foundation necessary to take what had been and make it something that truly could *be*, and she'd lost him. Somehow, in the course of their knowing each other in this modern time and despite the fact that they stood in front of each other with no impediments and no emotional obligations to anyone else, they had failed to actually *find* each other again. The vows she'd made to herself were null and void. Defunct.

What a hypocrite she had become.

This could go on no longer. It had to stop. This argumentative environment they had brought into being with barbed comments and then sought to hastily balance with superficial tender touches, a rapid coupling and a spare but shallow kind word could carry on no longer. She would see Ethan settled when they returned to the mortal realm. If possible, she would carry out her promise to Lugh. If she failed? Death waited. If she managed to hand Lachlan's brother over to the God of Revenge and Reincarnation?

Her sweaty palm slipped on a poorly chosen handhold and she nearly fell, recovering without Ethan's awareness.

Such a fall could have been a portent of failure as much as an affirmation of her choice. Either way, she knew what her final outcome would be.

Isibéal could no more condemn Ethan to commit his life to her than she could commit hers to him. Not when love played no part in the foundation of who they were. So she would relinquish her hold on him. She would give up the physical body she had longed for in order to see him free to make the choices that might make him happy. And she? She would give her physical body over to Lugh that he might ensure Ethan's safety from Sean.

Then she would move on to whatever afterlife the gods deemed appropriate.

Chapter 19

Ethan crouched low, all weight on his good foot, and leaned against the large stone monolith that provided him and Iz shelter as they regrouped for the final push to the portal. The temperature had begun to climb about an hour ago when they made it to the north side of the carnivorous durands' hunting grounds, and it hadn't stopped yet. If he had to guess, it hovered around triple digits right about now. He was hot and tired. No, not tired. Exhausted. The craving for a cold beer and a long nap, in that order, nearly overwhelmed him.

He glanced at Isibéal from the corner of one eye, taking in her withdrawn demeanor and her continued silence. No doubt she was tired, too, but this was different. More. Worse. She'd essentially refused to talk to him all day, and he didn't like it. He started to ask her what was bugging her so badly, but movement at the corner of his peripheral vision froze him in place.

"Did you see that?" Numb lips barely moved, so the question sounded as if it had been issued around a mouthful of mashed potatoes. She started to lean around the stone's edge and look, but he gripped her shoulder and stopped her. "Don't."

"Then how would you have me see?"

"There's something out there, Iz."

Beneath his hand, her muscles tensed.

Fine hairs all over his body stood on end as his hindbrain hummed like it had been hooked to a D-cell battery. Little shocks of awareness zinged down his neural pathways.

"We're at DEFCON CYA, and while the shit missile hasn't been fired at the fan yet, the target is definitely locked and loaded," he said under his breath, pressing the heels of his hands against his temples. "I have a feeling I am—we are—the target. I *hate* being the target."

Air moved, the scent of hot, dry skin and clean comfort carrying to him on the nearly nonexistent breeze.

Isibéal slipped in beside him as he moved closer to the stone. When she spoke, her voice mirrored his in both pitch and volume. "I'm quite sure I'll regret this, but do I need to know what 'DEFCON CYA' means? And what is a 'shit missile'?"

He couldn't help it. Man, he tried—pinched his nose, held his breath, tried to find his zen. All he ended up with was a ruptured blood vessel in one eye and a hell of a good laugh.

No inner peace on my watch.

"Well?" Isibéal leaned forward as if she intended to peer around the giant rock.

He didn't think, simply gripped her near elbow and pulled her into him, her nearly bare back pressed against his entirely bare chest. Leaning forward so his lips brushed the shell of her ear when he spoke, he fought to ignore the gooseflesh that rose on her arms...and his. "'DEFCON' is an acronym—a series of letters that stands for something. In this case, it's an acronym used by the US Government that stands for 'Defense Readiness Condition.'"

"Rather self-explanatory." She took a step forward, small but still enough to break the skin-to-skin contact he'd established and force him to release her. "And a 'shit missile' is certainly not what it sounds like." She looked up at him, authentic concern creating a small V between her eyebrows. "Is it?"

"No." Damn if he didn't smile so wide his cheeks hurt. "It's just a figure of speech. We say 'the shit is going to hit the fan' when things are about to get bad."

Her shoulders sagged, and she closed her eyes. "Contemporary figures of speech have proven to be my bane."

"It's common vernacular. You'll learn."

She stood and shifted her weight to her less damaged foot. "I've no need."

A whole different set of alarms sounded in his head. "Why *wouldn't* you need to understand common vernacular?"

She waved him off and peered around the stone's edge. "The portal—it's that mirage on the air, is it not?"

"Yeah. Iz, I'm sure I saw something out there." Ethan ran a hand around the back of his neck and rubbed at the prickly, invisible fingers of distress scraping over sensitive skin. "I'm just not feeling this whole 'dash to freedom' thing."

"I understand."

The weight of her voice struck him in the chest, saturated with emotion better suited to a eulogy than a mad dash to freedom. Beyond that, he had the distinct impression he was, and had been, missing something all morning. Sure, they'd argued. Then they hadn't spoken for a couple of hours. But she'd pissed him off. He'd needed the time to sort out the tangled mess he'd made of his head by trying to make sense of everything they'd been through over the past few days, from her profession that she was his wife to the little bit of castle demo they'd done to their trip to the Shadow Realm that resulted in not only her reincarnation in a body with a shelf life but also the best sex of his life. On a stone floor. *In hell.* Shaking his head, he crouched. They could argue later, preferably after they were back in the mortal realm. Alive.

Ethan had historically believed a person got what he earned, but he had to admit that, just then, there was almost nothing he wouldn't do, nothing he wouldn't give, for either an Easy Button or a pair of ruby slippers. Hell, he'd even slip on the blue and white gingham dress and carry a shaggy dog in a picnic basket if it meant he could click his heels together and end up in Kansas.

"There's no place like home," he whispered.

"Agreed," Isibéal murmured.

Ethan couldn't help smiling at how quickly she'd agreed instead of asking for clarification. It would take time, but she'd find her place in the modern world. Closing his eyes and resting his forehead against the sun-warmed stone, he rolled his head back and forth as he repeated the famous movie line over and over. Kansas never did appear, but he did get a pretty good layer of grit on his sweat-slicked skin.

Figures.

"I need a big red button." He didn't look at her, nor did he wait for her to ask what he meant. He volunteered the explanation. "A 'big red button' is what Westerners, people from the United States…um, land discovered after you, well, died…" He scrubbed a hand over his head. "The button is big. Red. It's something citizens of developed countries joke about—that our leaders have big red buttons they can push to blow up other countries. Make them explode. And disappear. With weapons. Really, really big weapons." Could he flub that *any* worse?

She didn't respond for a moment, seeming to take a second to sort out what he'd said. Then, "I assume it's this button which fires the shit missiles?"

His bark of laughter was as loud as it was unintentional.

Isibéal clapped a hand over his ankle and squeezed. "Shhh."

"Sorry," he choked out. "Sorry. You just… You can't drop comedy bombs without a little warning."

"I dare not ask."

"Yeah, probably wiser to leave that one alone."

Going to his knees, he moved in close to her and braced one hand on her shoulder for balance. She looked up at him with such sorrow that the very heart of him ached for her. He'd meant to protect her through this, to see her through, and he'd let her come to this point, whatever it was. He'd failed her. Again.

The need to soothe her, to be her refuge, wiped out every ridiculous concern he had, trumped his fear of what it might mean that he cared so much for her. *He* cared. *Him. Ethan.* Not the dregs of what was left of Lachlan or Lachlan's memories. That man was nothing but dust. He, Ethan, was real.

Her skin was hot against his palm as he cradled her face, her lips slightly chapped under the pad of his thumb. No matter. He wanted to show her that he, Ethan Kemp, cared, that he wanted to throw open her emotional closets and banish her skeletons. All he knew to do was start with a kiss and build to the words that were beginning to coalesce in his mind. Looking at them would scare him, so he didn't. That would come later.

He lowered his face to hers, and his lips whispered over hers, a phantom kiss that laid the foundation of the first promise he would make to her in this life, the first promise he would make as Ethan—the promise to care for her instead of cowering to his fears. He would put her first. Always and in all things.

Her eyes stayed locked on his, a flicker of something promising coming alive, burning at the deadened cold that had threatened to pull her under. This woman was not meant for the cold. She burned with vitality and life and humor and…love.

Ethan's heart leaped, driven by equal measures of fear and joy. He moved to deepen the kiss, and two things happened simultaneously. Either one alone had the power to stun him. Together? He was paralyzed, frozen where he stood.

First, clarity struck him, harsh and bright, blinding him as effectively as if he'd looked at the sun. He saw Isibéal, truly saw her, and it was as if he'd never seen her before. He saw her for who she was, saw all the hope and fear and faith she had carried as she waited for his return, saw what it had cost her to then fight her way back to him. The truth was exposed then, as well-defined as a film's negative. Only one image within the picture's frame mattered, standing out in sharp relief as everything surrounding that image was cast in shades of varying opacity.

Isibéal.

Second… Gods save them both. What came second was far more dangerous than realizing he'd lost his heart to the woman he'd loved across the ages. His fingers curled into her shoulders hard enough she protested with an inarticulate sound. "Shhh," he hissed, refusing to let her go even when she tried to jerk free. "Be still."

Neither holding her nor shushing her was done with the intent of pissing her off, nor was either act some misguided dominance play. Whatever had moved in his peripheral vision earlier had just moved again, but it was closer. *Much* closer.

Giving up the pretense of hiding behind the stone that had evolved from shade to shelter, he wrestled to free the two largest branches in the dead shrub at the monolith's base. "Listen to me, Iz. There are three…*things*…about to rush us. They're big and they're ugly. We're going to hope they're also dumb." He handed her the lighter of the two branches. "This is the best I can do to arm you. Swing high and hard if you have to."

Her eyes narrowed, sparking with ferocity as she wielded the impromptu weapon. "I will."

Pride in her bravery nearly overwhelmed him. He should have known she'd take on this fight with nothing less than a warrior's spirit. That was, after all, who she was. Who she'd *always* been.

Her gaze drilled into his, direct and unwavering, harboring infinitely more life than it had held moments before. "Ethan, I—"

He interrupted her with a swift kiss. "Later. We'll sort this out later."

She swallowed hard. "Okay."

Ethan hefted the heavier branch. "I'm going to draw them away from the portal. The minute they're distracted, you haul ass—*run*—as hard as you can straight to the portal. Go straight there, Iz. Don't argue," he snapped when she started to do just that. "You go. I'll follow right behind."

If I survive.

Isibéal tightened her grip on the thick branch Ethan had handed her. The desiccated wood could be wielded as either sword or bludgeon. No matter the method used, it would be sufficient to wound an opponent and, if the Morrigan was with her, to kill. She had no compunction about taking another's life in the event her or Ethan's life was threatened. Being murdered tended to change a person's view on violence.

Attack imminent, she sidled closer to Ethan and listened for the sounds of rushing feet, heavy breathing, shouted commands or open challenges. Neither sound nor word broke the void-like silence. Driven to near madness by anticipation, she snuck a peek around their columnar defense. Regret struck her so hard her vision swam.

Three demons stood no more than one hundred feet away, shoulder to shoulder. Their smooth skin was a blanched yellow that made each of their four onyx eyes—three across each wide forehead and one at the base of each throat—appear distinctive. A thick, curled horn grew above each ear and angled toward the back of each demon's bald head. They each wore tattered leather trews that were too short despite the demons' diminutive stature. Around their waists were broad belts adorned with weapons, pelts and what looked like rudimentary canteens.

The thought of water made her all the more aware that she had become dangerously thirsty.

As if he'd read her mind, Ethan whispered, "I'd kill one for its canteen alone."

Isibéal eased back around the stone and gripped her makeshift weapon even harder. "What are they exactly?"

"Not sure, but I know that color yellow isn't one Crayola would claim." He sniffed the air. "Whatever they are, they stink. Bad."

A snarl ripped the silence.

"Apparently they understand English, at least enough to find you offensive." She fought to keep the fear out of her voice, to tease him instead of pleading with him to promise he'd return to her as he always had done before. This man was not, after all, Lachlan.

"That's because I *am* offensive. It's a gift." Shifting his much larger branch to his dominant hand, he reached behind him and blindly fished around in the skeletal bush, retrieving a much smaller branch. He hoisted it as if its weight and balance were relevant. "It'll do."

"Ethan, I could help. You might need me to—"

"Get to the portal." His gaze hardened as it found hers and held it without compromise. "*That* is what I need you to do, Iz. No 'might' about it." He stood, his knees cracking as he found his rickety balance on his good foot. "Gods, I'm too old and broken to be tossing demons around."

"Ethan." The force of her pleading was as raw as it was real. She didn't care. She needed him to know what he was to her.

A sudden rush of footsteps interrupted the moment, each sole-to-ground impact sending out a subtle but undeniable promise of imminent violence.

Ethan reached out and she took his hand, grateful that he had the wherewithal to see her standing before the demons reached them. She spun the branch in her palm. It seemed ridiculous, an insignificant means of defense in the face of the demons' blades and whips and arrows.

"Where's your faith?"

He might have aimed for a lighter tone, might have been battle primed and prepared to take on the trio of ugly with nothing more than a pair of dead branches, but she was scared. Terrified, actually. The irrefutable truth of what was to come now hovered around them, an invisible mist heavy with regrets and words left unsaid.

Metal glinted in the pale sunlight.

Sword.

Shouting, giving inarticulate voice to her rage, Isibéal swung her branch at the demon's thick wrist. Dead wood met the top of it, and the demon barked in pain. Its knobby-knuckled, stout-fingered hand spasmed and dropped the sword.

Groin. Eyes. Joints.

Lachlan's self-defense training replayed through her mind and muscles. She let her body do what it had been trained to do, let the thrust and parry, strike and deflect movements be what they were. Her next swing, much lower this time, aimed for the thing's trunk-like legs. The branch connected with the outside of her opponent's knee, snapping the joint with a sickening *pop*. The leg bent inward in a totally unnatural angle, and he went down, literally crumpled where he stood, his shout of pain far more intense this time.

Behind her, Ethan had engaged the second demon, grappling with it as they each fought to gain the upper hand. The sounds of metal meeting dried wood was punctuated by fists hitting flesh and the sounds of protest equating to impact.

The third demon was nowhere to be seen.

Something latched to her ankle, claws piercing the skin, shredding muscle, destroying tendon. Pain ripped through her as if it were lightning and she the grounding rod. White burned out her vision. She blindly swung. Met air. Had her impromptu club ripped from her hand.

And she went down.

Dust billowed around her, filling her nose and eyes and mouth with grit. She'd never been more miserably aware of her thirst as she tried to scream her objections to being dropped where she stood. All that came out was a wheezy sound followed by a puff of silt. Her vocal box felt as if it had shriveled up and left nothing but the memory of its existence behind.

Claws dug deeper into her ankle.

She kicked out with her good leg, only to have it seized in the same fashion. Wounded, her vision beginning to clear, she clawed at the ground in an effort to pull herself free. Sought purchase with bleeding fingers in the unforgiving dirt. Anything she discovered—rocks, skeletal remains, dirt clods—she threw at the creature that held her captive.

A high-pitched whistle preceded the solid *thunk* of petrified wood connecting with a thick skull. The grip the thing had on her ankles relaxed, its eyes softened and lost focus as its mouth went slack. Then it tipped over like a claimed pawn on a chessboard.

Ethan panted heavily as he stood over the body of his enemy. Bruised and bloodied, the remnants of his large branch clutched in both hands, he looked like an avenging god of war laying waste to those who had broken faith. Three hop-steps forward and he reached her where she lay. Dropping the last piece of his bludgeon, he went to his knees and promptly gathered her in his arms.

She turned her face into his bare chest, ignoring the filth that covered him. Safe. She was safe. The realization triggered something in her, and she began to shake with surplus adrenaline that held a metallic taste—*fear*—and, beneath that, something more bitter—*anger*—and, over-laying it all, something faintly salty—tears. She didn't cry as many might, the response triggered by volatile emotion. Isibéal knew herself far better than that. Her tears were a direct result of her relief that Ethan had returned to her. Perhaps he was slightly battered, but he was certainly not beaten.

"Shh," he admonished, rocking her gently. "No tears."

"I'm n-not c-c-crying," she stuttered.

"No?" The smile in his voice settled across the adrenaline that still spread over her awareness. His effect on her, the warmth he brought her, was much like a spoonful of oil dropped in a cup of water. His strength was such that it would always rise above circumstance, would always come out on top and never settle for less than that.

Ethan grunted, the sound followed by a full-body spasm that hit him hard enough he almost dropped her. His arms tightened so hard she couldn't breathe.

She lifted her head, her intent to tease him about choking the life out of her. Before she managed, a sharp pain pierced her side below her ribs—a pain she knew, remembered. Hot. Wet. Not dangerous until it became numb.

Those arms that held her close, arms that represented safety and security and home, went lax.

Isibéal rolled free of Ethan's grasp, clutching her makeshift bandeau as she landed before him where he knelt. She scrambled to her knees, her hand automatically clutching the wound, her mind screaming its denial so loudly she couldn't hear her own wail.

Ethan swayed, disbelief decorating his face, his mouth hanging open in silent objection. Behind him, the owner of the sword that had been run through Ethan's side stepped back and kicked Ethan between the shoulder blades, driving the warlock to the ground.

Ethan landed in a macabre heap, closing his eyes and clamping his mouth shut as he fought the brutal agony inherent to the wound.

She fought not to retch as she rolled toward Ethan and reached for his hand. "No," she managed. "You stay with me. Don't leave me. Not now." A hard sob racked her. "Ethan Kemp, you stay with me!" Movement behind Ethan fueled her panic. Ignoring her wound and the associated pain, she flung herself at Ethan's prone form and covered what she could, shielding his body with hers.

A look of satisfaction accompanied the high color staining the aggressor's cheeks.

The other man stepped closer, placed a booted foot on her shoulder and pushed.

She couldn't hold on and ended up sprawled on her back in the dirt looking up at their attacker.

It wasn't the demon.

The suns created a strange nimbus around the man's head and shoulders. Insinuating himself between her and Ethan's prone form, he dropped the tip of the blade to the dirt and cocked his head to the side, studying her, as he leaned on the sword pommel.

Her mind rebelled. She had spent lifetimes hating this man, had craved vengeance against him every second of every day for destroying the lives of those closest to him. And here he was, poised to do it all over again.

"I believe I owe you a small token of gratitude for saving me the effort of the hunt. That you delivered Lachlan to me, again, is much appreciated, though you didn't exactly seek me out personally. My faithful servant did that. Did you never wonder where the third assailant disappeared to?" He tsked her in mock disapproval. Then he smiled down at her, the gesture benign save for the naked maliciousness banked in his eyes. "So I'll offer you a choice. One of you may die swiftly and one slowly. Which do you choose…sister?"

Chapter 20

Ethan blinked in and out of awareness. The lucid moments were the worst. He'd been a healer long enough to recognize and interpret the signs—sluggish heart rate, chills accompanied by sweating, narrowed vision, heavy and generally unresponsive limbs, numbness interrupted by debilitating pain followed by more pervasive numbness. He wasn't in trouble. No, not trouble. He'd passed that point long before his last visit with unconsciousness. It was far more accurate to say he was in such deep shit that even chest waders wouldn't get him through the thick of it.

He winked out again, blackness taking him and receding with no reference to, or respect for, time's passing. Fighting to hold on, he forced himself to focus on the things he could see and define, cataloging specifics so he might be able to identify changes after his next trip into the dark. He pushed himself to consider each blink as the equivalent of a snapshot. With his eyes closed, he would pick out the small things that made up his surroundings. He started then, working in chronological order that he might develop a timeline. Anything to keep his mind from ceding control to his failing body.

First image: the desert he lay in was beige on beige on beige, a monochromatic landscape that lacked visually interesting elements.

Second image: the demons he'd fought had been washed out, Technicolor versions of childhood nightmares, and he hadn't been able to take them too seriously.

Third image: the blood that seeped from the—likely mortal—wound in his side was black in the fading afternoon light.

Fourth image: the boots his assailant wore were a deep brown and inexplicably dust free.

But the woman… She was far more complex than a one-line definition.

He forced his eyelids to open a fraction.

It was enough.

The only true color in this world, she knelt in front of him, a brilliant gem deposited in a bucket of dull steel bearings. Just below her right rib cage, something bright red was smeared obscenely over her porcelain skin.

The realization she'd been wounded kicked him out of his experiment and set his heart racing. If she could tell him what had happened, he might be able to triage her from here. He tried to speak but didn't manage more than a slow, wheezing exhale.

Ominous, that.

The only time he'd ever heard it before was before death.

While he knew he was in trouble, he refused to accept

that his heart would tap out here, in the Shadow Realm, and leave his soul free for the taking.

He shifted a fraction. It was enough. Muscles protested by seizing up, shrinking against his tall frame until it seemed certain his bones would shatter. Pain burned through him as if someone had taken a blowtorch to his internal organs. The wound on his side wept.

The woman...the woman...the woman...

Isibéal.

She cried out to him, called him by his given name. "Ethan!"

Ethan.

A lifetime of memories crowded his consciousness, recollections incompatible with the life he knew as Ethan. The castle. Battles fought on horseback. Candlelight. Meals cooked over a fire. Dirt roads. Hand-sewn clothes. Buttons, not zippers. Custom-fit boots of the finest leather. Blacksmiths. Swords fit to his hand. Daggers slipped in his boots. Hunting parties. Meat hung in the smokehouse. A reflection of hair he didn't recognize and blue eyes he did.

And her.

She was there, this woman who knelt before him.

His heart swelled in his chest until he couldn't breathe.

The look on her face paralleled the untempered desire in her eyes. She gazed up at him as he sat astride his horse. He would leave for war, and she would see him off, as always. She had always been there.

Isibéal offered him her hand, and he, per tradition, had taken it. "Fight well, Assassin, and lay this conflict to rest. I have lit the candles in the keep's four towers. Those candles will burn every moment you are gone that you and your men may find your way back to those who await your return."

"Your faith honors me," he responded in a voice that was his but not his, then bent over her offered hand and kissed her fingertips one by one.

She smiled and whispered for his hearing alone, "Darling Lachlan. Husband mine. I love you more than is rational and far more than is sane."

Something inside his broken body settled into place, and understanding wove through his shattered consciousness.

This woman.

His woman.

Isibéal.

His *wife*.

She had loved him as the man he'd been then just as he knew she loved the man he was now. They were different but the same. The one constant was her love.

A man's voice registered then, coming from somewhere behind them. Blood gone sluggish in his veins froze. That voice…he knew that voice. It had been the one to take his wife from him when he lived as Lachlan, and he had to believe its owner would do the same to him as Ethan. There would be no remorse. That voice was death. Ethan's. And Isibéal's.

Sean.

Lachlan's blood brother; Ethan's soul's brother. One and the same.

Rage flooded his mind and spilled into his body, his substantial frame not remotely large enough to contain the heated fury that fueled a violence he felt compelled to carry out. Gathering what strength he had and forecasting as little of his intention as possible, he prepared to intercede. He would take Sean to the ground and afford Isibéal the opportunity to get to the portal. It would undoubtedly cost him his life. That Isibéal...his *wife*... would survive was enough. The afterlife would be acceptable if, and only if, he knew she lived.

A split second before he moved, a petite hand rested on his shoulder and pressed down.

His body relaxed under her touch, and his soul quieted. She calmed him, centered him, even now, and he realized that all he wanted was for her to hold him as he died. And he *was* dying. The way his heart skipped now and again and the fact that his hearing had gone tinny affirmed what he'd known but refused to accept.

Dying hadn't ever been something he'd worried about. Fact of life: if you were born, you were going to die. Period. He'd been born; ergo... But now he saw that logic for the cop-out it was and always had been. He'd lived on the periphery of true investment, never committing to much in life, doing what made him happy in the moment and never thinking about what came next. He'd lived a crowded yet solitary life within the busy work and social life he'd created, never allowing himself to go too far beyond his comfort zone, backing away from anything too dangerous, joking with anyone who pushed him and shutting down, and out, those who wouldn't leave well enough alone. And by *push* and *dangerous*, he really meant anything involving commitment. And love? Oh, hell no. Now? He was pissed beyond belief at all he'd missed from cowardice.

You always loved another woman.

His heart skipped for a different reason this time.

The truth.

His subconscious had always been a straightforward bastard. Smart, though.

Because despite his excuses and in spite of himself,

he loved Isibéal. He hadn't wanted to. Nor had he been able to accept that love wasn't bound by the confines of time and space as he understood them. Arrogance allowed him to believe that simply refusing to acknowledge everything related to his unwelcome emotions would change the outcome of his ultimate showdown with the truth. But in the end, the truth did what it did best. It prevailed. Ethan was wiser now—now that it was too late to do anything with the knowledge.

He'd been a fool.

A palm rested on his forehead before shifting to gently tunnel fingers through his hair. *Isibéal*. She comforted him now as she had always done, offering tender touches and whispered assurances he alone heard. Steadfast, she would stand by him to the end. She was loyal like that. That loyalty had cost her her life once before.

Ethan would be damned if he allowed it to happen again. Defending her obviously hadn't worked out so well for him. Pair that with his current situation and there were few options left that would see her safe. The choice most likely to succeed was also the one most likely to hurt her.

Better hurt than dead.

Wasn't she?

His heart skipped a long beat, and his focus wavered. There wasn't time for an internal debate. He'd act now and die with the burden that he'd hurt her but he would take his last breath with the knowledge that she lived. It would have to be enough.

A thousand regrets threatened to drag him down even as the darkness rose to greet him.

Ethan rallied, summoning the last of his strength to carry out his final task.

Break Isibéal's heart in order to save her life.

* * *

Isibéal tried to suppress her reaction when Ethan whispered something unintelligible. She failed.

Miserably.

Fear constricted her throat and made her mind thick even as it sporadically fired random nerves so she twitched like a palsy sufferer. The last thing she needed was for Sean to realize Ethan was coherent. Unsure what to do, she rested a hand on Ethan's forehead and murmured, "Rest easy." Then she turned her attention to Sean. "Why is Lugh angry with you?" She emphasized Lugh's name, nearly shouting it.

Sean reached out and slapped her so hard her lip split. "Are you mad?"

Beneath her hand, Ethan twitched.

She curled her fingers into his scalp and prayed to the Morrigan that he would trust her in this if nothing else. Dabbing the wound with the tip of her tongue, she arched an eyebrow. "Lugh's name upsets you. Why?"

Her brother-in-law's chest heaved, his breath coming in near gasps. Bouncing his left foot, he leaned on the sword in attempt to appear nonchalant, but he couldn't sustain his look of indifference. Fear seemed to seize him and he turned a full circle, his gaze active, seeking.

Isibéal hungered for a weapon, something with which to strike the bastard down.

Her fingertips tingled.

She went as still as the surface of a frozen lake. Nothing moved…nothing the eye could see. Yet beneath that sheet of ice, things were happening. Life went on. It was a foolish man who believed the truth dwelled solely in that which could be seen by the naked eye. Lucky for her, Sean was a capital fool.

The man she'd once loved like a brother rounded on

her fully, bending down to go nose to nose with her. "Do not use that name in my presence. Ever."

She slowly dragged a hand down her face to remove the drops of spittle. Then she repeated an insult she'd heard one Druid issue to another. "Your breath could knock the hair off a buffalo's ass."

He backhanded her again, striking her across the cheekbone this time. The ring he wore—the one that was once presented to the Assassin at his inauguration but had long been thought lost—sliced her cheek.

The wound bled freely and left her light-headed.

"Stop," Ethan whispered.

She gripped his hair and squeezed, pulling the strands tight. It was all the warning she could offer. Too little, too late.

Sean settled a foot on Ethan's skull just above his ear and pushed, grinding his cheek into the dirt. "Stay down, brother. It's the only hope our dear Isibéal has."

Ethan grunted an acknowledgment and remained sprawled at the dark warlock's feet.

"I've shown you mercy, sister, and given you the right to choose how you die." He rolled his foot across his brother's face so hard his neck popped in protest. "So choose. Now."

Isibéal scrambled away on hands and knees, a blood trail mapping her retreat. Hands splayed wide on the ground, her toes digging into the dirt, she positioned herself as close to the portal as she dared. There would be one chance to call for help and one chance to help herself. Neither option held much promise. No matter. She had to try or she would forever be prisoner to what might have been had she only been brave enough, strong enough, stubborn enough, to attempt the impossible.

Ethan's breath rattled out a death knell she'd heard before in others who had suffered mortal wounds.

Instinct screamed at her to save his life.

Common sense said he was already gone.

Compassion whispered she should spare him this suffering.

Love stood silent. Stoic. Waiting.

Isibéal let her shoulders roll forward as she dipped her chin to her chest. She looked defeated and she knew it. There was no help for appearances. Canting her head to the side, she peered through the sheet of her hair at the man she'd defied death for. Her options were many, her choices few. Only one answer would ever be the right answer, and as she let gravity pull her chin around until it was parallel with the ground, she was astounded she'd ever thought the other options held any merit at all.

She lurched to her feet, one hand pressed to her wound under the pretense of stanching the bleeding. Stumbling in a very authentic manner, she needed a moment to legitimately gain her footing. She took another moment to control her breathing before lifting her chin. Regardless of her choice, she wouldn't face Sean from a submissive position. It would feed his ego. As far as she was concerned, he could starve.

Positioning herself so the portal hovered behind her, she shoved her hair out of her face and opened herself to her fear, letting it peek out from behind downcast lashes. "The God of Revenge and Reincarnation gave me more choices than this when I met with him."

Sean took a threatening step toward her and settled his sword for the deathblow. Not against her neck, but Ethan's. "Say that name again and I'll take his head." A fresh line of blood trailed from the slice made by the sword's tip against tender skin.

The threat to Ethan was more than she could stand.

Isibéal threw her hands out and called on the fragile spark of magick she'd felt moments before. She commanded the sand she'd mixed with her blood, her words fierce and sharp. "By my command comes a wall of sand!"

A thick mass of wind-driven sand smashed into Sean, pummeling him until his clothes hung in tatters and every inch of exposed skin ran red. He raised his face to the sky, lifted his hands over his head and shouted, "Cease!"

The wind died and the sand immediately fell away, creating small dunes around his feet. He kicked through them as he came toward her. "You think you can beat me here, in a desert realm of my own design?" He laughed at her dumbfounded look. "Your death at my hand was witnessed, *sister*. Your loss did not bring him to his knees. Instead, he cast me out of the Realm of Man, sent me here to suffer my penance because he was too cowardly to kill me."

"He loved you," she shouted.

"All the more fool was he." Sean punted Ethan's prone form, flipping her husband onto his back. "Your sacrifice was worthless. Your death secured me *nothing*!"

"You would blame me for your failed coup?" she asked, stunned.

"No," he spat, resting the sword over Ethan's breastbone. Over his heart. "I blame him."

"Why?" she asked, desperate to keep him talking as she tried to find another way out.

"He...would not...die." Sean pressed the sword tip against Ethan's battered chest.

Isibéal watched in horror as it broke the skin.

Ethan didn't move.

"Take me," she demanded, stepping forward, arms wide-open.

Sean let his gaze trail over her body. "Oh, I intend to. Then I'll kill you."

Horror choked her then, and she realized that she could do nothing more to save Ethan, could only spare him the horror of a painful death. She would do anything for him. It was, after all, why she'd chosen love from all her options.

Stepping forward, palms down, she forced herself to hold Sean's gaze. "I choose a swift death for him."

"Beg."

She fell to her knees. "Please."

"Not as satisfying as I'd hoped." He pushed the sword in another fraction.

This time, Ethan grunted.

"What do you expect to gain from this?" she demanded.

"Revenge."

A deep voice, familiar and yet not, came from behind her. "Then perhaps you should have taken your issue up with me."

Lugh stepped from behind the stone monolith. "Grow and wind, seize and bind."

Ropy vines surged from the barren earth, winding around Sean. He struggled violently, hacking at them with his sword. Several chunks of the terrifying plant fell away, but in mere moments it had done as commanded by the God of Revenge and Reincarnation, first seizing and then binding him where he stood.

Isibéal rushed to Ethan's side. His skin had grown cold, his breaths fast and shallow. "Help him."

"I was not created to 'help.'" Lugh wandered over to Sean. "Hello, friend."

Isibéal ignored the two men, instead turning her attention to her husband. Drawing Ethan into her arms, she rocked him as she had done earlier, whispering a combination of pleas and curses into his hair. "Don't leave me, Ethan. Not now. I only just found you." He didn't respond. She shook his massive form gently. "You open your eyes, Ethan Kemp. Now!" No answer.

This went on for what felt like forever and then Ethan did the very thing she'd ordered him not to do. His breath rattled out in a rush…and he left her.

Grief welled up, a wall so dense and dark she couldn't imagine giving it sound. But she did. The wail that erupted from her made the earth beneath her tremble. She screamed at the setting suns and cursed the empty sky as she clutched Ethan… What she held in her arms was not Ethan, but his body. She clutched the shell of the man to her breast and prayed that sorrow would truly drown her. As she breathed in and out against her will, she realized that her pleas had fallen on deaf ears. Madness clawed at her mind then, shredding it as time had never been able to do.

Strong arms came around her, pulling her into a living chest.

Hope surged and she struggled to face the one who held her.

Lugh.

"Be still," he ordered.

She curled her fingers into claws and raked his face with her nails.

"May the gods save you from a grieving woman," he said over his shoulder to Sean and then snorted. "Or not."

Facing her, he shook her hard enough her teeth rattled. "Seriously, Isibéal. Stop with the screeching. You're scaring off the durands."

"Durands?" she asked through numb lips.

"My pets." At her wide-eyed look, he shrugged. "Don't knock it. They're great for keeping pests away."

A hysterical laugh escaped her.

He nodded. "Better."

Then he looked at Ethan. "That, I can manage."

Isibéal watched from outside her body as she raised her hand and slapped the god hard enough to snap his chin to the side. "He's not a 'that.'"

Lugh set her down and got in her face. "I owe you a debt of gratitude for retrieving this deceiver for me," he said softly, jerking his thumb toward Sean. "What might the God of Revenge and *Reincarnation* do for you?"

Her heart beat against her chest like a lead-winged hummingbird. "Bring him back to me."

"You know what that will cost him."

She blanched at the memory, swallowed hard and whispered, "Let me take it for him. The pain, I mean. Let me take the pain."

Lugh looked at her like she was a worm to his giant bird of prey. "Would you?"

"Yes." She gripped his near wrist. "Yes."

Lugh gently removed her hand and crossed to Ethan. Crouching next to her husband's body, the god scooped up a small fistful of dirt and began to speak.

Words reached her sporadically, short words or pieces of phrases Lugh chanted as he let the sand sift over Ethan's forehead. The ritual closed with Lugh pressing his dusty palm to the pile of dirt that had collected on Ethan's forehead and now dribbled into his hairline. The god rose, looked at her and gave a sharp nod. "Should be good to go."

She raced to Ethan's still form and carefully retrieved his hand. "What now?"

"Patience, Isibéal." He started toward Sean and stopped to look back at her. "Honorable, you offering to suffer for him. But it isn't necessary. I didn't have to create the body. That's the painful part. He should be fine." Rounding on the bound man, the god bent low and severed the base of each vine that held Sean. One by one, the trunks disappeared. Those vines that remained and secured her foresworn brother-in-law held fast. Lugh looked at Sean, a brutally cold, emotionally vacant look settled in his eyes. "You and I haven't even begun."

A wind kicked up a small, dusty tornado. The swirling mass moved over the two men and then completely collapsed.

They were gone, leaving her alone in the desert with nothing but the body of her husband and shallow magick she had to hold in reserve. Ethan would be safe so long as she lived.

A hand gripped Isibéal's ankle and yanked.

She screamed, kicking back as hard as she could.

"Son of a bitch!" Ethan shouted, cupping his face. Blood poured from his hands. "You broke my damned nose."

She screamed again and tripped as she rushed toward him. Forced to scramble the rest of the way to him, she managed to throw herself, laughing and sobbing, into his open arms. Nothing could stop her from raining kisses all over his face, even his fabricated protests that she was smothering him.

Gripping her shoulders, he held her at arm's length. "I died."

"Been there," she answered, mopping her face.

His face softened. "You brought me back."

"Lugh—"

His hands tightened on her shoulders as he repeated, "You brought me back."

"There was never any other choice, Ethan." She framed his face with her hands and stared at him for several moments before speaking the words she'd longed to give him. "I love you."

She yelped in surprise as he hauled her close and buried his face in her hair. "You always have, though I've often not deserved it. I'm a lucky bastard."

She smiled into the warmth of his neck. "Yes, you are."

Once again, he held her away from him and stared into her face. "Two things."

Her heart leaped. "Okay."

"First, did you really tell Sean his breath could knock the hair off a buffalo's ass?"

That gave her pause. Brow creased, she nodded.

He grinned. "I love you."

This time her heart stopped. "Because I told Sean he had bad breath?"

"Nope. That was totally a bonus. The love thing was my second point."

"Say it again," she pleaded, her voice thick with a thousand emotions clamoring for release.

His face was solemn. "You'll never have to beg me for those words. I vow to love you over a thousand lifetimes... wife."

The first storm of emotions trailed down her face, carving paths through the layers of dirt. "Why?"

"Because you chose love." He leaned in to kiss her, pausing just above her lips. "And so did I."

* * * * *

MILLS & BOON®

n o c t u r n e™

AN EXHILARATING UNDERWORLD OF DARK DESIRES

A sneak peek at next month's titles...

In stores from 6th April 2017:

- **Taming the Hunter** – Michele Hauf
- **Bewitching the Dragon** – Jane Kindred

Just can't wait?
Buy our books online before they hit the shops!
www.millsandboon.co.uk

Also available as eBooks.

Join Britain's BIGGEST Romance Book Club

- **EXCLUSIVE offers every month**
- **FREE delivery direct to your door**
- **NEVER MISS a title**
- **EARN Bonus Book points**

Call Customer Services
0844 844 1358*

or visit
nillsandboon.co.uk/subscriptions

* This call will cost you 7 pence per minute plus your
phone company's price per minute access charge.